Dead Right

CATE NOBLE

ZEBRA BOOKS
Kensington Publishing Corp.
http://www.kensingtonbooks.com

ZEBRA BOOKS are published by

Kensington Publishing Corp.
850 Third Avenue
New York, NY 10022

All Kensington titles, imprints, and distributed lines are
available at special quantity discounts for bulk purchases
for sales promotion, premiums, fund-raising, educational, or
institutional use.

Special book excerpts or customized printings can also be created to fit specific needs. For details, write or phone the office
of the Kensington Special Sales Manager: Attn. Special Sales
Department. Kensington Publishing Corp., 850 Third Avenue,
New York, NY 10022. Phone: 1-800-221-2647.

Zebra and the Z logo Reg. U.S. Pat. & TM Off.

ISBN-13: 978-0-8217-7633-9
ISBN-10: 0-8217-7633-9

First Printing: February 2009
10 9 8 7 6 5 4 3 2 1

Printed in the United States of America

To **Michael John Desmond**
Strong, Brave, Gifted

and

To **Jackson Nolen Desmond**
Sweet, Adorable, and Endlessly Clever

I have been blessed beyond words.

Acknowledgments

A tip of the hat to Kate Duffy and Robin Rue.

Major thanks to my "special" consulting team: Karen Kearney, Lori Harris, and Nolen Holzapfel.

A shout out to my peeps and fellow writers: Jenn Stark and Kay Lockner.

And one more for Nolen: Life grew brighter when you entered.

All mistakes and liberties are mine. Hey, give me an inch . . .

Chapter 1

Western Thailand Jungle
March 2
(Four Months Ago)

The voices in his head were back.

"You no forget blood chit."

Dante Johnson forced his swollen eyelids open, confirming he was alone in the dark basement cell. That he'd only imagined the Thai orderly Ping's chop-chop voice.

He lifted his head, groaned. His ears rang like a couple of bell towers. A familiar calling card. He tried to move, but nearly blacked out again.

So what had hit him this time? Flashback, premonition, seizure? Or just another sucker punch courtesy of this damn malaria relapse?

As crappy as he felt, he at least knew the guards hadn't beaten him while he was passed out. *That* had a totally different feel.

He sucked in a shallow breath. Relax, damn it. Think of the ocean. The sun. Think of waves lapping against his sailboat. He could practically feel it. The tropical breeze. The sweat on his skin as he chopped up that bitch's body and fed it to the sharks. Yeah . . . that was it.

The sweetness of the dream beckoned and he was almost asleep when Ping's voice echoed in his head once more. *"You no forget—"*

The blood chit.

Oh, shit!

Ignoring the protest of bruised ribs, he struggled to sit up. What the hell time was it and how long had he been out? Had the guard already been by for the three o'clock cell check?

He craned his neck toward the barred window high on the wall. Even though it still looked middle-of-night dark outside, the difference between 2 a.m. and 4 was huge. Life or death huge.

Rain slashed the glass. The unseasonable monsoons that cursed the area the past week hadn't let up. Conspicuously absent, though, was the metallic *scrape-drag* of a dozen shovels.

The graves were finished.

Can't worry about that now.

"Think," he muttered. "What's the last thing I remember?"

He struggled to focus. Earlier tonight he'd been outside, digging in the mud. Digging his own grave. Then he'd passed out, coming to just in time to receive slacker's pay: thirty lashes.

No, after that. After he'd been returned to his cell. Ping had come by . . . to consummate their deal. Their goddamned deal.

He started scratching furiously around in the dirt floor.

After negotiating an escape plan that seemed to have half a chance, had he blown it mere hours before his scheduled execution? If he'd screwed this up—

The cuts crisscrossing his fingertips stung as he dug, angry recriminations continuing to ricochet helter-skelter in his head.

After what seemed like two eternities, his fingers connected with first the shackle key, then the short-bladed knife. At least he'd had enough sense to hide them when Ping left.

A sudden dizziness scrambled his stomach. Lunging for the bucket, he vomited.

When his stomach was empty, he collapsed against the wall. The pounding in his head metronomed in sync with the storm as cramps wracked his insides.

In another part of the building, a door slammed, the sound muffled and distant. Completely alert, Dante leaned forward, listening for a second slam that would confirm the guard was making rounds.

He caught himself making a deal with God, then retracted it. His prayers had long gone unanswered. Yet when the second door slammed, he silently rejoiced. Maybe he had a chance after all.

Splaying his legs out in front, he unlocked the ankle manacle, made certain it opened freely. The four-foot chain allowed movement between his bunk and the slop bucket while restricting him to one corner of the six-by-eight cell.

He slumped to one side and leaned against the foot of the bunk. Then he dropped his head to his chest, hoping he looked passed out as the longest minutes of his life ticked tortuously by.

Time stretched and skewed as one worst-case scenario after another kaleidoscoped on his mind's IMAX, beginning with the idiotic deal with Ping.

His gut instincts about the situation had been all over the board. He couldn't lock on to any single outcome. One moment he'd see himself free; the next he'd get a feeling that Ping was lying. Then there was a premonition of death. Ping's death, he hoped, since the vision usually followed thoughts of the orderly. But that wasn't always the case.

It was crazy. *He* was crazy.

Trusting Ping—hell, anyone, had goatfuck written all over it. The guards had set up Dante before; allowed him to break out only to be captured and tortured—for sport.

But thoughts of escape had continued to consume him. That, and payback. In fact, most days vengeance beat out survival. The idea of getting even with the woman who had done this to him, who was responsible for his capture and the death of his friends, took on epic proportions in Dante's dreams. He lived to make sure she paid. With her life.

Down the hall, another door slammed, louder.

Footsteps shuffled closer, stopped. Perfect silence fell over the imperfect setting. This was it. He counted seconds. But nothing happened.

Perspiration pocked his forehead, his cheeks. Damn it, why hadn't the guard come directly into the cell? Was he screwing with Dante? Preparing a surprise of his own?

Or was he waiting on a second guard? Oh, sweet Mary, no! Two would ruin everything.

More silence.

And more.

Please, God, please . . .

A key grated in the lock. First time *that* sound had ever brought relief.

His fingers tightened around the handle of the crude knife concealed against his pant leg as the tremors began again. He swallowed the bile rising in his throat, felt his head swim.

The door swung open and banged against the wall.

"Get up, asswipe," the guard ordered in Pidgin English that made Ping sound like an aristocrat.

Dante forced himself not to react.

"You not look so hot," the guard went on. "Maybe you need treatment. Me get doctor."

The guard laughed at his own sick joke. During his prior escape, Dante had noted the building's sign translated to medical asylum. *Right.*

On the upside, since the facility wasn't technically a prison, security was Neanderthal; the guards used shackles, drugs, and just plain viciousness to keep order. They expected token resistance but not an outright fight since the prisoners were always subdued.

Through slitted eyes, Dante watched a beam of light bounce along the floor, knew the guard swept the cell with a megamillion-watt spotlight, a favored trick to temporarily blind and disorient a prisoner.

He heard a scraping noise and guessed the guard had set his light on the ledge near the door. Next came a hollow, slapping sound, like wood striking a fleshy palm. The guard had brought in the long pole used to shove food trays closer. A sizable, sharp nail protruded from one end of the pole.

At Dante's continued silence, the guard made a *tsk* sound. Dante's muscles clenched as he sensed the guard moving in close enough to jab.

Now.

Jesus! The nail punctured deep into his thigh. Ignoring the pain, he sprang to life and grabbed the pole. Then he rammed it straight back into the guard's spleen, before jerking it up and into the Adam's apple in a swift one-two. The guard doubled over as he dropped to his knees, trying to suck in enough air to shout.

Dante regretted that the sorry-ass knife wasn't sharp enough to slit the man's throat. Acting quickly, he tackled the guard, taking him the rest of the way to the floor while plunging the shank into his gut and twisting it. The handle broke, leaving the blade embedded beneath the ribcage.

The guard coughed, spitting up blood as Dante maneuvered more fully across the man's back, half-straddling, half-lying on him.

The guard tried to buck, only to cry out as the shank cut deeper.

"I fucking kill you!" The words were barely a hiss as the guard struggled for breath.

"Go ahead. Try." Dante purposely egged him on, framing the guard's head between his hands and twisting to the left.

Attempting to counter the move, the guard yanked his head sharply to the right.

Just like I wanted. Swiftly going right, too, Dante jerked his wrists and used the guard's own momentum to break his neck. Vertebrae cracked as the guard's muscles contracted and released.

Rolling away, he climbed to his feet. The urge to puke left him pitching to one side. Damn it, he didn't have time to be sick. It wouldn't be long before someone noticed the guard hadn't returned and came to investigate.

Gritting his teeth, he lurched out of the cell and down the dimly lit hall toward the rickety ladder at the far end. According to Ping, the cellar's crude exit was used to smuggle in prostitutes to service the guards.

Halfway there, the hallway narrowed. His vision tunneled crookedly the way it did before he had a flashback. Jesus, not now.

He struggled to stay in the present moment. Sometimes he had episodes that blacked out entire days. Weeks. Based on dates Ping gave, he estimated he'd been held eighteen months. But where had all that time gone?

Doesn't matter. Stay focused. If he lost it now, he was as good as dead.

But what about the others? Voices boomed in his head as two faces swam before his eyes.

Max.

Harry.

He'd been told his two partners—men who were like brothers—had died in the ambush. And he'd believed it. He'd seen their dead bodies, recalled the stench of burnt flesh.

But recently . . . the flashbacks, the incoherent memories. They made him doubt everything he'd believed to be true. Beginning with his capture. He'd been in Cambodia, right? How the fuck had he ended up in Thailand? And Max. He remembered Max. They'd been in adjoining cells—somewhere. Not here, though.

Here, Dante had been kept isolated in the basement cell, allowed outside only recently to dig graves. According to Ping, his fellow gravediggers were political prisoners, Burmese militiamen captured in border disputes. Ping had insisted Dante was the only American there.

But what if the orderly had lied?

What if Max and Harry were alive? Were here, but held elsewhere? Perhaps another floor of this building?

The possibility tore at Dante, but he couldn't be stupid. If they had survived, then he was their only hope at a rescue. And that meant he needed to get the hell out of here.

"I'll be back for you," he swore.

At the top of the ladder, he opened the trap door and crawled out. The rain came down in translucent walls as he flattened himself to the stone foundation.

Squinting, he got his bearings. During his last ill-fated attempt, he'd memorized the facility's grounds. Little appeared to have changed. A single guard would be hunkered down inside the front gate's shack, trying to stay dry.

The area surrounding the main gate was well lit, but the rest of the compound was blanketed in uneven shadows.

Staying low, he rushed across the yard toward the rear of the property. A twelve-foot-high chain link fence topped with barbed wire surrounded the perimeter.

He headed straight for the delivery gate tucked in the far corner, right next to a maintenance shed. As Ping had promised, the light above the gate was out.

The short sprint left Dante winded. He cursed his lack of strength, knew it was more than the malaria relapse. A primary objective during his captivity, to keep in shape to escape, had been nearly impossible here. The guards had caught him doing push-ups once and broken his wrist. *Now pushie up.*

Inside the shed was the small metal table Ping had described. Dante felt along the underside, but found nothing. He bent lower to peer beneath, seeing little.

Ping was to have left a flashlight and a gate key. Damn it, where were they? Had the orderly been unable to get here? Or had he been caught by one of the guards? Were they on to both of them already?

The thought was terrifying. Was this like the last time? Was Dante about to be fucked over again?

He checked outside, but the stormy darkness was impervious. What did it hide? *Just go for it.* If it was over, then so be it. Bring on the bullets.

He jogged to the gate hoping Ping had left it unlocked. But the padlock held fast. His hands shook as he yanked on it again. Christ, didn't he deserve even the smallest break?

He looked straight up, rain stinging his eyes. From here the fence looked fifty feet high. The barbed wire on top mocked him.

"Yeah, well, fuck you, too. I'm not quitting."

Grabbing the chain links, he hooked his fingers into the spaces above his head. Getting a toehold, he started climbing.

His muscles felt like melted putty, as if they didn't want to work. His battered sides screamed in agony. *Doesn't matter. Keep going.* He concentrated on moving six inches at a time. Up. Stop. Up.

Almost there.

Near the top, his foot slipped. He battled to hold on as the fence buckled and swayed. Dizziness had him seeing double. Grunting, he caught his toe once more and shoved upright, steadied. He was now eye level with the barbed wire.

He closed his fists over it. The razor edges bit into his palms. Ignoring the pain, he tried to dive over it. Instead he tumbled full into the wire.

Barbs ripped into his shoulder and arms, and then chewed up his back, slicing away skin as he rolled across and fell straight down.

He slammed flat on the ground, knocking the air from his lungs. Pain gyrated down his back. His legs refused to move and for a moment he thought he was paralyzed.

Funneling his anger, he managed to catch his breath and roll onto his side. From there he pushed onto his hands and knees.

He crawled, desperate to make the jungle. The thick foul mud sucked at his hands, swallowing up to his wrists, making ten yards feel like ten miles.

Would he make it? Or would the guards find him bogged down in this godforsaken field?

The rain let up just as he reached the trees. He pulled himself up as the moon broke free and illuminated a path. A tiny spark of hope swelled as he shoved off. *Maybe.* Just maybe he'd win this round.

He pushed on. Vines snagged his bare feet, tripping him as he headed deeper into the jungle. Cover was crucial.

"Move it, move it," he chanted, concentrating on putting distance between him and the prison.

When another wave of nausea swamped him, he grabbed for a branch, using it for support as he threw up.

Done, he straightened. He was shaking so bad, he had to lift his knees with his hands. His muscles were giving out now.

That's when he heard them.

Dogs baying.

Shit! They were after him!

He tried to run and nearly collapsed when something

sharp sliced into his foot, jamming straight up his heel. He pressed on.

Ahead he could hear water thundering. The river. Ping had warned it would be flooded beyond its banks. Crossing would be treacherous, if not impossible.

Behind him, the sound of the dogs remained steady.

The animals would have a problem tracking in the rain, but by now there were likely four or five guards searching, too. Guards who were more familiar with the area and who didn't have to stop to puke every eight feet.

Unexpectedly, he hit a clearing. Dante stumbled back, chest heaving. One more step and he'd have fallen into the floodwaters.

The ebony river roared as if hungry. He looked up. The moon, which had moments before seemed a blessing, now worked only in the guards' favor.

He scrambled toward a bush and tried to study the crumbling bank.

Hearing a noise, he glanced back over his shoulder. A flashlight beam stabbed the night. He'd been spotted.

Dante ducked, half-expecting to be hit with a barrage of bullets. Except the guards would consider that too humane.

Undoubtedly, they had found the man he'd killed. Which meant the rest of the guards wanted him alive. So they could kill him very slowly.

Two shots sounded, both fired into the air. A signal to move in.

Game over.

The dogs circled in closer, their snarling growls a living, breathing surround sound. Though the beasts still couldn't pick up his scent, the guards taunted them into a frenzy, keeping them ready for a savage release.

As Dante edged away, the guard shouted, *"Ngót!"*
Halt!

"Never." Dante plunged into the river.

Rapid-fire shots chased him. Muddy water rushed up
his nose. Exhausted muscles locked up in the frigid
water. The current claimed him, spinning him in circles.

He heard shouting, followed by a splash. One of the
dogs had jumped in to pursue him. Or had been thrown
in. The animal's howl faded as the water sucked Dante
under a second time.

He kicked, managing to break the surface long enough
to gasp air.

There was no fighting this. His only hope was to
remain buoyant until he was downriver and could get to
the bank again.

But could he survive that long? The guards would fan
out and—

Pain exploded in his skull as something—a log? a
bullet?—slammed into the back of his head, fractur-
ing awareness into agonizing splinters of reality.

He expected to see his life flash pathetically before his
eyes, but all remained dark.

Cold.

Hopeless.

And his last conscious memory was of a woman
laughing.

Chapter 2

Western Thailand Jungle
March 2
(Four Months Ago)

As he had every morning for the last year, Ping trudged along one of the jungle paths toward the prison. Despite the recent rains, the paths were less muddy than the road. More private, too.

His thoughts scurried like the rats his wife's cat chased from the food bins. This surprised him, considering he'd had no sleep last night.

He had stayed at his brother's until late, and afterward, on a liquor-induced whim, he'd returned to the prison grounds, hiding outside the guard shack in the predawn hours. Morbid curiosity—*no guilt!*—had him eavesdropping on the radio calls.

He'd crept away after hearing that the guards had the prisoner cornered at the river, that they planned to let the dogs drive him back. The order to take him alive had been chilling.

That the prisoner had even gotten free as sick as he was astonished Ping. He hadn't even bothered to hide the gate key, certain the plan wouldn't work.

He slogged through a puddle, ignoring the pinches of conscience, something his brother had claimed Ping had a lot of practice at. *Hah!* Didn't his brother realize Ping was doing this to *appease* his guilt? To make right his old mistakes?

Sure, he'd done so at the prisoner's expense, but Mr. Dante knew the risks. Okay, maybe not all of them, but enough. Even before Ping's deceit was factored in, the odds for success were horrid. Like he'd told his brother, he felt no allegiance to the American. If Mr. Dante were even half the criminal they said, he deserved whatever befell him.

And it was not as if Mr. Dante was—how had he termed it?—*at the top of his game.* The stupid saying almost made sense. This had been a game to everyone. Except Mr. Dante.

When Ping had delivered the final evening meal yesterday, he'd been alarmed at just how sick the prisoner was, and had been aghast to learn the man still wanted to proceed with their plan.

It shouldn't have surprised him. The prisoner's incredible stamina provoked the guards, who seemed to delight in abusing him even as they took extreme care that he did not die.

Someone had a special interest in keeping Mr. Dante alive. Or at least that was the impression Ping had gotten from the warden when approached about this job.

"Befriend him, but not in an obvious manner," the warden had suggested. *"Show some pity, or perhaps ask*

about his family, his traditions. Then wait and see if he recruits you. Take care none of the guards notice. This arrangement is strictly between us: boss and esteemed employee."

Ping had been flattered at first. "Esteemed employee" meant favors: like being assured a higher-paying position at the prison's new location.

Though it was forbidden to discuss their jobs, Ping had heard rumors the prison was closing; had even seen a few signs himself.

For one, they were executing most of the prisoners. Like the treacherous Burmese soldiers who were rumored to have kidnapped young Thai males and forced them back across the border with bombs strapped to their bodies. Ping would gladly spit on their graves.

There were other hints of an impending move: boxes, late-night transports of other prisoners.

Except when Ping had quietly investigated, he'd learned no prisons were being built within a fifty-mile radius. And there were no existing buildings that could be used.

That's when he realized he was being manipulated. The warden was using him. Ping had been recruited for this job for one reason: He spoke some English.

The warden had assumed that Ping's English skills meant he had enough knowledge of Western ways to trick Mr. Dante into striking a deal. *"Think of something clever,"* the warden had said. *"Let him think you're unhappy with the guards here. Or sympathetic to the West."*

In truth, Ping's knowledge of the West included only one area: blood chits. But he hadn't told the warden that.

Growing up, Ping heard about chits from an uncle

who'd worked with the Australians during both World Wars. His uncle—who'd also insisted Ping and his brother learn to speak English to land better jobs—*hah!* if cleaning out shit buckets was better—had told wondrous stories about chits.

Given in exchange for assisting U.S. military pilots downed or captured in enemy territories, a blood chit could be redeemed for any wish, courtesy of the magic genie, Uncle Sam. The lucky holder of such a chit could ask for anything. *An-ee-thing!*

Ping rubbed his hands together. He was going to be a rich man. Because if Mr. Dante was as important as he suspected, the reward would be greater, right?

While talk of the prisoners was even more strictly forbidden, Ping had already figured out much on his own. Mr. Dante had to be a high-ranking, U.S. military spy, probably working with the dog-faced Burmese militiamen who'd been captured. Why else keep him at a prison "hospital" whispered to be a brainwashing center? Or brain removal center judging by the jars he'd once glimpsed in a lab upstairs.

Ping suspected Mr. Dante once had a female accomplice, who'd betrayed him. He'd overheard the guards laugh about the pornographic videos that were frequently shown to the prisoner before he was tortured.

That had to be bad; knowing you were betrayed by your own sorry cock.

Befriending the prisoner hadn't been easy. Mr. Dante generally kept quiet, refusing to speak. Until one day Ping asked about chits. That got his attention.

As Ping had recounted first one, then another of his uncle's stories, Mr. Dante unexpectedly confirmed their veracity. After that, Ping could scarcely control his excitement and peppered him with hushed questions at every chance: What exactly could one demand as a reward? And how quickly could it be paid?

From there, their conversations flowed naturally toward the obvious. Yes, Mr. Dante would give Ping a blood chit in exchange for help breaking free. Yes, Ping and his entire family—thank the heavens his wife's parents were dead—would be whisked out of Thailand and relocated to the United States. Yes, Ping would also be provided with citizenship, a house, and a job.

Finally Ping had exchanged a homemade knife and shackle key for a handwritten chit, smeared with a drop of Mr. Dante's blood. The scrap of paper held a name—Travis Franks—and a very long international phone number.

"Call no matter what," the prisoner emphasized. "Explain our deal. Even if I do not make it, the blood smear will provide DNA and they will offer a reward."

Not that Ping had disclosed any of *that* to the warden. No, the warden had fully believed the story that Mr. Dante had picked up on Ping's dislike of one of the guards who had threatened to dunk Ping's head in a slop bucket.

Hah! In truth, he disliked all the guards. They treated the orderlies almost as bad as they treated prisoners.

The rain picked up just as he stepped clear of the jungle. It dawned on him that this would be his final journey to this place. He should be skipping like a child. Instead he tugged his jacket close and ignored the scolding voice in his head that sounded suspiciously like his wife's nagging. *Hah!* So what if he collected his reward from the warden before sneaking off to cash in the chit? That didn't make him evil. No, it proved he was smart.

This was his chance at a better life. The life he'd dreamed of since childhood. Even his brother—who now held the precious chit—was starting to believe. More, his brother had agreed to try and find Ping's son, who'd taken off years ago after a terrible argument.

At thirteen, the boy had fallen in with a bad crowd, then had tried to fight Ping. Ping had been drinking that night, too, had nearly killed his son. This was an opportunity to reach out. His wife claimed money couldn't buy love— but wouldn't it make a nice down payment on apologies?

Having reached the prison, he shoved aside his thoughts. At the front gate, security seemed tighter. A grim-faced guard waved him through. He hurried toward the building that housed both the warden's office and the infirmary.

Just ahead would be the mass gravesite. His feet slowed. Had the executions taken place at sunrise as planned? Was Mr. Dante now buried there, too? Or had they kept him alive to torture some more? He shivered.

Rounding the corner, he tried to avert his eyes, but couldn't. When he'd left yesterday, that section of ground had been wide open. But now it was covered in mounded soil. He spotted a few guards, heads bowed against the rain, their shovels propped against a tree.

Holding his stomach, Ping moved on.

Inside the office building, the air was tense. Charged. Ping's nerves tingled as he removed his sopping hat and approached the guard sitting rigidly at a front desk.

Embarrassed by the water dripping from his clothes and conscious of the mud on his shoes, Ping bowed lower than usual. He hesitated, catching himself before blurting his words out in English. He'd been practicing so much lately he'd grown careless.

"The warden is expecting me," he said in Thai.

The guard picked up the phone. "He is here." Silence. "Yes, I will handle it." The guard hung up, his face expressionless. "The warden is busy. He asked that you wait."

Ping tried to mask his disappointment with a nod, another bow. He did not want to stay, but felt he had no choice.

The guard stood and motioned him to follow. "He said it is better if no one sees you."

Ping gulped and mentally shoved away the tentacles of shame. How much did the guard know about his deal with the warden?

Probably nothing, he reasoned. After all, the warden had supplied the knife and key, even warned him that a guard might be injured in order to make Mr. Dante's escape seem realistic. The warden had also promised that Ping would not be implicated in any of it, and would be paid regardless of the outcome. He'd had nothing to lose.

A short distance down the hall, the guard stopped next to an office. Ping quietly ducked inside.

Actually it wasn't an office. More like an examination room, he decided as he took in the single straight-back chair shoved against one wall. The room smelled of disinfectant, and water puddled in a corner near a drain. The guard looked pointedly at Ping's wet clothes.

"Will the warden be long?" Ping asked, increasingly uneasy. "I can come back later."

"Let me check." The guard shut the door.

Alone, Ping paced the room, but the back-and-forth motion didn't help him escape the growing bad feeling in his abdomen. A feeling he knew was more than his hangover.

As minutes piled up, his resolve weakened.

Maybe his brother was right. Maybe Ping *was* being greedy. The reward the warden had offered was a pittance compared to the chit's value. Besides, if the United States was willing to pay grandly for information about Mr. Dante, what would they offer in exchange for the other things Ping had heard? The darkest of secrets?

Hah! If he played his cards just right, maybe he wouldn't have to work ever again. His brother either. The two of them could open a bar, near the ocean in California. Water and whiskey. That wouldn't be like work. He brightened, excited by this new angle.

Footsteps approached as the guard returned.

Ping now hoped the warden was still tied up. He'd act disappointed and promise to come back in the afternoon. Then he'd race home, get his wife, and leave to find his brother.

He slid onto the edge of the chair, in a hurry for the door to open.

When it did, all he saw was the barrel of a handgun. He stood, started to speak. Too late, he noted the guard's stance, feet spread.

Two shots were fired, the sound oddly muffled.

Heat seared Ping's chest as he dropped to one knee. It took a moment for the pain to register. Denial was short-lived.

He blinked, realized he was on the floor, that the guard watched. The pain was wracking now; breathing difficult. He thought of his wife; he missed her already. And he regretted that his last words to his son had been bitter with renouncement. And his brother. Their dreams . . . California.

Ping coughed, his vision dimming. He tried to focus, but the white wall, the white floors were now indistinct.

He spotted something black on the floor and concentrated on it, as if by clinging to something here in this room he could stave off death.

His sight cleared momentarily, and he started weeping as he realized what he saw.

The drain.

Now he understood what it was for.

Chapter 3

Western Thailand Jungle
Uncertain Date
(Four Months Ago)

The wheels on the bus go round and round.

Dante opened his eyes. Closed them. Who the hell was singing? *Round and round.*

Nobody . . . the voice was in his head.

Wheels.

Cart.

Potholes.

"Oh fuck!" His face slammed against wood, busting his cheekbone, the pain sharp enough to jar him completely awake. He was lying in the back of a wooden cart. Face-down in a pool of vomit and worse. The smells gagged him, but he couldn't move.

Too weak.

Too . . . sick.

A tired-sounding man chattered in Thai. It was familiar. Why?

A woman's voice interrupted. They were arguing. About him?

Think.

The old man had hauled him out of the river. His wife had disapproved. The couple had argued then. Dante promised money. Thai *bhats.* Gold. Anything.

When had that been? Today? Yesterday? Last week?

Dizziness had him closing his eyes. Everything ached. His skull. His leg. His arms. What had happened to him?

He groaned as full recall mowed over him.

The prison.

He had escaped, had made it to the river and been swept away. He had a blotchy memory of scrambling onto a log. Of clinging to it until daylight and beyond. But for how long? Exactly how far had he made it?

Jesus—he had killed a man. The guards would be searching, they wouldn't give up or give in. He needed to get away. Could he really trust this old man?

Dante tried to raise his head to speak, but couldn't. He heard laughter again, a woman's voice.

Then blackness swallowed him.

"Trust me?" The woman's tongue swirled against his erection. Her teeth nipped, scraped maddeningly against his hard shaft. Her lips parted with a moan as she tried to take his entire length into her mouth, down her throat.

Dante couldn't—didn't—move. Afraid that if he exhaled, he'd come. And he wanted this to last and last. Cat going down on him was supreme ecstasy.

Her hot, greedy mouth tried to take him in fully. Failing, she sucked harder, her fist milking him at the same time.

*"I won't stop until I get it all," she purred. Her tongue
flicked at the sensitive spot just beneath the head. Then
she gently, playfully nipped again. "How do you eat an
elephant?"*

He groaned. One bite at a time.

The cart hit another hole.

Dante came up from the nightmare, spitting mad. He
hated that after all this time, he still remembered exactly
how it ended, knew exactly how it felt. How she'd drive
him to the brink and deny him release over and over.
Until he was practically mad with the need to fuck her.

In the end, she'd fucked him. Royally.

Traitorous bitch. Harry had warned him.

Harry.

Max.

Their memories spilled into consciousness. Christ, he
had to get up, get moving. Had to save his friends.

Dante rolled onto his back. The fire-bright sun seared
his retinas, hammering nails into his skull. He turned
his head to the side and threw up yet again. His vision
grew dim and he fought to stay conscious.

Harry. Max. He was their only hope. If they were
alive . . .

Your friends are dead.

"No." He remembered Max clearly. Super Max. He'd
been invincible.

Bullets had bounced off his chest. *His* chest, not Max's.
Damn it, Dante had been invincible, too, in those strange
hallucinogenic dreams. Jesus, what he wouldn't give for
it to be true.

"Must . . . help," Dante croaked. "American. Embassy."

The old woman shouted as the cart lurched to a stop.

He could hear other voices now, realized they hadn't stopped for him. The voices grew louder. While he couldn't follow words, the no-nonsense tone scared the shit out of him. He attempted to sit up. Had to . . . get away.

Rough hands clasped Dante's shoulder, forced him back down to the floor of the cart. He tried to concentrate. There were two men, both in uniforms. Police? Or soldiers?

His mind fumbled to make excuses. He'd been hiking. Got lost. "Need hospital," he rasped.

The soldiers continued to ignore him, talking again to the older couple. More arguing.

"A-merry-can," the old woman singsonged.

"American," Dante repeated. "American." He shouted now, trying to be heard.

Seconds later, he was grasped by the ankles and dragged from the cart. His head thumped across the wood before slamming painfully against the ground.

Too late he realized his mistake. *American.* The prison had probably issued the Thai equivalent of an APB: for one sick American escapee. The uniforms. These weren't soldiers. They were fucking guards.

And God help him . . . he'd die before he let them take him back.

Chapter 4

A Northern Bangkok District
March 10
(Four Months Ago)

The crowded, mazelike walkways surrounding the open-air market in this outer *khet* reminded Rocco Taylor of the canned sardines his grandfather used to bring along on childhood fishing trips. The tightly packed bodies, the pungent oily smell.

"One man's bait is another man's lunch," Grandpa would say.

He wondered if Gramps would say that after being served fish head soup. Or chum chowder, as Rocco's men called it.

God knows he'd choked down more than his share of that and other crap these past four weeks while trolling the backwaters of the Malay seas in search of drug merchants. Which in the backwaters of Malaysia pretty much meant every vessel.

This was his third trip in less than a year. The straits were more crowded than ever, as the growing thirst for illegal recreational drugs outstripped supply, most particularly in areas with stringent drug eradication programs. *Just say no* raised prices and demand. Hell, if the drug cartels could, they'd run the stuff out via submarine. Slimy bastards.

Rocco knew too well the evil their kind spawned. His sixteen-year-old nephew had been in and out of rehab four times in as many years, making it even harder to turn a blind eye while the stuff was blatantly trafficked.

For unlike the DEA and their international ilk, Rocco and his men weren't after the routine suppliers. Their target was much, much smaller. One man. A highly elusive smuggler rumored to run nothing but SugarCane, the CIA's uncreative code name for an outrageously potent grade of designer opium that allegedly financed a nasty enclave of terrorists.

Allegedly, as in no one was talking.

If 'Cane brought as much per ounce as he'd been told, then the terrorists co-oping its production certainly had more than enough money to buy a lot of silence. That, or the brass's latest top-secret source was feeding them bullshit—yet another clever story designed to keep the forces of justice in this post-9/11 world distracted.

He stopped short. Damn, that even sounded cynical to his own ears. Maybe Maddy was right.

Maddy. He whipped open his cell phone, hit her speed-dial number, but then closed it before the number completely dialed. Damn it, she wasn't his girlfriend anymore. Which meant he had no right to expect forgiveness for calling her in the middle of the night—or to expect a purring welcome when he sneaked into her warm bed unannounced.

So why keep her in speed dial? Self-torment?

The truth was he and Maddy had broken up numerous times before, but the longest they'd lasted had been two weeks. One or the other of them—Maddy—always caved.

Except this time. It had been two fucking months.

She hadn't come running back and wasn't exactly tossing him any opportunities to make up either. Did that mean she'd found someone else?

Give the big dumbass a prize. Of course that's what it meant. The woman was gorgeous, sexy, smart. Driven.

She'd been perfect for him. Because she also worked for the Agency, he didn't get hit with questions he couldn't answer. Likewise, she didn't whine when he took off with a duffle bag in hand, pulling a Houdini for days or weeks. Maddy was one of the few women he'd ever dated who truly understood and tolerated what he did.

But not the only one . . .

Shit. Therein lay the real truth; the real reason he and Maddy could never be together forever. He was still hung up on another woman.

Another woman who hated his guts and probably wished he was dead.

Yeah . . . he was cynical all right. He forced his thoughts back to the present, back to his last assignment: chasing that highly elusive smuggler.

As bad as Rocco wanted to capture the man, he seriously had to wonder if they were chasing ghosts—make-believe bad guys. A highly probable scenario seeing as his team had come up empty-handed again and again.

Rather than exhaust their welcome—the various Southeast Asian governments were helpful one moment, hostile and accusatory the next—Rocco and his men had been ordered out. Or almost out.

They'd been headed to New Zealand for a little R & R, rest and recon, when Rocco's boss called with an urgent request.

Those were never good.

He had dreaded telling his team that leave was likely being canceled so they could chase another wild goose.

But as it turned out, only Rocco's leave got canceled. Delayed actually. He'd been asked to do a favor—the kind you couldn't refuse.

That Travis Franks, now his boss's boss's boss, had wanted to talk with Rocco personally was the first clue that this *favor* was very important and highly sensitive. Probably borderline illegal.

"A man using the name 'Artel B. B. Quaid' is being held in a remote Bangkok jail."

Rocco had scarcely believed Travis. Artel B. B. Quaid— B. B. for Benton Brownleigh or Bubba Brothers— depending on who you asked—was an obscure alias created by Rocco's late best friend and fellow CIA operative, Dante Johnson.

More than an alias and private joke, use of the name with both middle initials also signaled danger. Extreme danger. As in *S-O-right-fucking-now-S* danger.

Depending on context, it could mean the operative himself was in grave trouble or he was warning that his counterparts were at risk.

Context was crucial and in this instance they had none. They barely had a description: Caucasian, dark-haired, male, claiming to be American though he had no papers, no identification.

Worse, the man was reportedly delusional, supposedly from illness. Drugs, Rocco would bet. And if he'd made this trip for nothing, he'd make certain *Mr. Quaid* paid.

Because whoever the hell he was, he damn sure wasn't Dante.

Just thinking of his late friend twisted a knife in Rocco's chest. He'd known Dante since childhood. They'd built forts together, they'd fished together. Then they'd joined the Army together. Special Forces.

Following the escalation of hostilities in the Middle East, the CIA had recruited both men. Back then, the two rarely went on a mission without the other, and had saved each other more times than either recalled.

Unfortunately, he hadn't been on the team a year and a half ago when Dante and two other agents, Max Duncan and Harry Gambrel, were killed in Cambodia. *I should have been there.*

To think that if it hadn't been for Harry, Rocco would have been on that mission, too, didn't sit well. Never would. And he didn't give a rat's ass if he was dissing the dead either. Harry Gambrel had been a motherfucker. Period.

Rocco crossed a street, shelving the mental yakking. Blending into the crowd as best he could at six-two, he backtracked a few blocks then turned west, stopping several times to assure that his trail was unremarkable. An old habit he found himself doing even on dates.

Satisfied he wasn't being followed, he proceeded more directly to the small jail where Mr. Quaid was currently housed. Locating the prisoner's whereabouts hadn't been easy as records weren't fully computerized here. Or even accurate, especially in the smaller provincial jails that were privately run and seriously overcrowded.

Compounding those problems was the fact that one of Bangkok's larger, more notorious prisons had recently burned down, meaning their incarcerated had been farmed out among local jails like this one as well.

Travis Franks had purposely not asked any official questions about Mr. Quaid, opting instead to have him checked out in person. Too often a prisoner *disappeared* after the State Department expressed interest. This time they hadn't requested so much as a photograph, hadn't even acknowledged the fellow as a pimple on anyone's ass.

Still, Rocco had expected a little more information to be forthcoming from Travis. More than the prisoner was scheduled to have his foot amputated because of gangrene. But then Travis had gone uncharacteristically silent the last two days, not answering e-mails or phone calls.

Rocco had heard through the grapevine that all wasn't rosy at the Franks household; that Travis had even scheduled an unheard-of vacation in an attempt to save his marriage.

Maybe he was off bonking his wife—which was why Rocco hadn't pressed it. More likely, though, it was simply a case of too-fucking-busy syndrome. That and congressional hearings were two reasons Rocco had no interest in climbing the management ladder. He was and always would be a field operative. Born to sneak, raised to break rules, as Gramps said.

He hurried his steps, now eager to get this business finished. His instincts said Mr. Quaid was probably just another fool trying to avoid a Thai prison sentence. All those nasty things they said about prisons here were true. And worse. Destroying papers and IDs then claiming to be an American was an amateur's trick. And a useless one.

If the name hadn't sent up a red flag on a top-secret computer in a basement in Langley, the Embassy personnel would have eventually handled the matter, informing the poor sap that there weren't any get-out-of-jail-free cards when it came to foreign legal systems. When in Rome, obey Roman laws!

Travis wanted Rocco to question the man on how he'd come up with that particular name. Had the man somehow gotten ahold of one of Dante's old undercover IDs? Or had this person worked with Dante before, perhaps as a snitch? Or with some other snitch who had? Snitches of a feather . . .

The Agency was, as expected, interested in recovering their late operative's assets. *Reliable sources* were in high demand these days.

Rocco secretly hoped for more. If the man had, in fact, worked for Dante, maybe he could provide a clue as to what had gone wrong eighteen months ago. The details were scant, the unanswered questions anything but. How had Minh Tran's terrorists found Rocco's friends? Travis Franks believed Tran had somehow scored inside, highly classified information. Translation: They had a mole. Hell, maybe Mr. Quaid was even *it*.

Sure, it was a long shot, but in this business, long shots were the norm. The name of the game was patience and thoroughness. Turn every stone. Every pebble. Every dog turd. Yeah, lots of dog turds.

Of course, it would be his dumb luck that the prisoner was already dead. Getting a foot amputated was the equivalent of a death sentence. If the infection hadn't killed him, the surgery would. Prison surgery in this part of the world had a ninety-percent-plus mortality rate. Rocco would have preferred a bullet in the head, thanks.

His interpreter, a local contact arranged by Travis, met him a block from the jail. Rocco briefed the man, giving him only the barest of information about the prisoner and none about himself. That was one nice thing about Travis's sources: they never asked questions. Because they were paid well not to.

At the jail, the interpreter played it perfectly, demanding to speak to the director regarding the American prisoner. Rocco remained mute, tried to look important. It was all a head game.

The bluff worked. When the BMOC appeared, he looked suspiciously at Rocco before speaking.

"He wants to know why you want to see Mr. Quaid," the interpreter said. "He asks if you're his legal counselor."

Rocco shook his head and eased open his jacket to show he was unarmed. Then he reached into the breast pocket and discreetly withdrew a nice thick stack of Thai *bhats*. He handed the money to the interpreter.

"Tell him I won't be long."

In most third world countries, bribes were not only customary, but expected. And size mattered. Borrowing a play from Travis Franks's book, Rocco made sure to bring along plenty of cash, not only for this, but also to provide the guard with inspiration to look the other way if he decided to teach *Mr. Quaid* a lesson about using a dead man's alias.

Rocco glanced at his shoes while the money disappeared. Not that it mattered. It would take a slow-mo instant replay zoom to prove the police chief had taken the cash. The guy could give Penn and Teller a run for the money.

The interpreter smiled. "He said you'll have to see the prisoner in his cell. Mr. Quaid is too ill to walk."

"Ask him what Mr. Quaid is charged with and how he came to be arrested."

The two men bantered rapid fire, then his interpreter bowed. "Mr. Quaid assaulted an officer who had asked to see his identification papers. An elderly couple fished him out of a river north of here and he promised them a reward for their help. The police suspect he escaped from another prison, perhaps even crossed the border from Burma. But with the influx of new prisoners, the chief has not had time to make proper inquiries."

The explanation cast even more doubt on the prisoner being helpful. If it weren't for the peculiar name . . . "Let's get on with it then."

"You'll also have to be patted down," his interpreter added.

After the weapons check turned up nothing—when in Roman police stations, you also don't break the law— Rocco was offered a paper face mask and latex gloves before being led down a hall to the cell wing.

His interpreter refused to go all the way. Rocco didn't blame him.

The place was noisy and vile, not that Thai jails had a reputation for being otherwise. Despair hung in the air like noxious smog. The mask did nothing to block it, nor the horrid stench of unwashed bodies and open sewage holes.

On top of that, they stopped at the worst-smelling cell. Mr. Quaid and his infection were rank.

The guard yelled and waved back the other prisoners, before pointing at the unmoving body on a cot at the rear of the cell. Rocco pressed the mask more closely against his mouth as he stared at the back of the prisoner's head.

"Is he alive?"

The guard didn't even blink, not understanding English. Rocco made a few gestures. "Can he speak?"

The guard shouted a command in Thai. One of Quaid's cell mates kicked the cot, but the prisoner didn't respond, didn't so much as move.

Great. He'd come all this way to visit a freakin' corpse. Dead, the man was useless.

Rocco started to turn away, then stopped when he spotted the slightest movement from beneath the blanket.

"Mr. Quaid," he had to shout to be heard above the din. "I'd like to speak with you."

The response, spoken so soft he could barely hear, shocked him. "Rocco?"

Had he imagined it?

Rocco grabbed the bars, then turned to the guard. "I need to see him." He pointed to his eyes, then to the prisoner. "I need to see his face!"

Once more the guard shouted at the other prisoners, who simply kicked the cot again. The man groaned, clearly in pain.

But slowly, slowly, he rolled over and turned his head toward Rocco before opening his eyes.

Jesus. Mary. And Joseph.

It was Dante.

Dante.

Dante alive.

Rage strong-armed Rocco's disbelief. He didn't know how the hell this was possible.

"Hold on, man!" He had his cell phone open and

punched in Travis's speed dial, not bothering to check for a signal. Rocco *always* got a signal. It was a running joke; stand next to him and . . . The number was taking forever to ring through. *Don't fail me now.* "Answer, damn it!"

Travis's voice mail picked up. Swearing, Rocco dialed his home phone. His hands shook. *Jesus. Jesus. Jesus. Hurry!*

Travis's wife picked up. "Sandy?" The connection was terrible. "I hate to bother you, but this is an emergency. I need to talk to Travis."

The guard started shouting now, making it even harder to hear Sandy's response. Rocco pressed the phone closer. "What was that?"

"He's in the hospital." Sandy started sobbing. "Accident . . . coma," was all Rocco heard.

Stunned, he turned back to the prisoner. *Dante.* "I'm sorry, Sandy. I'll call back later."

He stepped closer to the guard.

"I need in there," Rocco tried to signal. Damn it, he needed that interpreter down here right now.

The guard ignored him and instead waved his arms to signal that the allotted time was up.

"No. I have to talk to him." More gestures.

The guard shook his head and pointed up the hall. Two men carrying a stretcher were working their way toward them.

Rocco's sign language became more frantic. He pointed to Dante then toward the stretcher and shook his head.

The guard answered with his own hand signals. Pointing to Dante, then down to his own foot, the guard made a sawing motion. Then he pinched his nose to indicate a foul smell and tipped his head toward Dante once again.

Oh. Hell. No.

"You're not amputating anything. He's an American!" Rocco motioned to the stretcher and shook his head vehemently as he slashed his arms downward. "No fucking way!"

The guard scowled, ready to pull rank.

Tough. Rocco tugged out his remaining stash of *bahts*. The guard's eyes widened as he waved the wad of money.

"Yeah and there's plenty more where this came from." Rocco moved to block the cell's door as the others drew close. "Now go get your boss. He's an American! *American!* And he's coming with me!"

Chapter 5

Dante zipped the black canvas duffel bag shut but made no attempt to lift it from the hospital bed. *Have to sit.*

He stepped backward until he felt the edge of the chair hit his legs. Then he collapsed. The dizziness, slight nausea, passed quickly this time, leaving him mentally fuzzy and physically exhausted. At least he hadn't blacked out. Score one for him.

He'd been told he'd feel shitty if he cold-turkeyed off all medications at once. Actually, he'd been advised to wean off them slowly to avoid possible severe side effects. Like death.

Babies *weaned*. Real men barfed their brains out and sucked it up. Besides, if what they'd done to him in Thailand hadn't killed him . . .

Don't even go there.

He rubbed his sweaty palms on his thighs. He'd found

that focusing on the tactile kept him centered. The jeans he wore were brand-new-stiff. Same with the shirt. The clothes hung on his frame, emphasizing the weight he'd lost.

Rocco—God bless him—had brought in a bag filled with personal items weeks ago, long before it even dawned on Dante that he literally had nothing. And damned if he was walking out of here in the hospital gown he'd worn in.

He'd been told he reentered the States, strapped to a gurney on a secret military transport, more dead than alive. Eaten up with infection and dysentery, he'd then contracted pneumonia. All that on top of malaria put his odds of survival at about a gnat's ass above zero.

That he'd actually been deemed too sick for surgery had likely saved his foot. When the megadoses of super-antibiotics they pumped/shot into every vein and orifice finally kicked in, they'd worked a true miracle and allowed him to keep all body parts.

While he was far from recovered, he at least felt he was starting to heal. Being sick and tired of being sick and tired was no longer good enough. Damn it, he wanted his strength back.

Hell, he wanted his life back. *His* things. *His* stuff. And he was more than willing to work for it. When the physical therapist had pushed Dante to do "just two more" leg lifts—Jesus, he used to do a hundred no sweat—Dante thought of cruising the Blue Ridge Parkway on his Harley. And did four more.

When chills had him feeling like his body was encased in ice, he'd imagine himself in the driveway of his town house, getting sunburned while washing his classic '77 CJ-7 Jeep Renegade on a screaming hot day.

And in the middle of the night, after fighting his way free of the horrors in his mind, he'd think about sailing away. Man, boat, ocean.

None of which, *newsflash,* would ever happen now. Not after what he'd learned in the last few days.

When he'd been declared dead a year and a half ago, with no next of kin, the state of Virginia had assumed possession of his town house, bank accounts, and personal belongings, most of which had been sold off.

He'd tried telling himself it was no big deal. The Agency, under the guise of protecting his true identity, had offered a decent settlement. He had a butt load of money, sitting in the bank. And living was all that mattered, right?

Wrong.

Dante craved the familiar. He found himself recalling things he hadn't thought of in years. Sure, he could get a new Harley, another Jeep; but what about the pictures of his folks? Or the model boats he and his dad had spent hours on?

His parents had been dead for more than twelve years, and while Dante hadn't looked at those mementos since their funeral, it had been nice to know they were all boxed up, ready to drag out someday. Unfortunately, as *nonvaluable personal effects,* those boxes had been carted off to the landfill.

The reality was he could never go home. Period.

He had to deal with it and move on. Today. Because he no longer trusted the Agency and their so-called medical staff, he'd decided to take matters into his own hands. First up, was getting out of this place.

While he'd never admit it to *them,* he was finding it increasingly impossible to tolerate being here. It reminded him of prison. The hospital there. He'd had it with being medicated; with being pricked, prodded, examined, and questioned. And requestioned. Jesus, they had him second-guessing himself now.

Instead of badgering Dante, why weren't they looking for Max and Harry? Or were they waiting for him to *conjure* up that solution, too?

He knew Rocco was out shaking the bushes, but at great personal cost. His friend had already made two unofficial trips back, was probably there again now. But so far, Rocco had found nothing.

The place they believed Dante had been held was razed; no one knew anything about it. Or more likely were too scared, had probably been warned against speaking with any Westerners. Even Ping was nowhere to be found.

And instead of getting a medal for rescuing Dante, Rocco had found himself skating on emaciated ice. He'd apparently pissed off some high-ranking government baboon by enlisting a *verboten* contact to help extricate Dante from prison and whisk him off to Manila. It was believed that contact, Diego Marques, a criminal and info broker wanted by a host of countries, subsequently leaked word of an anonymous prisoner's escape back to the Thai government.

Personally, Dante sided with Rocco. He was grateful his friend had done *whatever*, legal or not, to spring him. Particularly since the only other person at the Agency who even knew about Rocco's mission at the time, Travis Franks, had been critically injured in an automobile accident. Ultimately, Travis would have pulled the same strings Rocco had, except he would have done so without triggering a much dreaded diplomatic incident.

The State Department and Thailand were currently locked in a private pissing contest. The Thai government refused to acknowledge or look into the matter until the United States gave them full information on the escapee. *What escapee?*

The lack of solid answers frustrated Dante even more than the feeble excuses he'd been offered.

Max, Harry, and Dante had all been declared dead after matching DNA was taken from three decomposed corpses found in a shallow grave in northwest Cambodia. "Someone" had accepted a Cambodian lab's DNA *proof*, without demanding independent testing. Then because the bodies had been exposed to a virulent form of tuberculosis while in the morgue, they'd been quarantined, cremated, and disposed of overseas. And all the while Dante was in Thailand in prison. How the fuck had that happened?

The thought of Max and Harry suffering the same fate drove Dante crazy. Damn it, he'd go find them himself. And after that he'd find the sons of bitches—and the bitch—responsible. And make them pay.

Those types of goals meant concentrating on rebuilding his body, his stamina. It meant eating whether he was hungry or not; working out whether it hurt or not. Swallowing his pride even if he choked.

Oh, and no more head shrinking, no more tests. *No more drugs.*

Dante had decided to take Rocco up on the offer to use his condo while he was out of town. In fact, Rocco's girlfriend, Maddy, an Agency analyst, was on her way to pick up Dante now. Besides being Rocco's on-again, off-again lover, Madison Kohlmeyer had generously offered to help Dante backstop his new identity.

His new name. *Dante Johnson, R.I.P.* To the outside world, he was now Dan Hogan, recently discharged from the Army.

Dante had resisted at first. The new social security number seemed yet another reminder that he'd lost his past. Then he'd realized a new identity worked well with his bigger plans. His bigger schemes. Like the one where he'd find Cat and make her pay. His new wet dream was seeing that first horrified moment when Cat saw he was there to collect payback.

From outside, a truck blasted its horn. The ringing in his ears started up again, adding a new dimension to his headache.

"Knock, knock."

Dante sat up straight. He'd been expecting this visit.

Dr. Erin Houston, one of the psychologists appointed to his case, breezed into the room. The petite redhead's gaze took in the duffel bag before shifting to his shiny new Nikes.

"Checking out, are we?"

"Don't play dumb." Dante pushed to his feet. "Nurse Nancy already explained her obligation to rat me out."

"That's SOP when a patient decides to discharge themselves against their doctor's advice."

"I suppose I should be grateful she called you, instead of Dr. Evil."

Dr. Stanley Winchette was a senior CIA psychiatrist who'd taken a "special interest" in Dante's case. The man looked and acted like he'd stepped out of a fifties cold war time capsule. His condescending attitude had been the last straw.

"Um, Dr. Winchette is off this weekend."

"Off performing lobotomies? Give him my regards."

Erin pushed her shoulder-length hair behind one ear. "Dante, I know this hasn't been easy. What you've been through, that you survived, is remarkable."

"And what exactly have I been through, Doc? Wait, don't tell me. I'm psychic, remember? They think I was held by some terrorists, right? So who are they blaming this week? Or is it still Minh Tran?" Minh Tran was the Osama bin Laden of Southeast Asia.

"Where you were held and by whom are some of the questions we're trying to answer. But we can't do that without your help."

"My help? Right." He'd been over this dozens of times. With Erin, with Dr. Winchette, with the Agency's internal investigators. Damn it! He'd been held for eighteen months. It was difficult to sort through, to recall. Especially when the majority seemed to have been wiped from his memory. Or replaced with chunks of time that didn't quite fit. Had he been sick? Drugged? Who the hell knew . . .

Despite claims to the contrary, nothing they'd done here had helped Dante patch those holes. To find solid answers. In fact, once Dr. Winchette got involved, the focus shifted from resolution to experiments. *Let's talk about those other things you can do.*

Dante circled toward the window and looked down at the small parking lot. It was a struggle to keep his temper in check. Where the hell was Maddy?

He started to count to ten, and then stopped, recalling his new motto: No more playing by the rules. He was pissed and he didn't give a flying fuck whom it offended.

He turned and met her gaze. "Let's be honest, Doc. All anyone here wants my help with is those experiments."

Dr. Houston's cheeks reddened, indicating that she knew what he meant.

While in intensive care, Dante apparently had had some extraordinary premonitions. Though he had no memory of it, a nurse had noticed he jabbered about which doctor lurked in the hall, what tests they wanted to run, and what the results would be. And he was right every time. The phenomena stopped when he regained consciousness. Or so they thought.

After he'd been moved to a regular room, he'd been given a dozen supposedly fictitious case files to read— under the auspices of retraining—and asked to deduce the outcomes.

Yesterday morning he'd learned that two of those cases were actually unsolved murders and that skeletal remains had been unearthed exactly where he had said.

How had he known that?

And why the hell couldn't he come up with other answers—like where he'd been held. Or where Max and Harry were? Dante had wanted to delve into the prison flashbacks more, which he felt held real clues. But Dr. Evil dismissed those flashbacks as unreliable, insisting they set up studies that could be readily verified.

Studies that included induced comas to replicate conditions from ICU. *What part of "go fuck yourself" don't you understand, Winchette?*

"Dr. Winchette believes those experiments, as you call them, are crucial to unlocking the blocks in your mind," Dr. Houston said.

"And do you agree with everything Dr. Winchette says?"

She blinked. "Off the records? No." Her mouth tightened. He sensed there was much she didn't agree with, though she was too professional to share it inappropriately. Her innate integrity—so blatantly lacking in Winchette—had earned Dante's respect.

She looked directly in his eyes. "Level with me. Would you stay if Winchette was removed from your case?"

He shook his head. "He's already off my case. I'm checking out, remember?"

"What could I do to convince you to continue working with me, then?"

"For starters, you could get the case files I was promised on my missing friends. And on Catalina Dion."

"That will take time—"

The door opened. "Man, they don't look too happy at the nurses' station. Who'd you piss off today? Oops!" Maddy stopped short when she saw Dr. Houston and started to back out of the room. "Sorry."

"It's okay." Dante motioned Maddy forward. "We're finished." He nodded to Dr. Houston as he grabbed the duffel bag.

"Wait," Dr. Houston interrupted. "There's only one file I can access right now. The others will take me a day or so to get." She looked pointedly at Maddy, then back at Dante.

Maddy read between the lines. "I'll step down the hall."

When they were alone, Dr. Houston continued. "I can get the file on Ms. Dion from Dr. Winchette's office. The others will—"

Dante felt as if he could breathe fire. "Winchette's had Cat's file all along? That . . ." *Lying bastard.* What else had he hidden?

"You were betrayed by a woman you'd once loved. I think he was trying to be sensitive to your pain."

Dante laughed harshly. "Yeah, I'm sure that was it. Next time you see him, explain that sex isn't the same as love."

Dr. Houston looked puzzled. "Are you saying you didn't propose to her?"

God, he wanted to deny it. Except that made *him* a lying bastard.

"I had bought a ring. Had thought about a proposal, maybe mentioned it to a buddy. But never to Cat. And trust me; I retracted said thought a couple thousand times in prison."

"Are you aware she was rumored to be involved with another member of your team?"

"Max Duncan." Dante rubbed his neck, ignoring the tension gathering in his spine. Max and Cat's history was old news. The two had worked and supposedly played together long before Dante came on the scene. And why any of this mattered . . .

Shit. He knew. He met Dr. Houston's gaze. "I just figured out why Winchette's been holding on to Cat's file. There's nothing in it I don't already know. And obviously the Agency has no better idea of where she is than I do."

"That's not true." Dr. Houston stuffed her hands in her coat pockets.

Dante's blood pressure spiked, setting off a new ringing in his ears. Jesus, how could he have been so dense. "They know where she's at. They've known the whole time I've been here, haven't they?"

"It's not what you're thinking."

He lurched forward and grabbed his bag again. "Oh, so you read minds, too. You might want to keep that under your hat in this place."

Score. He saw anger flash in her eyes just before she glanced away. *Counting to ten, Doc?*

But when she met his gaze again, her eyes held compassion. "Actually, Catalina Dion died a little over a year ago."

Chapter 6

Key West, Florida
July 2
(Present Day)

Dante's sneakers slapped the pavement as he rounded the corner of Duval and Front streets. Running downtown, dodging sunburned tourists in the blistering heat of the afternoon, while breathing exhaust fumes spewed from cars and RVs, might not appeal to most, but to him it was heaven.

Of course, his definition of heaven was still fairly liberal. *Waking up* topped the list as it implied sleep.

Most nights remained lose-lose situations. Insomnia plagued him. And when he did slip off to sleep, *she* haunted his dreams. He'd mourned for Max and Harry, which had helped. But Catalina's death left him feeling cheated, burned.

A traffic light forced him and twenty tourists to pause. The urge to slap his hands over his ears to block their chatter was strong. As soon as the light changed, he bolted.

While the hearing thing had gotten better since leaving

the hospital, there were still times when it jumped entire octaves, as if the internal volume in his head had been magnified and he was suddenly tapping into the collective stream of consciousness.

Unfortunately, it wasn't free-floating enlightenment he picked up on. It was more like tuning into psychic static. It was the reason he avoided crowds.

An overzealous hawker, dressed as Uncle Sam while peddling overpriced fireworks, stepped into his path and tried to hand him a brochure. He shot the guy a look and passed on. The whole Independence Day thing kind of stuck in his craw right now.

The muscle in his right foot ached as it always did after a good run, but he ignored it. Pain was proof he had both feet; proof he had survived.

And contrary to the latest psych eval he'd just received, pain proved he could feel something other than anger. Hey, he felt other things. Resentment, mistrust. Oh, and what about his unquenched thirst for vengeance?

Useless bunch of butt wads.

He knew the Agency's game. They'd use Dr. Winchette's report to ground him; to try to coerce him to play along. *Wasn't happening.*

Slowing to a jog, he cut across a vacant parking lot, before slipping down an overgrown drive that led into the ramshackle marina he temporarily called home.

In its day, the marina, aptly named *Paradise Lost*, had been one of Key West's busiest. Until a pair of hurricanes two summers ago destroyed most of the docks. Zoning problems delayed rebuilding and then the owner had heart surgery and decided to leave the place as-is, using it as an overblown home-base/fix-it shop, much to the chagrin of eager land developers.

The marina's broken-down charm appealed to Dante. That, and the peace and quiet. Though right now, the peace was being shattered by a certain yapping mutt.

"Yo, handsome." The familiar female voice, raspy from decades of menthol cigarettes, sounded even harsher thanks to a recent bout of bronchitis.

He directed his attention to the sunbather perched atop the cabin of *El Capitan*, a forty-foot trawler. Iris and her husband, Truman, a former Vietnam vet, had owned the marina for more than fifty years. Dante had met them a month earlier, after finally tracking down his late father's thirty-foot sailboat.

Of all the things he'd lost during his incarceration, the boat was the only one he'd truly regretted losing. Sold at auction, it had traded hands several times before Maddy, that absolute doll, tracked it to *Paradise Lost* and learned it was one of the few vessels to have actually survived the storms.

By the time Dante had showed up, Truman, having lost interest in its restoration, had been more than willing to sell. He'd also offered free dockage in exchange for *Dan Hogan's* handyman skills.

"Afternoon, Iris." Dante wiped the sweat from his brow onto his sleeve, the only dry spot on his T-shirt. "How you feeling?"

Iris raised her hands, shielding her eyes with the paperback she'd been reading. Then she went into a coughing spell.

"Oh, I'm just peachy," she grumbled when she finally

caught her breath. "You got company. D-dog ain't too happy."

Dante glanced at the lone stretch of cobbled-together dock that led out to the deepwater canal where his boat was moored.

Who the hell had the Agency sent this time? Steve Elliott, his new boss, had blocked his resignation, insisting instead on a leave of absence. As if that made a difference. They both knew he'd never fit in again.

Those who knew the truth at the Agency treated Dante guardedly now. He was tainted. He knew it. They all knew it. And the distrust widened each time he was interviewed about what he couldn't recollect.

It hadn't been like that at first. He'd been welcomed with open arms. But as he healed and was debriefed, that welcome cooled, became more formal.

Bottom line: He'd been in enemy hands too long to ever be completely trusted. Refusing to undergo further *tests* or *one more round* of questioning hadn't won any points either.

Subsequently, he'd seemed to have become the scapegoat for every unexplained leak, real or imagined.

"Thanks for the warning, Iris." Dante started to turn away, but she stopped him.

"Easy, Dano! This guy introduced himself as a friend. Said he preferred to wait at your slip—that you wouldn't mind. I promised to kick his ass three ways to next Sunday if he's a salesman or something."

Or something. "Not if I beat you to it."

She held up a pair of Army surplus binoculars. "I've been keeping an eye on him, just in case. And D-dog hasn't let him near the boat." She winked. "We got your back."

The words, well meant, were a sad commentary on his life. "How did I survive before I met you?"

"Dunno. Maybe having friends like that one helped." She tipped her head in the direction of his boat and fanned herself in an exaggerated fashion. "He's a big 'un. Hot looking, too. I can barely concentrate on this novel now."

Relief and surprise leached the tension from Dante's shoulders. If he'd wanted proof of identity, he'd just gotten it. Rocco Taylor had that effect on all women. "Don't let Truman hear you say that."

Iris gave him an eye roll. "*Puh-leese*. I'm married, not blind. And speaking of my lord and master"—another eye roll, this one more lighthearted—"Truman mentioned that you're done with PT. Does that mean you'll be leaving us soon?"

Truman and Iris believed *Dan Hogan*, ex–Special Forces, had been injured while fighting overseas. Not exactly a lie.

Dante had completed his work-mandated physical therapy six weeks ago in Virginia, but he hadn't been satisfied and had continued to work with a trainer while staying at the marina. High-calorie, high-fat, supersized meals helped him regain weight. Daily sessions at the gym, plus a run, plus a swim, made sure the fast food didn't turn to flab.

The extra effort had paid off, too. His body and the boat were both nearly restored. Ready to execute.

"I'll be around another week or two." He shrugged, not wanting to commit. "Got to finish the teak. The rest depends on the weather." Among other things.

Iris cleared her throat then settled back in her chair, effectively dismissing him. "In that case, I'll pray for a storm. I like having you around, kid."

Dante headed for his boat, grateful he didn't have to reply. For some reason mild forms of affection felt uncomfortable; he preferred black and white. Love or hate. Words such as "like" gave him a rash.

He focused on seeing Rocco again. Though they'd exchanged e-mails and talked by phone, this would be the first time they'd been face to face in three months. This unannounced visit must mean his friend's *sentence* had been commuted.

When Rocco's superiors learned of his covert trips back into Thailand, searching for information on Max and Harry despite directives to the contrary, they'd taken a collective dump and banished him to a remote region of Afghanistan. The Agency's equivalent of scrubbing toilets with your toothbrush.

As Dante stepped onto the last section of dock, D-dog, perched like a flea-bitten gargoyle on the ship's deck, switched from barking to growling. An unsociable terrier-mixed mutt, the dog had the personality of a crab with entitlement issues.

The man sitting on the bait cooler a few yards from where Dante's boat was moored looked up and grinned before climbing to his feet.

Dante held out a hand.

Rocco ignored the gesture, wrapping him in a bear hug instead. "Jesus, you look great! You smell like crap, though. You lose your key to the bathhouse?"

"Nice to see you, too." This man had saved Dante's life more than once over the years. Rocco claimed it was payback, but in Dante's book the only thing that mattered was who scored last. Rocco was definitely on top. "When did you get back?"

"A few days ago. Been buried with damn reports."

"I thought the digital revolution was supposed to eradi-cate all that."

"Government pipe dream."

Dante swung onto the boat and went below deck to grab two beers. When he returned, Rocco was still on the dock.

"Permission to board?"

Dante held out a bottle. "We're not that formal."

"I was talking to the mutt." Rocco lifted his backpack and climbed aboard. "What's his name?"

"D-dog. Use your imagination."

"How long you had him?"

"Too long."

"I might borrow him later for a run on the beach. Chicks dig scruffy-looking mutts." D-dog scampered closer, tail wagging. Rocco bent to pet him. "Isn't that right, little fella?"

Teeth bared, D-dog lunged. Snapped. Missed.

Rocco straightened. "Dude! What's his problem?"

"He hates men. Me included." Dante eyed the dog and pointed toward the bow. D-dog flattened his ears and stood his ground until Dante stomped his foot. Then, still growling, he trotted off. "He acts friendly just to throw you off. Sucks you in closer for the kill."

"Why keep him?"

"The owner's wife thinks he's cute; with women he goes marshmallow."

"We talking about that little old lady who threatened to kick my ass when I arrived?"

"Don't underestimate Iris. And don't use the O word in front of her either."

"She'll clean my clock, huh?"

"To stay on her good side, I worked out an arrangement with the mutt: I buy food, he sticks around and growls if anyone comes close."

"Hmm. If he digs females, he may still be useful jogging. Can he fetch?"

"No. I'm telling you, the dog's worthless." Dante shoved aside cans of marine varnish and solvent, clearing a bench for Rocco to sit on. Then he took a seat opposite. "Since when did you need a prop to meet women?"

"Since Maddy left. She broke my heart."

"Maddy broke your ego." As good as those two had been together, Dante knew Rocco's heart wasn't really available. "Maybe it's time to move on."

Nodding, Rocco ran a hand across a freshly sanded rail. "Speaking of moving on: The boat looks good. Hell of an improvement over the pictures you sent. Still planning to sail off into the sunset? Start a handyman biz in the islands?"

Dante snorted. "Assuming they unflag my passport. Bastards had no right to do that."

"You're preaching to the choir."

"Well, they can tail my ass all they want." He stared out over the water. "I'm going back."

Rocco was silent a moment. "I want to believe as much as you do that Harry and Max may still be out there, but—"

"I know. Nothing indicates either of them survived." Though Rocco's last trip back to Southeast Asia yielded an eyewitness who claimed to have seen the explosion and dead bodies, overall it raised more questions.

"And I know that's not the same as doing it yourself," Rocco agreed. "I just want to remind you that in certain places over there, you're still considered an escapee. If you're caught in Thailand again, you'll never see daylight. Lady Luck lifted her skirts once. Even I wouldn't ask for seconds." Rocco raised his beer, but didn't drink. "That's not going to stop you, is it?"

"It's a matter of honor."

"Yours or theirs?"

"I admit it—there's an element of both. How else do I clear my name? It doesn't seem the Agency has any interest in finding the people responsible unless I first agree to *work*, carte blanche, with Dr. Evil and Company."

"And Company." Rocco wagged his brows. "Did you ever put in a good word for me with that hottie, Houston?"

"She got transferred to another case." Winchette had been pissed to learn Dr. Houston had made good on the promised files. Dante had left when she did.

"Seriously, have you considered telling them what they want to hear? Just to make it go away?"

"You mean play along?" Dante asked.

"If it gets you back in the field, yes. It keeps you in the loop—gives you access to certain resources."

"I don't want to be the Agency's resident psychic."

"So offer them a deal," Rocco went on. "Tell them you'll bend a few spoons *after* they sign off on your medical fitness release."

"I wish it were that easy. Unfortunately, it's not something I can turn on and off. And I think those seizures fried my circuitry."

After agreeing to another round of tests, Dante had suffered a couple grand mal seizures. While short-lived, they seemed to have disrupted his flashbacks. They also left yet another black mark on his medical record.

"The real pisser is that that damn Winchette thinks I'm

purposely suppressing my abilities. Bastard's refusing to
sign off on my psychological evaluation." Which effectively
hampered Dante in certain job markets, while leaving
others—say, a career as a convenience store clerk—wide
open.

"I'm telling you, you don't need his stinking evaluation." Rocco leaned forward, lowered his voice. "Travis
can get you cleared like that." He snapped his fingers.

Dante disagreed. "Helping me would be career suicide. Besides I haven't talked with him since leaving the
hospital. I, uh, know he's had problems of his own."

After recovering from the car wreck, Travis's wife had
reportedly walked out on him.

"Well, you didn't hear this from me, but Travis is as-
sembling a new team. Black ops. Just like the old days."

Dante paused. The old days. Max, Harry, Rocco, and
Cat. Jesus, he didn't want to go there.

Travis putting together a team explained how and why
Rocco had been sprung from Afghanistan. Travis was notorious with pulling strings.

"What makes you think he'd even consider me?"

"Underneath that heavy mantle of career aspirations,
he's still one of us." Rocco retrieved his backpack and unzipped it. "I saw him yesterday, by the way. He sent this.
Along with his regards." He withdrew a paper sack.

Inside were two plastic cups and a bottle of Chinaco
Emperador, a rare seven-year-old tequila. Twisting away
the top with a flourish, Rocco splashed a generous amount
into each cup. He passed one to Dante then held his cup
aloft. "This is from Travis, too: 'To lost brothers.'"

"Salud." Dante downed half the tequila before Rocco
cut in.

"You didn't let me finish. 'And to brothers found.'"

"Shit."

"There's a Hallmark moment."

Dante emptied the cup, held it out for a refill. He toasted Travis, and then chased the tequila with beer. He grimaced. He needed to pick a poison. "How long you in town for?"

"I've got a late morning flight to Guantanamo. Travis thinks it's best if I stay out of Langley's crosshairs for a while. I've basically got one night to get drunk and find a willing wench to help me forget my sorrows."

Dante drained his beer and jettisoned the bottle, barely hitting the trashcan. "Let me shower, then we'll blow this place and head downtown."

Two pitchers of beer later, they were shooting pool at a popular biker bar a few blocks from the marina. Dante was glad to quit talking shop. The subject left him raw.

Two blondes ambled over to the pool table. One smiled and winked, while the other giggled.

"Called." Rocco nodded toward the right corner. He wasn't talking about the pocket.

They quickly become a foursome, and over the course of the next few hours, Dante learned that Amber and Leslie were college students from Ohio.

"We heard Key West has the best fireworks," Amber said.

While Rocco and Amber's mutual interest threw off plenty of sparks, Leslie was upfront about just breaking off an engagement. Her lack of interest suited Dante.

But as the evening progressed, he had a harder time

following the conversation, his thoughts drifting back to what Rocco said about Travis's new team. As the crowd in the bar swelled, the noise level amplified. Dante's other senses seemed to sharpen as well. The overstimulation put him on edge, left him wanting to pick a fight.

Wrong way to feel in this place, especially on a Friday night.

When the women left to find the ladies' room, Rocco gave Dante a loopy grin. "I'm staying at the Oceanside. They've got a bar poolside. Why don't we take the party back there?"

Dante shook his head, realized just how much he'd had to drink. "You go on. I've had enough for one night."

"You're gonna pass up the opportunity to get laid?"

"Leslie left a fiancé in Ohio."

"Oh. Well, those two chicks at the bar have been eyeing you all night. You could do one of them. Maybe both."

Dante's gaze flicked toward the bar. When he first hit the Keys, he'd found that nameless, meaningless sex was just that. Meaningless.

"I think it's you they want," Dante said.

"Yeah, right. Admit it. You're wussing out on me. See if I care."

"Like you'll miss me when Amber's back." Dante stood. "Call when you're back from Gitmo. And tell Amber and Leslie that it was real."

Outside, the streets were busy. Dante drifted past a couple of young Turks who seemed determined to harass the bar's bouncer.

Away from the crowds, his hearing returned to normal and the tension in his neck eased.

It was barely one o'clock by the time he reached the

quiet, dark marina. Truman and Iris always turned in early, always slept late. Dante envied their predictability. The orderliness of their existence. Iris claimed their simple life was a result of burnout, that they'd raised too much hell too early.

He looked up at the sky, taking in the stars. A sailor's sky. The restlessness inside him swelled.

Why was he sticking around? His personal trainer had agreed he was as fit as he was going to get. And he'd already taken steps to procure a fake ID and passport. Perhaps it was time to start laying in supplies, get ready to shove off.

Except, damn it, part of him wanted to contact Travis. Scratch that.

He wanted Travis to contact him.

Rocco had a point about being in the loop, but it was more complex than that.

Lost in thought, Dante made his way across the lawn, toward the dock. As he passed the bathhouse, the ancient pay phone mounted beside it started ringing.

He slowed, waited for it to stop. While he used the phone periodically for outgoing calls, it—like all pay phones— rang occasionally with a wrong number. Usually after a few rings it quit.

This time it didn't.

Not wanting the noise to disturb Truman and Iris, he reached for the receiver. His hand froze in midmotion.

The scent of a woman's cologne permeated the air, the fragrance thick, unmistakable. It was a scent he hadn't smelled since . . .

He closed his eyes.

Cat.

She'd worn a signature scent. Dante used to complain that to smell it made him hard.

Now it nauseated him.

Anger heated his skin as the incessant ringing continued, growing louder, buzzing, roaring, like a beast inside his skull.

It brought it all back home. The flashbacks. The memories.

He recalled the video he'd been forced to watch in prison of her. She'd boldly stripped naked, clearly bent on seducing some off-camera lover while bragging about betraying Dante.

Or had she claimed to betray Max? Hell, maybe he wasn't even remembering that part correctly anymore.

He stepped in closer to the telephone, found the scent of cologne even stronger. As if she'd just walked away after using the phone. Perhaps tucked it between her neck and shoulder.

What the hell? This was crazy. Catalina Dion was dead. She couldn't have been here tonight.

Except how else did he explain the cologne? Wishful thinking?

He snatched the receiver up, squeezing it.

The ringing ceased immediately, leaving a tangible silence in the night.

A silence that lasted three seconds.

Then his boat exploded.

God, just like . . .

Chapter 7

West Cambodian Jungle
September 20
(Twenty-Two Months Ago)

"What the hell was Max thinking, taking off this late?"
Harry Gambrel snapped.

Dante glanced up from the stick he whittled. It was hard
to tell whether *this late* was meant literally—it was barely
10 p.m.—or relatively—the last few hours of their mission. The closer they got to wrapping a job, the shorter
Harry's fuse.

They were holed up in a two-room, mud wall shack, a
mile south of their final destination. From there they'd head
home. To another bleak fall.

"Relax. He'll be back soon." A curl of wood drifted to
the floor as Dante drew his knife downward again. If Rocco
were here, they'd be playing cards. Harry preferred to pace.

"If we don't make it to the extraction point by morning,
we're in deep shit."

"We'll either make it or get word out to postpone. Depends on what Max learns."

"What do you know about his so-called source? And how come we're just now hearing about it?"

"I trust Max. Thanks to his sources, we got a real lead on Minh Tran."

Tran had been a key player in Southeast Asia's illegal arms pipeline for years, moving across borders, between countries with ease. More recently, though, he'd joined an elite group of smugglers that specialized in chemicals and bioweapons. And while the United States and her Allies had been aggressively shutting them down, the ones left were getting protection from certain third world dictators.

Harry wasn't satisfied. "Yeah? Am I the only one who finds it a tad too coincidental that Tran got tipped off before we got there?"

Dante's knife paused. "What are you implying?"

"Hell! I don't know. I guess I'm just pissed Tran got away. And I'm tired of this place."

"We're all pissed. And we're all tired."

"Fuck. I know. Guess I'll hit the rack. Wake me when it's my watch." Harry disappeared into the next room.

Dante checked the time, then slipped outside to do a perimeter check. The temperature had dropped. The stars he'd seen earlier were obscured with clouds. He scanned the thick jungle with night vision binocs, spotting nothing unusual.

While he hadn't told Harry this, Dante had decided they'd move on to the extraction point as soon as Max returned. Providing, of course, he had no news.

They'd been in Cambodia nearly six weeks and Dante

was as ready as Harry to leave. Eager to know if Cat had responded to the birthday card he'd sent in care of Remi St. James's firm. The wondering, the second-guessing, made time here seem eternal.

Damn it, he missed Cat. Which surprised him considering they'd spent more time apart than together. She'd definitely gotten under his skin; dominating his thoughts when he let his guard down.

He'd really thought they'd had something special, too. An understanding that didn't require a commitment. Didn't require words like "love" or "I promise." She hadn't liked hearing that . . . and they'd agreed to disagree.

But after he'd cooled off, he'd felt like he'd made the biggest mistake of his life. And it was more than just the sex—not that that hadn't been spectacular. Sex with Cat had been his new religion. Now he felt excommunicated.

Memories of her lurked everywhere. Songs held hidden meanings. Hell, he couldn't eat without recalling the way she'd stare almost reverently at her plate before picking up her fork. He'd thought she was praying. *Just appreciating the abundance, the beauty of my food,* she'd say.

God, he really missed that, her raucous appreciation of practically everything. She loved the fucking air she breathed! She loved being out in the sun almost more than he did. They'd parasailed, ridden horses, biked, jogged. They did anything and everything . . . except talk. Really talk.

Hi, honey, how was your day? Kill anybody good?

Oh, man, you should have seen the freakin' fireball when it blew. Made me wish you were there, too.

Shit. Getting mushy had been taboo. In his world, intimate talk meant phone sex.

But life without her was unbearably bleak. He decided he wanted more. Decided to take the gamble. Jesus, he'd even decided to apologize. Okay, beg.

But when he'd tried to call—he'd found her cell number was disconnected. Ouch. He finally broke down and asked Max for her new number, only to learn Max didn't have it either. Which had launched one of those what-the-fuck-did-you-do-to-her conversations.

In a weak moment, Dante had even bought a diamond ring and written a long, please-come-back-to-me-I'll-do-anything e-mail. He'd agonized over sending it, had deleted sappy parts only to replace them with even sappier fare. Then he'd hit SEND and immediately regretted it. That started a whole new cycle of agony and recrimination.

Ultimately, the e-mail was returned. MAIL DAEMON: UNDELIVERABLE.

Being here, now, with lots of time to think, made him contemplate the future. Something he avoided since he generally expected to die in a hail of bullets, preferably after doing something brave. His parents' lifelong dream had been to sail around the world after they retired. That dream died prematurely in a car wreck that killed them. Was that why Dante never planned for a future? Why he lived in the now?

Back inside the shack, he began whittling another stick. With two, he could gouge out his eyes.

Three raps at the door alerted him before Max Duncan, dressed all in black, slipped inside.

"It's darker than the devil's asshole out there," Max said.

"I'll take your word for it. About the devil's arse. Got anything?"

"My guy says Tran's in Thailand. Maybe headed for Burma."

Dante grunted. "Pretty wide area."

"Yeah. Apparently Tran knows someone's on him now, so he's gone underground."

"We figured as much. Look, the sooner we leave, the sooner he'll feel safe enough to resume."

"We'll get him next time then."

Dante nodded. "Wake Harry. Let's pack up."

Max disappeared into the next room, just before the ceiling exploded.

Dante slammed to the ground, ears thumping from the rocket blast. He was vaguely aware that his clothes were on fire. He rolled, landing beneath the table as a second shell hit, collapsing the walls. Thick smoke stung his eyes. The chemical smell choked his lungs.

"Max! Harry!" Dante tried to kick free, but the rubble had his legs pinned. Orange flames surrounded him.

"Dante, I'm— No!" Max's shout turned to a scream of agony.

That went on and on and on . . .

Chapter 8

Key West, Florida
July 3
(Present Day)

Dante twisted away from the explosion. Blazing bits of debris stung his neck, burned his skin. A red-hot rage seared through his alcohol buzz.

A split second before the actual blast, he'd *known*. In his mind, he'd seen the fireball even before it had happened. Just like it happened.

The cloying scent of cologne taunted him. *Catch me if you can.*

He didn't care what any fucking file said. Catalina Dion was as alive as he was. He knew it. Felt it. And if it took the rest of his days, he'd find her and get answers. For this. For everything.

He turned, his shoulders stiffening as he took in the sight before him. The scene matched his *vision* perfectly.

His boat, half the dock—were gone. Orange-glow flames leaped into the air, illuminating the water, the darkness. Beyond the reach of the flames, the sky swallowed up the billowing black smoke.

A smaller, secondary explosion ripped through the night. The nearly empty gas tank.

A whining caught his ear. Jesus! "D-dog!"

He dashed out onto what remained of the dock and dove into the water, swimming as fast as he could toward the wreckage.

When he reached what seemed like the center of the debris, he stopped, treading water as he listened.

Shit! Where was the damn dog?

"D-dog?" He whistled. "Come 'ere, boy!"

He heard an answering bark, saw a small figure breaking the water up ahead, to the left. He swam toward the animal.

D-dog growled as Dante eased one arm beneath the dog's stomach. "I got you, boy."

It was the first time the animal had ever allowed his touch.

Towing the dog, he sidestroked toward shore. He had to negotiate around the larger pieces of floating wreckage, some of which were still burning and putting off smoke heavy with chemicals.

Sirens screamed as emergency vehicles roared up the drive. A small crowd had already gathered at the far end of the sea wall.

Spotting Truman and Iris among them, Dante called out.

"There he is," Truman pointed.

As soon as his feet brushed sand, he stood.

Truman waded out to meet him. "Holy crap! I thought you were dead. You okay?"

"Fine." Dante nodded toward the dog. "He's hurt, though. I need to get him to a vet."

A fireman came up as they were climbing out. "Anyone else on board?"

"No. Just the dog."

Iris gasped at the sight of the injured animal, then started coughing and wheezing. "Let me get dressed," she croaked. "I'll drive."

"You're in no shape . . ." Truman's voice faded as he took off after her.

Before Dante could stop him, the fireman reached to take the dog. D-dog growled.

The fireman stepped back but seemed unfazed by the aggressive behavior. "Donna Kramer's good with animals. I'll get her over here." He turned and looked at the knot of emergency workers. "Hey, Donna," he yelled. "I got another dog for you."

A few seconds later, Donna, obviously an EMT, appeared.

"Careful," the fireman warned. "He's in bite mode."

Yet when Donna extended her hand, D-dog quieted and after several seconds allowed her to take him from Dante.

"Guess he likes women," she quipped, offering an amused smile.

"It'll be the death of him," the fireman replied.

You have no idea, Dante thought grimly.

Donna placed D-dog on a gurney, giving Dante his first look at the animal's injuries. The fur was burned off the left hindquarter, the skin beneath raw. A jagged cut snaked down his back.

Meeting Dante's concerned gaze, Donna shook her head. "This is pretty bad. I'm not sure if he's going to make it."

"Just tell me where I can take him."

"My dad's the emergency vet hereabouts. I'll handle getting him over to the clinic."

"I appreciate that, but I'll—"

She tipped her head toward an approaching officer. "Actually, you need to stay here to answer questions."

"You're right. Thanks. Tell your dad to do whatever it takes. I'm good for it." Dante watched her leave, then turned back and took in the panorama.

In the eerie shimmer of sodium spotlights, the scene looked surreal. With the flames fully extinguished, the space where his boat had been was a black void.

His gut tightened as the full impact of loss hit. Jesus! All his hard work, his last—only—tie to his father—just gone. Another kick in the teeth.

"Excuse me, Dan Hogan? This your boat, sir?"

Dante turned to the officer who'd asked the question. *That's not my name.* "Yeah, it was mine."

"My name is Chris Furbs. I'm an investigator with the fire department. Any idea what happened?"

"No. I'd been downtown with a friend and was just coming in when it blew."

"I understand from the marina owner that you were restoring the boat," Furbs said. "What can you tell me about the solvents and paints on board—or on the dock?"

Dante rattled off a list of products. Any combination could easily be responsible for the fire, and for now it was easier to let everyone believe that chemicals had caused the explosion.

Of course, once Furbs did some digging, it was going to get tricky explaining the sophisticated device that had undoubtedly been utilized as a detonator.

"Much personal property on board?"

Dante took a quick mental inventory of his worldly possessions. Any really important papers, like his currently useless passport and insurance policies, were locked up in a bank deposit box.

"Hand tools, but nothing really valuable. Clothes and toiletries are in the bathhouse."

And since he used a local coffee shop for Internet access, he kept his laptop in his truck. He'd had his keys, his wallet, and his cell phone with him.

Shit! He patted down his pockets. No phone. He probably lost it when he dove in. Not that it would have survived the dunking.

Furbs asked a few additional questions and then assured Dante he'd return in the morning. "It's too dark tonight, but I've taped off the scene to keep everyone out until I can get back in the morning and complete my investigation."

That meant Dante had to complete his own before then.

As Furbs turned to leave, he motioned toward Dante's arm. "Maybe you should get that looked at."

Glancing down, Dante realized he had a long gash on his upper arm. "I will."

Once the emergency personnel wrapped up and took off, the marina cleared out quickly. Dante made his way back to where Truman and Iris stood. "I will pay to have everything rebuilt," he began.

"Don't worry about it," Truman said. "It needed tearing down anyway. I'm just sorry about the boat. I know what it meant to you." He nodded toward the trawler. "You're welcome to sleep over at our place tonight."

Sleep was the last thing Dante wanted. "Thanks. But I'll be fine."

"Change your mind, you know what door to knock on," Truman said before he and Iris headed back to their boat.

Dante turned toward the dock.

"Wait up!" Hearing Rocco's voice, he paused.

Upon reaching him, his friend bent forward and sucked in air, clearly having run from Front Street.

"Too much tequila, too little beer." Rocco straightened, then surveyed the scene. "Tell me that wasn't your boat."

"No can do."

"Damn! We heard the explosion downtown, but weren't sure what it was. The bartender had a scanner, heard them mention this address. You okay?"

"Yeah. I'm fine. A scratch or two maybe."

"Any idea what caused it?"

"A little C-4."

"A little what?" Rocco cocked his head. "This was deliberate?"

"Yeah. And this is going to sound crazy, but . . ." Dante told him about the phone and the cologne.

"Whoa. You're saying Cat Dion was here? Tonight? That she's alive?"

"That or someone wearing her cologne."

"Sounds vindictive as hell. No offense, but did you really break her heart that badly?"

If Dante had been asked that question two years ago, his first answer would have been that Cat had broken his heart. Prison changed all that. "She didn't have a heart."

"Maybe what you smelled was something similar to what she wore."

"No. This stuff was unique. Cat was the only woman I

ever smelled it on." Dante made his way to the bathhouse, an ancient wood frame structure built in the fifties.

Rocco followed. He sniffed the air and then snapped his fingers. "Wait a minute. I can still smell it, faintly. I remember this stuff now. Flowery as hell. You could smell her coming and going."

"When she wanted you to. As distinctive as it was, she was careful where and when she wore it."

"You know, maybe it's the liquor, but I can't get my mind around it. First the video of Cat while you're in prison, now this?"

"Yeah, I know." The whole thing reeked of overkill. A setup? "If somebody's fucking with me, they know Cat and I were an item."

"It wasn't exactly secret. After the Belarus job, you two never worked together."

After the Belarus job, Dante and Cat had gone off alone, to Anguilla. He changed subjects. "Whoever it was knows I wasn't killed overseas."

Rocco studied the pay phone mounted to the wall of the bathhouse. "I don't suppose we'd get lucky in the fingerprint department?"

"I doubt it. Besides, I picked up the phone to answer it."

"Do you think that was the trigger?"

Dante had given that some thought. "Perhaps, but someone would have to be watching to know when to dial the number. It didn't start ringing until I hit there." He pointed.

"Any chance you were followed from downtown?" Rocco asked.

He recalled how much they'd had to drink. "Maybe. Dumbass move."

"That makes two of us."

Dante retraced his steps, then stared out at the water, looking around for likely vantage points. The place was remote, hidden. He pointed to the line of mangroves opposite the marina. "My money says she came in by boat, probably swam up and attached a detonator to the hull. She could have watched the whole thing from out there."

Shifting sideways, Rocco surveyed the waterway from a different angle. "There were several ways a craft could have come in."

"Powered by an electric motor, the approach would have been virtually silent."

"And since D-dog wouldn't have let a man get anywhere near the boat . . . Uh-oh." Rocco looked around. "Did the dog survive?"

"He's at the vet's. It doesn't look good."

"Ah, hell. Iris know?"

Nodding, Dante turned back to study the distance from the dock to the phone. A blotch of red on the wood siding next to the phone caught his eye. Blood?

Up closer, he saw the blotch was actually an upside-down broken heart. Drawn in lipstick.

Dante touched the edge, found it still fresh enough to smear.

"Son of a bitch." Any doubt he'd had about who was behind the explosion evaporated. A surge of fresh adrenaline hit his veins like a heady elixir of vengeance.

"What is that?" Rocco pointed to the mark.

"Cat's telltale. From our last job."

"Who else but you two knew it?"

"No one. It was a secret sign." That they missed each other. "Personal."

The fact it was drawn upside down was the equivalent of being flipped off.

A formal declaration of war.

One that, this time, Dante was damn well going to answer.

Chapter 9

Juarez International Airport, Mexico City
July 3
(Present Day)

The customs agent glanced at her passport and ticket. According to those papers, she was Luzia Gomez, en route to Cabo San Lucas.

Even though she'd passed through a similar checkpoint on an earlier flight, Catalina felt uneasy. Being out in the open, unarmed, and bottlenecked at a queue left her feeling like a walking bull's-eye. Her skin crawled as she imagined someone tracking her movements through the scope of a rifle.

Which was ridiculous. Her enemies wanted, no, *needed*, her alive.

She watched the agent's supercilious gaze skim up, then down, dismissing her. She knew what he saw: questionable hygiene, messy hair, frumpy clothes, slumped shoulders. And it worked every time. He handed back her papers without giving Luzia Who? a second thought.

"Por favor." The words weren't directed to her, the man's attention already focused on the pretty, impatient blonde directly behind her.

Men were so bloody predictable.

A plain-looking woman—not ugly, because that frequently rated a second glance—slowly turned invisible beside a beautiful one. Make it a large-breasted beautiful woman and the transition time sped up. Toss in a sheer, low-cut blouse and bingo! The plain-looking woman disintegrated.

Once upon a time, Cat had turned her share of heads, had commanded the same reaction the blonde did. Hell, she probably still could, if it weren't for—

Enough. What was up with all the self-indulgent bullshit today? Wrong time of the month? She hiked her backpack farther up on her shoulder. Hell, what month was it even? June? July?

The past forty-eight hours had been a blur of juggling too many commitments with too little sleep. Which also explained the migraine that threatened. She resisted the urge to massage her temples. Show any weakness and bang! You're dead.

She needed to keep her attention on the crowd, on her surroundings. If what she'd been told was true, if the wrong people were indeed on to her—

Stop. You're exhausted.

God, she hated that voice. *Tell me something I don't know.*

You're also an emotional basket case.

Don't hold back now. If you really think I'm a gutless coward, just say so.

And you're grieving.

"I am not," she muttered under her breath.

It's okay to feel.

No. It wasn't. *Feeling* got her in trouble every time.

She straightened, hauling her errant opinions back in line as she checked the time—3:27 a.m.—added an hour for Eastern Standard. Had it happened yet?

She considered making a phone call. Except it would do no good. There was no undoing what she'd set in motion, no washing the stain of death from her hands.

More favor than debt, it was too long owed. She hadn't been able to refuse even though it had crushed her to be part of it.

"Atención!" An amplified voice began droning over the PA system, announcing several gate changes. One of them was Cat's flight.

She didn't react, continuing to move with the crowd, her eyes sweeping from side to side, memorizing faces. Then she ducked into a newsstand and stalled for several minutes before reversing her track. No one gave her a second glance.

She made her way to the reassigned gate feeling fairly certain she was safe, at least for the moment. Beyond that it was a crap shoot. How big a *crap* she didn't know yet.

That was the problem.

It had only been a few hours since she'd gotten the news: "They're looking for you again."

She had immediately taken offensive action; changed her flight. And though she felt relatively secure at the moment, she didn't dare go home now. If someone picked up her trail later, she damn sure didn't want to lead them back to Rio.

Not for the first time, she wished she had more

information, an outside source of solid intel. Staying out of the loop, while safer, carried the price of ignorance. And putting out feelers of her own, after what she'd done, was too risky. They'd be watching for that.

The sad truth was she had no contacts left; none she trusted anyway. They had all died; at least the ones she'd cared about. The rest—her enemies—couldn't die soon enough.

She moved along the corridor, part of her brain monitoring her surroundings, while the other part rehashed what she knew about the current threat.

The details had been sketchy. An electronic copy of her death certificate had been accessed twice in the past month. Both hits had been traced back to CIA derivatives. Or *Cocksuckers in Action,* as Giselle used to call them.

Giselle.

God, she missed her friend. Another sin to lie at the Cocksuckers' door. Sadly, the bearer of the news, Remi's longtime butler and aide, Alfred, would no longer be of help either, leaving Cat to puzzle over the meaning all alone.

So what was the CIA sticking Cat with this time? In death, she'd become a highly decorated criminal. They'd supposedly closed a few big cases by pinning the onus on her. Couldn't go into a Senate committee meeting with a shortfall on the desperado quota.

Thankfully, she'd *died* before they could declare her a terrorist. "Enemy combatant" meant they could do anything. Torture. Murder. Oh, sure, they distanced themselves from that last one. Plausible deniability and all that. But it was still the New Inquisition and God help the witches.

You sound bitter.

Damn right I'm bitter. They drew first blood. They sold her out; *they killed Giselle.*

No, Viktor Zadovsky killed Giselle.

Cat shook her head, weary of the internal debate. Zadovsky had made it clear who'd sold her and Giselle out. And she'd overheard more than one of his arguments with his contact. There was no doubt in Cat's mind who was responsible.

The thought of the CIA even suspecting she was alive made her shudder. Her primary objective in life was to make sure that never happened.

No, your primary objective is to protect your son.

The thought was sobering in its clarity. And painful, given that she couldn't go to him right now. If protecting her son meant staying away from him for a while, then so be it. This wasn't like the last time, when they'd been torn apart against her will.

This time their separation was Cat's choice. She was going to Cabo until she felt certain her trail was cold. With the recent swell of upscale resorts, she could find work there as a housekeeper. Accepting under-the-table cash at less than the going rate would mean working longer hours, but that wouldn't matter. She'd need the distraction.

Just the thought of not seeing Marco for that long sent spasms ripping into her heart. Would he forget her? It was bad enough he didn't even know she was his mother, but at least by posing as a volunteer at the orphanage when she wasn't working, Cat was able to tuck him in every night. To see him every morning.

She blinked away the moisture in her eyes and forced

her thoughts back to her surroundings. Just ahead was her reassigned gate. A knot of unhappy-looking passengers milled near the counter.

She tensed, ready to flee. Her gaze swept over the area, quickly memorizing new faces, comparing others. The faces that pinged her radar were ones she'd passed along the way; people who appeared to be legitimate passengers.

"Delayed due to mechanical problems," an airline clerk was announcing. The revised departure time was two hours later.

No one in the crowd seemed expectant. All seemed either perturbed by the news or resigned to the fact that such delays were part of modern-day travel.

Still, Cat moved on. As was her habit, she'd wait elsewhere until her flight actually began boarding. But not so far that she was unable to keep an eye on this gate.

A short distance up, she spotted a bank of pay telephones and resisted the urge to move straight to one. Better to watch and wait first.

Taking a corner seat, she pulled a crinkled book of crosswords from her backpack. The cracked spine automatically fell open to a puzzle with a few words filled in.

Cat could care less which ten-letter word, starting with S, meant "the state of being old." But erasing and rewriting the word SENESCENCE gave the appearance of absorption. It also gave her a moment to quasirelax.

The throbbing behind her eyes had steadily grown worse. The last thing she needed was a full-blown migraine. Even if she'd had a prescription medication with her—not that she'd been to a doctor recently—she wouldn't have risked taking it. Couldn't risk having her senses dulled.

Self-pity returned, buzzing like hungry mosquitoes

feasting on her brain. God, she had a sorry life. Marco was the sole exception. But outside of him, there was far too little sunshine. Far too little freedom. Way too many snakes and landmines.

You could change that, her mind taunted. *Sell your secrets to the highest bidder.*

She ignored the insidious voice of temptation. She'd considered that option before—what, maybe a thousand times? Unfortunately, it wasn't that simple; that easy. Or even moral, if anyone was counting these days.

Try feeding your son morals, the voice taunted.

The paper ripped. Cat stared at the hole she'd just made with her overly frantic erasures.

Get a grip.

Keeping her head bowed, she turned to a fresh page and penciled in a few squares until she regained her equilibrium. Then she put the booklet back and moved to the pay phones.

It was almost seven in Rio. Sister Dores would be up.

Sliding the prepaid card through the reader, she punched in the numbers and waited for the connection to click and clack across the airwaves, bouncing off how many spy satellites along the way.

The orphanage couldn't afford its own phone, instead sharing a line with the church office.

That was another problem she didn't want to think about. With the local parishes consolidating to save money, the *Orphanage de Saint Maria* was being closed at the end of the year. Cat and her son would have to go elsewhere.

The phone finally started to ring. She felt the sting of guilt over what she was about to ask.

No, the guilt you're feeling is about what you did earlier.

Cat rubbed her temples, praying that Sister Dores would answer quickly.

The nun, bless her, wouldn't question Cat's need to disappear for a while. Though Sister Dores didn't know the details, she understood that Cat was hiding from a troubled past; a past that could cost Marco's life if the wrong people found out about him.

Sister Dores had even helped set up a series of subterfuges. "Lying to save another's life is not a sin," the nun had once told Cat.

Marco Lopez was purportedly abandoned at the orphanage by his addict mother, who'd died in the streets—a real-life scenario Sister Dores dealt with regularly. The lawyer who did pro bono work for the church handled the details of securing a birth certificate based on the nun's affidavit.

Marco's age had been fudged. He wasn't fourteen months old, he was really sixteen. That his true birth name was changed didn't bother Cat. In a maudlin postpartum moment, Cat had named him after his father. Another big mistake.

The longer the phone rang, the more concerned Cat grew. With thirteen babies, most of whom had been sick before Cat left—and only Sister Lolita and another woman who occasionally volunteered—Sister Dores had her hands full.

There were many times that Cat wished she could stay at the orphanage full time and help more. Except she had to save for relocating again. And the children often needed extras. Without Cat's help, things like medicines couldn't always be purchased on a timely basis.

That meant when Cat got to Cabo, she'd have to work

three times as hard if she hoped to have extra money to send back to the orphanage.

Sister Dores finally answered.

"It's me," Cat said.

"I prayed it was."

Picking up on the nun's anxiety, she sat up straight. "What's wrong? Is Marco—"

"He is fine. Are you on your way back?"

"Yes." She would explain about having to go to Cabo San Lucas in a few minutes. Right now . . . "Your voice sounds funny. I can tell something has happened."

There was a pause. "It can wait."

Oh no, it couldn't. Cat's mind had already painted a catastrophic scenario: Her enemies had found Marco. "You would have me suffer while I worry about the worst?"

Sister Dores relented. "It's not what you're thinking."

"Then what?"

"Father Silvestri came by yesterday. The diocese is accelerating their plans. He wants the children moved to Saint Bernadette's right away. Since they're all sick, he relented slightly. But he made it clear we must be moved before the end of the month."

The end of the month. Cat's spirits plummeted. She had counted on having more time.

"We knew this was coming," Cat said, trying to ease the distress she heard in the nun's voice. "It's just sooner than I'd planned."

Sister Dores sighed now. "I'm afraid there's more. Father Silvestri brought a couple with him. I was at the market and Sister Lolita let the couple see the children. They fell in love with Marco."

"No!" Cat felt her cheeks flame and bent closer to the phone to hide her face. "How dare she!"

"It is not her fault; she doesn't know. She acted out of her concern with helping the children find homes."

"I have to change my flight." God, what would that cost her? "But I will get back as soon as I can. It might be late tomorrow, but I will be there! Do not let anyone take him! Do you hear me?"

"Shhh." Sister Dores tried to calm her. "You are angry."

"I was born angry," she snapped. "Remember?"

"Yes. And I also remember that you sometimes act rashly when you are mad."

Cat huddled close to the phone, gulping in air, wishing that she could cry or scream. Except she couldn't afford that either. "Then I promise, this time I will try to act more judiciously."

"Good," Sister Dores went on. "Because I would ask that you think—just think—about what Marco is being offered here. Is a life of hiding, of poverty, fair to him? And what if something happens to you?"

"We already have an agreement on that." If Cat ever went more than seven days without contacting Sister Dores, the nun was to assume the worst.

"The fact that an agreement like that is even necessary speaks loudly of the potential for danger," Sister Dores said. "Have you thought about what would happen if that danger strikes after you and Marco move away and I'm not around?"

It was the question Cat avoided. She knew the horrible potential downside, had faced it before.

"You think I like living this way?" Cat could hear

her own voice crack with strain and hated that she was lashing out.

"Of course not! But your past haunts your son every bit as much as it does you." Sister Dores made a tortured sound. "You know how I feel about you and Marco. But we both know this can't go on much longer. Given that . . ." The nun expelled a heavy breath. "Given that, perhaps it is time you considered what's best for Marco. To let him have a normal life with a family who would love him."

Chapter 10

Key West, Florida
July 3
(Present Day)

Dante stayed at the Oceanside with Rocco, grabbing maybe two hours of sleep. The rest of the time his mind paced. He'd spent the past hour on the balcony staring out at the Atlantic even though it was still dark.

Watching the boat blow had been a cruel form of déjà vu.

After accepting that he'd lost everything, to find his father's project boat here in Key West, as untouched as when Dante had first inherited it, had been an almost religious experience. Having a tangible connection to his past helped him make peace.

Its loss now was so personal, he ached. Seeing the boat destroyed reopened old wounds. Made his longing for a little tit for tat even sharper. The question was who's tit? Was Catalina Dion really behind this? And was she working solo?

No, he'd guess she'd had help. Perhaps from another

enemy of his? So would they come after him again when they realized he hadn't died in the blast? He'd initially thought the ringing phone was merely a distraction. Now he wondered if the explosion had been delay-set to to allow him to get onto the boat before it blew.

Last night he'd stopped and stood there for a full half-minute before answering the phone. Did they know enough about his habits—that he typically ignored the phone—and set the charge to allow him time to mosey on down the dock? Hell, maybe they'd even dialed the wrong numbers in the past to observe his reaction.

The issue of whether Cat was really alive or not was moot. Deaths could be faked for any number of reasons. Look how many months everyone thought he'd been dead.

He could guess her motive. If Cat knew Dante was alive, she'd have to know he'd come looking for her. Those videos she'd made were self-damning.

He heard the door open. Rocco stumbled up behind him.

Dante checked the time. "Are you ready to roll?"

Rocco yawned. "Yeah. Got any aspirin?"

"I'll grab some when I stop for a disposable water-proof camera. You checked e-mail yet?"

Earlier, Rocco had sent a cryptic e-mail to Travis Franks, requesting a postponement of his trip to Guantanamo.

"No reply. I just sent a second message telling him I've been delayed. If he's got a problem with that, he'll call."

It was still dark when the two men returned to the marina. Truman kept an assortment of dive gear, including underwater flashlights, in the boathouse. Dante slipped into the water without a sound. Rocco followed. It was critical they get in and out, search the wreckage before the fire department did.

The majority of the boat had sunk right beside the dock. The bow was largely intact; making it apparent the explosive had been planted near the stern. Rocco snapped pictures with the waterproof camera while Dante concentrated on gathering evidence.

It didn't take long to wrap up. After hitting a fast-food drive-through for coffee and the biscuit special, they went back to the motel.

Inside Dante held up his mesh gear bag. Among other things, he'd recovered what appeared to be the detonator. Bits of wire and part of a watch. "I'm glad I found this before someone else did."

Rocco grabbed a second biscuit. "You said the fire investigator asked about chemicals on board?"

"Yeah, I'll make it a point to tell him that I stored varnish and mineral spirits in the back of the boat."

"Along with some oily rags. Spontaneous Combustion 101."

"Let's hope that discourages him from sending off any samples to be analyzed."

Rocco pointed to his own collection of debris. "I tried to get a variety of charred wood. With luck, at least one of them has traces of accelerant. I'll get these into a lab. Maybe I can get them to expedite it since it was a domestic bombing, and technically, you're still an Agency employee. What next?"

"Back to basics," Dante said. "Cat supposedly died in France. So that's where I'll start."

"I know a guy who can hack into a couple of overseas servers. He's a complete nerd, doesn't even own a phone, so as soon as I'm done with this"—Rocco waved his biscuit—"I'll e-mail him."

"Thanks."

"Have you decided where you'll go now? The offer stands to stay at my place." Rocco still had his condo in Alexandria, Virginia.

"Appreciate it. But I'm not going to hide. For the time being, I think I'll stick around here."

By two that afternoon, Dante was settled into a small, furnished duplex not far from the marina. He'd rented both sides to avoid neighbors. Moving had been easy. Two suitcases. One briefcase. A fast trip to Wal-Mart had replaced what little he'd lost, including his cell phone.

The real work had been locating and installing security enhancements. The duplex had an alarm system, but they'd piggybacked closed-circuit cameras along with a second, more elaborate alarm.

While Rocco worked on locating information on Cat, Dante returned to *Paradise Lost*. On his way there, the fire investigator called.

"I was at the marina this morning," Chris Furbs said. "The owner said the boat wasn't covered under any of his policies."

Dante knew Furbs was politely probing the question of insurance fraud. "That's correct. Technically, the vessel wasn't seaworthy yet. So I hadn't insured it privately either. Its biggest value was sentimental."

"Then I'm closing the case as an accident. Probable cause: spontaneous combustion. If you need a copy of the report, call this number."

At the marina, Dante headed for the bathhouse, wanting to look for clues in daylight. He stopped when he saw the void where his boat used to be. Low tide had exposed part of the mast.

"Hey," Truman called out a greeting as he walked up. "I was going to call you. The fire investigator came by earlier."

"I just spoke with him."

Truman nodded toward the wreckage. "It must be hard. Seeing her scuttled."

"It's tough." Dante squinted at the sun glinting off the waves. "I made arrangements to have her salvaged and hauled off."

"I appreciate that," Truman said. "But you didn't have to deal with it right away. And I know this may be too soon, but I've got a buddy who's a boat broker in Nantucket. I'm sure he'd be glad to poke around and find another like her. It won't have the same sentimental value, but I hate to see you give up your dream. And Iris is already fretting about you leaving."

The older man's words touched Dante in ways he wasn't ready to acknowledge. It also made him regret the subterfuge. Truman and Iris thought Dante dreamed of sailing around the world. That had actually been another of his father's dreams. A father-and-son trip of a lifetime.

Dante turned his back to the mangled docks. "I'll keep your buddy in mind."

He stayed a little longer, then took off. He'd barely driven away from the marina when Iris called. "Truman said you came by while I was napping." She coughed. "I'm worried about D-dog. And I feel too dang crappy to go see him."

"I wouldn't sweat it. I talked to the vet earlier and he said he's a tough old mutt to have made it this far." Dante was paraphrasing a bit. Besides the cut and burns, D-dog had suffered a broken leg, which had required surgery. He hoped that, for Iris's sake, the dog survived. He hadn't realized exactly how fond the older woman was of the little beast.

"I know, I called them, too," she said. "Vet also said the first twenty-four hours were critical."

"Look, if it will make you feel better, I'll swing by and check on him personally. I'm not too far from there now. I can call you back."

"That would be great. But do me a favor first."

Iris's *favor* meant driving through Dunkin' Donuts. When Dante arrived at the vet's, the receptionist recognized his name and waved him through the doors, then had to dash back to answer the phone. "Sorry, we're short-handed today. Your dog is just down the hall. Third door on the left. I'll get Brenda."

"He's not my dog," Dante muttered to the empty hall.

He found D-dog alone in the infirmary, in an elevated cage. The dog's back half was fully bandaged, and he had a large plastic cone around his neck. The dog raised his head when Dante came in, scraping the side of the cage with the plastic.

"Ouch. I take it that means no Conehead jokes."

D-dog bared his teeth and growled.

"Easy Frankenpup. I came bearing gifts." Dante held up the donut box. "These are from Iris."

He flipped the box open as he stepped up to the cage, then he dropped a round glazed hole toward D-dog's open mouth, his aim perfect. "Not that you'd miss one wearing that funnel." He offered a second one then set the box aside. "Let's see how those do on your stomach. You start barfing, I'm outta here."

D-dog looked at the box, then back at Dante. Actually it was more like pointing his cone. Followed by more growls.

"Just give it a sec." Dante bent down to eye level with the dog. "I wish you could tell me what happened, boy. You saw her, didn't you? Probably smelled that sweet perfume and wet yourself."

The door opened just then. A perky brunette stepped inside. "Am I intruding?"

He straightened. "Hardly."

"I'm Brenda, Dr. Kramer's partner."

"Dan. Hogan."

She pointed to the donut box. "Don't tell me you brought those for him."

D-dog lowered his cone to his paws and started whining.

"Okay, one more." Brenda picked up a donut hole and opened the cage door.

D-dog gently took the food. Then he licked the sugar glaze from her fingertips. Brenda patted his nose. "You poor little thing."

Dante winked at the dog, voice low. "Your secret's safe with me, faker."

"What was that?" Brenda turned back around.

"I said I think he feels safe here. So what's his prognosis?"

"His white cell count is still elevated and his red count is down, but that's to be expected." Brenda gave D-dog a final scratch behind the ear. "And of course, that he's eating again is a good sign. He's not out of the woods, but I feel cautiously optimistic that he's made it this far."

They talked for a few minutes, and between the three

of them, they polished off the donut holes. Before leaving, Dante paid the bill and asked the receptionist to keep his credit card information on file.

"I'm going to be in and out of town for a while, but when he's ready to be released, call here." He gave Iris's phone number. "And if the dog needs follow-up or any kind of medicine, charge it to me as well."

Outside, he called Iris and filled her in.

"I feel so much better." Her voice grew muffled as she wheezed and coughed. "Now what are you and that hunky friend of yours doing tomorrow night for supper? And what the hell is that beeping noise?"

"Call waiting." Dante glanced at the display. PRIVATE CALLER. Probably Rocco. "I need to take this call, Iris."

"Bye then. We'll expect you tomorrow at six," she said before disconnecting.

Dante switched to the other call.

"I hear you had a little excitement." It was Travis Franks. He had obviously talked with Rocco.

"Bad news travels fast."

"Yeah, the speed of gloom amazes. You free for a late lunch?"

The question caught him off guard. "Lunch? You're in town?"

"At the airport. Private charter. I know Taylor's still here. I want to meet with both of you."

"I'll be there in fifteen." After disconnecting, he called Rocco.

"Damn," Rocco said. "I talked with him earlier and he brushed me off. Said he'd call back. Something's up. Hope it's good."

"I've learned to expect the worst. Fewer surprises,"

Dante said. "Order pizza for delivery. Travis and I will be there shortly."

The three men had once worked closely together. Travis had been a senior field agent when Dante and Rocco came on board ten years ago. Their paths diverged when Travis fast-tracked up the management chain.

Before that, though, they had been a team. Equals. Brothers.

In fact, their original *band of brothers* had been Travis, Dante, Rocco, and Harry. Harry Gambrel came on right after Dante did, but Travis left the group shortly thereafter. Things seemed to disintegrate after that. As if Travis had been the glue. Or cushion.

When Harry and Rocco bumped heads, fists actually, over a personal matter—damn women—Max Duncan had been brought in to ease the situation. That had been what—three, four years ago?

But Max's presence hadn't helped. And when that last disastrous assignment in Southeast Asia had required only a three-man team, Dante had suggested Max replace Harry. Instead, he'd replaced Rocco.

And while the decision to leave Rocco behind had never sat well with Dante, in retrospect he felt grateful. And selfish. But at least Rocco was here now. Truth be told, Rocco was probably a hell of a lot more supportive of finding Max and Harry than Harry would have been in a reverse situation.

Both men carried grudges, but Harry's had an edge. An edge he'd welcome if the SOB were still alive.

At Key West International Airport, Dante spotted Travis curbside. No luggage, briefcase only. He leaned on a cane.

Travis's leg had required multiple surgeries after his

car accident. Dante could empathize with the physical therapy routine the other man undoubtedly had to endure.

"You look good." The two men spoke in unison as Dante pulled back out into traffic.

"Liar," Travis said. "I know exactly how feeble I look. On the other hand, the sun and sand obviously agree with you."

"They agreed better when I had my boat."

"You should be grateful you weren't onboard when she blew."

Dante glanced sideways. "I've had it up to here with the you-should-be's. It's bullshit. And the only thing that will make it better is payback."

"Then I might have a proposition you'll be interested in. But first fill me in on the whole story. Rocco gave me the two-sentence, what-a-cluster-fuck version."

As he drove to his apartment, Dante explained the events leading up to the explosion.

Travis nodded. "Rocco mentioned you recovered some evidence. Anything significant?"

"Maybe a piece of the detonator." At Dante's new digs the conversation ceased momentarily as they climbed out.

"Describe the detonator," Travis went on.

"You can see it for yourself inside. We've got it bagged."

"I've got a lab that can process it overnight. If it's what I think it is, we'll want to move fast—"

Rocco opened the door just then. He pointed at Travis's cane. "Still not ready for a sprint, I see."

"Depends. What's the prize? Man, is that pizza I smell? I skipped breakfast and I'm starved."

Inside, they each got a plate and piled it high before

moving into the living room to eat and talk. The kitchen table was better suited to elves.

Dante waited until Travis had polished off three slices, then he handed him the plastic bag containing the detonator. "Finish what you were saying earlier. If the evidence is what you think it is?"

Travis put on a pair of glasses, then held the bag up, making *hmm* noises as he studied the contents. "The lab will have to confirm it, but this looks like the same-style detonator used in a bomb that killed two MI6 agents five weeks ago. And a Mossad operative a month before that. Both agencies are sniffing around now."

Dante had worked with operatives from both the British and the Israeli intelligence services. "Can you get any intel from them?"

"No, and I don't want to make an inquiry because I'd like to keep this incident off the radar. I'm just not sure how long it will stay that way."

The reason for Travis's unannounced visit became clear. Dante grimaced. "You still think there's a leak."

"I've begun to suspect that my car accident may not have been an accident," Travis said. "I think someone knew I'd sent Rocco to Bangkok. They might have thought I knew more about your imprisonment than I do."

Rocco swore, and then turned to Dante. "I think he's trying to tell you not to take this personally."

"Actually, you both need to take it very personally," Travis said. "From what I can tell, you're the last operatives who worked with Catalina Dion that are still alive. The British and Israeli agents who were killed had also worked with Cat in the past."

"Worked with her?" Dante asked. "Or slept with her?"

Travis met his gaze and shrugged. "That's one theory. Except Rocco doesn't fit the bill."

"If you're implying the bomb was meant for both of us," Rocco said. "That puts a different spin on it."

"Maybe." Pulling off his glasses and rubbing his eyes, Travis leaned back in his chair and looked at Rocco. "Our perp could have gotten to Dante anytime over the past four weeks. Anyone know you were coming here?"

"Nada. It was so last minute, I didn't even tell him." Rocco tilted his head toward Dante.

"Then your arrival may have been coincidental," Travis said.

"Is anyone on the suspect list besides Cat Dion?" Dante asked.

"I don't have a list. Yet. If Cat's really involved, big if, she's an underling. But she can lead us to the top dog. That's where we'll get answers," Travis said. "I haven't discussed my suspicions with anyone inside the Agency, by the way, and I intend to keep it that way. Until you help me find the leak and plug it." He looked pointedly at Dante.

"Me?" Dante snorted. "The least trusted person at the Agency?"

"*I* trust you," Travis said. "And the fact you're already out of the loop is perfect. I know Rocco has been trying to get you back in, but you're more valuable to me outside. If Catalina Dion is alive, I want you to find her before MI6 or the Mossad get wind of this. Custody will be everything."

"I want first crack at questioning her," Dante said.

"Agreed. What else?"

"I want my passport cleared."

"You know nothing indicates Max and Harry are

alive," Travis said after a moment's silence. "And believe me, I've exhausted every search option at my disposal."

"Nothing indicated I was alive either."

"And I'll carry that SNAFU to my grave."

"It wasn't your fault," Dante said.

Rocco shook his head. "I know exactly how T feels."

"Do this job first," Travis went on. "And I'll make certain that you get a chance to go back to Thailand, with the team of your choice."

"Agreed," Dante said. "I want Rocco to work with me on this. For starters, we'll need the old case files. Anything Cat worked on."

Grabbing his briefcase, Travis withdrew a sheet of paper. "Look over this list and tell me if I've got them all."

Rocco shifted to read over Dante's shoulder. "It looks complete to me," Dante said a few minutes later.

"Your memory's better than mine," Rocco said. "I'd forgotten some of them, like that fuckup in Belarus."

"Interesting you should mention that job. Max and Harry were on that one, too," Travis noted. "If memory serves me right, I believe Belarus was also the last time Cat worked directly for the Agency."

Shoving the paper aside, Dante exchanged glances with Rocco and Travis. "Your memory is perfect. Cat was offered another job after that, but she turned it down. Once we slept together, we agreed our personal and business lives had to be separated."

Chapter 11

Minsk, Belarus
September 29
(Thirty-Four Months Ago)

Surveillance stunk. Dante hated it. Especially on mornings like this when the sun was bright and everyone else in the world was outside. Enjoying themselves. Except him. "Pay no attention to the frozen corpse," he muttered.

He was holed up, alone—save for his bad attitude—on the second floor of an ancient building that the Agency—through a mind-boggling array of channels—owned under a variety of business fronts. The place was currently being renovated, which meant no heat, no electric.

"No coffee."

He logged the time, then resumed his watch. Though temperatures were only in the forties, the outside patio of the café directly across the street was crowded. Patrons sat with faces upturned, as if invisible solar panels in their foreheads could absorb the early morning rays, storing up the memory for those times when the sun wouldn't be seen for weeks.

The crowd was self-segregating. University students scattered along the edge, closest to the congested street, while faculty huddled in the corners near the building. The common, working stiffs were scattered in between but still sorted themselves by rank and file. Supervisors here. Line workers there.

This particular coffee shop was the new, the in, the hot, blending Starbucks panache with a flirtacious wait staff known to pamper their customers. Thus each waiter or waitress built a loyal following. Which made it easy for Cat to sit in Max's section each time, provided he was working that day.

She'd established a routine that included morning coffee here Monday through Saturday. To the casual observer she was yet another brilliant but overworked student, juggling a full class load and an internship at *Institut Predpriyatiya*.

The *Institut* was notorious for sapping the energy and creativity from bright, young interns, and then discarding their dried husks when they failed to maintain an outrageous performance level. Of course, those who did survive until graduation were in high demand by Mother Russia and beyond—the beyond being the choice that paid better.

Training his binoculars back on Cat, Dante watched as Max, the newest member of the team, pointed over her shoulder to something in the newspaper she read. She glanced up at Max, offering a wide smile and a comment. If Dante had been fluent in Russian, he could have read her lips. Max laughed at whatever she'd said. A joke perhaps? *I dunno, how many Outer Siberians does it take to change a lightbulb?*

Max moved on to flirt in a similar fashion with the redhead at the next table. Dante refocused on Cat. Had she already passed it? He shook his head. No matter how closely he watched, he had yet to catch the actual handoff of the microchip.

Once a week or so she would deliver to Max digital reports that included photos, voice recordings, and on rare occasions, computer files. There were lots of drawings, too, crude sketches actually because, while Cat had a photographic memory, she had little artistic talent.

Long suspected as a cover for secret government experiments, the *Institut* had tight security, so anything she managed to get out was miraculous. Her current assignment included memorizing the lab's physical inventory; no small task since the supplies were decentralized and scattered among a half-dozen locations.

People smarter than Dante and equipped with sophisticated software could take those lists of seemingly innocuous supplies, chemicals, and equipment and determine with great accuracy where and in what form they might appear next.

Unfortunately, because there'd been no way for Cat to get out actual samples of the specific chemicals or biological agents, the Agency had been unable to tie the *Institut* to any of the biochem weapons used in recent terrorist activity. Which to Dante's way of thinking was secondary to shutting them down.

The higher-ups didn't agree. Lately the CIA's interest in the *Institut* seemed to center obsessively on the experiments being carried out by the notorious Dr. Viktor Zadovsky.

Depending on whom you talked to, Zadovsky was either a genius or a certifiable madman. One moment he was credited with creating invisibility, the next it was total mind control. Even his failures caused ripples to buzz through the scientific network.

Though Zadovsky was one of a handful of scientists that governments around the world would pay through their noses to get on their payroll, few countries could afford a prima-donna genius used to having every whim met.

That was rapidly changing. With the economic destabilization that had occurred since the Soviet Union's breakup, the brainiacs weren't so loyal. Money talked and they listened.

Of all of them, Zadovsky could virtually name his price. While the United States was ready to top any offer, their generous overtures had been outright snubbed. Apparently, back in the Cold War days, Zadovsky's grandparents had been named as possible spies in a leaked propaganda document. While the report had been quickly discredited, Zadovsky's grandfather felt he never got rid of the onus, was always watched. Young Zadovsky was consequently raised with a U.S. = evil, Russian = good mentality.

Getting someone inside the *Institut* was a coup in itself. Cat's status as a contract agent removed any direct tie to the Agency, a plus in operations such as this. She posed as the great-granddaughter of Zadovsky's grandfather's closest friend, an impervious alias since the real granddaughter was in protective custody and cooperating with the CIA.

Cat played the role well, which meant she got more than a dismissive glance from the high and mighty Dr. Zadovsky. In fact, he'd taken her on as an administrative assistant, even suggested she might travel with him. Wink, wink. Which proved that despite the off-the-chart IQ and multiple PhDs, under the sterile lab coat Zadovsky was a lecher.

Of course Zadovsky wanted her. He'd have to be a blind gay monk not to. Cat was fucking gorgeous. From her short, platinum blond curls, to her lithe 36D frame, she exuded a kittenish sexuality.

Dante watched as she picked up her coffee mug, her lips pursing as she blew across the brew's surface before taking a sip. Knowing better than to torment himself with images of her doing that to his body, he lowered the binoculars and scanned the broader area.

Nothing caught his eye. The cars were the same as usual. Traffic had increased as people went to work.

He turned up the collar on his coat and shifted slightly to the right before picking up the binoculars to check the café again. The waiters were being attentive as ever, catching new customers as they sat, making last calls with their customers who began to pack up.

Still in flirty-waiter mode, Max touched the shoulder of another brunette before moving away to treat Cat with more of the same.

Dante frowned. Was there any truth to the rumors that Cat and Max had been lovers once? Rocco claimed no, that he'd heard they were only friends, but given what Dante saw through the binoculars, he couldn't help wondering.

A bus rumbled around the corner, adding its exhaust to the morning fog. Almost on cue, half the café emptied. Morning rush officially started as the bus pulled away.

Back at the café's still busy patio, Max began clearing tables. Dante focused the binoculars on his hands.

Max signaled "all clear," then "received."

Good. Cat had given him a report today.

Just as Dante was about to lower the binocs, Max gave a third signal. "Urgent." Another waiter came by and Max turned away.

Dante watched a few more minutes before hurriedly gathering his gear. In the two months they'd been doing this, this was the first time Max had used that signal.

What the hell was up?

Urgent wasn't life or death. It also wasn't *danger*. So it had been important that Max keep up his front as a foreign exchange student and complete his shift at the café and then attend class at the university.

Dante wondered if Cat had discovered a way to smuggle out actual samples. Hell, maybe she'd found an actual clutch of bioweapons. Langley would love solid proof of what went on behind those locked doors.

When Max reached the apartment outside of town three hours later, Dante and Rocco were playing seven-card stud.

"About damn time." Dante folded his cards and glared at Max.

"Someone miss their nap?"

Rocco looked as if he wanted to laugh at Max's retort, but didn't.

Instead he held out his hand for the microchip. "Let's see what's got everyone so excited." The team's computer and electronics whiz, Rocco handled the weekly decryptions. "Be back in a few."

As Rocco disappeared into the other room, Dante moved to the heavily draped window facing the alley. "You sure you're clean?" He carefully peered out through a crack in the wood shutter—saw nothing.

"Why? Am I that bad?" Max pretended to sniff his armpit before flipping him off. "Of course I'm clean. I took extra precautions, too."

"Extra, why?"

"Tabby said something's up, that we should be ready."

Tabby was one of Max's nicknames for Cat. They avoided using each other's real names even in secure environments. Dante pushed away the annoyance he felt whenever the other man called her that.

"Ready for what?" Dante pressed.

"Hell if I know. It's not like we could talk freely at the café. But I did notice she was more subdued than usual."

"Could have fooled me. You two looked pretty cozy."

"You want to tell me what your fucking problem is, man?"

Dante opened and shut his mouth. He was busted. Shit. "Forget I said that."

"No. I'm not forgetting. You've been like this since we started this job. I thought it was the old treat-the-new-guy-like-crap-initiation routine. But you know what I finally figured out?" Max didn't wait for an answer. "Your attitude takes a nosedive right after I meet with Tabby."

Dante recalled the way Cat had smiled at Max. Jesus. She was messing with his head. He let out a harsh breath. "Let's just drop it."

"Let's don't." Max stepped closer, his chest puffed out. "I'm sick of being caught in the middle."

Dante reached up to shove him away, but instead he grabbed the other man's jacket. "Middle of what?"

"You two. She's jonesing for you." He shook his head.

"Though for the fucking life of me I can't imagine what the hell she sees in you. First thing she wants to know each time is how you're doing. When I'm the one putting my ass out there. You get to hide out in buildings, watching."

"She asked about me?" Dante almost cracked a smile.

"Yeah. Now let go of my lapels before I kick your ass."

Dante stepped backward. "Damn it. I need to leave." He was an emotional liability, putting everyone else here at risk.

"No, you just need to admit you're hot for her, but that being a pro, you'll stuff it till later. Until the job is done."

"Easy for you to say . . ." Dante shut his mouth. Talking didn't make it any better.

"I take that back. What you need is to accept that Tabby and I are close friends. That I'd kill for her and nothing will ever change that." At the look Dante shot him, Max offered a weak chuckle. "Oh, I get it. What you really want to know is if we've ever been lovers. Right?"

Behind them, Rocco cleared his throat. "Uh? Should I come back?"

Grateful for the interruption, Dante turned away and motioned Rocco closer. "We're done. What's on the disk?"

"I'm still decrypting parts of it, but I just read her report. A couple things: First, she saw Dr. Z's infamous notebook. She was in his office when he got called away for a lab fire. He left his notebook open on his desk."

"Holy shit." It was Zadovsky's so-called recipe book that allowed third world countries to stock their arms pantries with frightening biothreats. At a hefty price tag.

More, Zadovsky was rumored to profit again and again

as he developed permutations that rendered weapons made by his competitors obsolete.

"What'd she get?" Dante asked.

"How the fuck should I know?" Rocco said. "The parts that aren't high math are in Russian. She only got through a couple pages but she sketched out everything she saw."

Once again, Dante recalled Cat's special gift, her photographic memory. He'd watched her demonstrate it once. After flipping through a 300-page book rapidly, she parroted back pages on demand. Yet another reason she was perfect for this job.

Rocco went on. "Here's the real kicker. She thinks they're getting ready to move the lab again, and that they'll make a couple deliveries before packing it up."

"Finally some action," Max said.

Dante ignored him. "Have you contacted Mr. T?" Travis, their boss, would be very interested in this.

Zadovsky frequently changed locations, making it virtually impossible to keep spies inside his lab. That Zadovsky had already been in Belarus longer than usual had been attributed to his wife's pregnancy.

But now that Zadovsky's son was four months old—

"I just hung up from T," Rocco said. "He wants Assman to get this data out of here tonight."

Assman was Rocco's nickname for the fourth member of their team, Harry Gambrel. Harry's ghostlike stealthiness made him an ideal courier. But since Rocco and Harry barely tolerated one another, Harry was staying elsewhere. Not a good situation.

Rocco turned back to Max. "T wants you to get a message to Tabby. He wants that recipe book. The whole fucking enchilada. At any cost."

"Does he know how difficult that will be?" Max asked. "Tabby getting access yesterday was an anomaly. It could be weeks before another opportunity arises."

"And we don't have that kind of time," Dante pointed out. "Not if the lab is being moved."

Rocco stuffed his hands in his front pockets. "It was suggested we create another diversion at the lab."

"Getting inside to do that will be impossible. People are there twenty-four/seven," Max said.

"What do we know about his personal schedule?" Dante asked.

"He doesn't have one," Rocco said. "The man's a paranoid workaholic."

"Then perhaps we need to create a diversion at his residence," Dante suggested. "Something his wife would call him home for."

Chapter 12

The telephone on Viktor Zadovsky's desk seemed to grow louder, more demanding, with each ring. It didn't help that there were actually two lines ringing simultaneously.

On the intercom would be his secretary, Bohdana, which angered him. When he said he did not want to be disturbed, he meant it. She could be so bright about some things.

The second line was a private number that only a select few had. And instead of leaving a message, the caller was hanging up and redialing. It didn't take much to deduce who it was. Or what he was calling about.

One more reason to ignore *that* line.

Viktor continued perusing the supplies requisition item by item, initialing each line after quizzing the nervous male lab assistant who sat across from his desk.

"And you're sure this is needed in such quantity?" It didn't matter that the item was as benign as denatured alcohol. The tone of his query flustered the assistant and enforced the message that Viktor had his eye on everything. Everything.

Viktor knew they all talked about his idiosyncrasies behind his back and he went out of his way to make certain they had plenty to discuss. Controlled gossip.

The phone quit ringing, both lines hushing in unison. *Finally.* Quietude exploded, emphasizing the rustle of paper, the muffled tick of the clock on his credenza. He relaxed.

Until the door to his office suddenly flew open, smacking the wall with a loud *bam*. Viktor's startled assistant jumped to his feet, scattering the files that had been on his lap.

Viktor charged forward, but stopped short when he recognized the man who had burst in unannounced. He felt the warmth of guilt rising in his cheeks. Did the man know?

An indignant Bohdana charged in right behind, nearly plowing into the man's backside. "Sir! How dare you!" she hissed, grabbing his arm. "I told you! Dr. Zadovsky is with someone. You must leave at once."

The man casually shook off Bohdana's flapping hands. "Hey, Doc. You want to help me out here?"

Victor didn't respond, counting in his head. *Eleven seconds, twelve seconds.*

The metallic clack of a round being chambered in a gun got everyone's attention. Viktor's lab assistant whimpered and sank back down in the chair, his face pale. If the imbecile fainted . . .

"Still got your posse, I see." The interloper raised his

hands as he spoke over one shoulder. "Hello, Karl. Long time, no shoot."

Karl Romanov, Viktor's bodyguard/personal aide, shoved the man's shoulder with the barrel of his gun. "I vouldn't press your luck, Mr. Peabody." That last word was spat out with a don't-tempt-me-to-use-your-real-name sneer.

"Oh, come on now," the man responded with a forced laugh. "I wanted to surprise my old friend. Poor choice of tactics, I see."

This last was clearly said for the benefit of Viktor's confused lab assistant and secretary. Make like it had been a joke. How original.

Karl looked to Viktor for direction. It was reassuring to know that in certain circumstances words were unnecessary. With only a slight nod, *Mr. Peabody's* brain would be splatter. Wouldn't his employees have a field day with that one?

"A poor choice, indeed." Viktor's glance went from his lab assistant to his secretary. "That will be all."

His harried assistant scrabbled to the floor, gathering his papers before following Bohdana out. Karl waited a few moments then left, too, pulling the door closed in such a way that there was little doubt he'd be right outside.

"What do you think you're doing storming in here like that?" Viktor moved behind his desk, but didn't sit.

"If you'd answer your goddamn phone. I've been trying to reach you for three days."

"I've been under the weather."

"You look fine to me."

"Yes. And as one might imagine, I'm running quite

behind here, so?" He rolled his hand, as if he were too busy to even finish the sentence. *What is so urgent you have to bother me in person?*

But beneath Viktor's lab coat, sweat pooled under his arms. And beneath his skin, his pulse thundered.

"We have a situation. Somebody blew up Dante Johnson's sailboat a couple days ago."

Act surprised. "He . . . he is dead?"

"No. But whoever's responsible has fucked up everything. We can't get near him now."

Actually, the fuck-up occurred prior to the explosion. But of course he couldn't say that.

"It's just a delay," Viktor offered instead. "Give it time; let the smoke clear."

"We've given it too much time already. I shouldn't have let you talk me out of killing him two years ago."

"He proved far more valuable alive. Look at the strides that were made."

"If they were really strides, why can't you replicate them?"

"Idiot!" Viktor began cursing in Russian. "You have no idea what is involved in these processes."

"Maybe I don't. But our mutual friend does."

"Do you expect me to be impressed?"

"I expect you to remember that without our friend's disinformation campaign, we couldn't move about as freely. Despite our little deal, I still have to answer to him. And he's not happy to hear the timeline is wavering again."

"Have you told our *friend* that some of the delays are his own fault? The last two shipments of opium derivatives were contaminated."

"He is working that through the supplier."

"You might also point out that we gave him a five-year window going in. Based on that, we're actually ahead of schedule. I would have thought he'd be pleased to learn I've restarted human trials."

"He's pleased all right. But now he's demanding copies of the preliminary studies."

"If he thinks to double-cross me—"

"With whom? You're light-years ahead of everyone else."

"Then remind your friend of that. Remind him these things take time." *Remind him my work is mine.*

The man tugged out a cigarette, but didn't light it. "Level with me, Doc. Exactly how close are you?"

"Less than six months."

"You said that four months ago."

"There were unforeseen problems associated with moving our last facility. We're still not up to full capacity." Viktor pointed to his overflowing IN basket, as if it held answers. "Now finish telling me about Dante Johnson. You had planned to make a move against him yourself?"

"Hardly. A few key players are still on high alert, watching out for him. I had planned to wait until he took off in that damn boat. People disappear on the high seas all the time." The man twirled the cigarette now. "Unfortunately, this explosion has refocused attention on his case. Which is the real reason for my visit. We've been ordered to stay underground until the fallout settles. Too many questions being asked. We're to remain incommunicado until he gives the all clear."

Viktor bristled. He didn't *take* orders. Except . . . With the others lying low, he could move about more discreetly.

He let out a dramatic sigh. Then he lowered his voice, feigning compliance.

"Very well, then. Actually, this may work to our collective advantage. If I'm not being constantly interrupted, I can concentrate on finishing up these projects. Perhaps ahead of schedule."

At those words, the man brightened. "Then I will leave you to it. By the way, I need an advance from the slush fund. I'll get nothing from our friend until this blows over."

Again, Viktor kept his features slack. "I've got thirty-five thousand Euros in the safe. More than that will require a transfer."

"What you've got is fine. I'd rather we didn't create a paper trail right now."

Viktor moved to the safe built into his credenza. Early in their relationship, he had learned the other man was easily distracted by cash. Withdrawing a heavy envelope, Viktor straightened. "Here. How will I know when it's safe to contact you?"

The other man pocketed the envelope. "I'll be in touch via our usual methods." By that the man meant their maze of coded, untraceable e-mails. "You do the same, you hear?"

When the man left, Viktor slid back into his chair, mentally and emotionally exhausted.

He couldn't keep this up much longer. The complex tangle of webs that were his life were tangling, knotting, collapsing. And to think that barely twelve months ago he'd been on top of the world—

There was a brisk rapping at his door.

"Yes." He sat up and grabbed a file, pretended to study it. It was Karl. "He arrived by taxi. I'm having him tailed."

"Let me know when he leaves town."

"Do you want him followed?"

"No. I don't want to spook him. And I don't want to spread our resources too thin at this time. Any word from Grigori?"

"Nothing new."

"Very well. Keep me posted."

"Yes, sir."

"And Karl." Viktor waited until the former KGB agent faced him again. "Next time make it less than twelve seconds."

Both men knew that short of Karl shadowing Viktor— which he would do if asked—twelve seconds was damn good.

When Karl left, Viktor summoned Bohdana, who bravely held back tears as he berated her. There had probably been little she could have done differently, but it wasn't in his nature to show mercy.

After she left, Viktor locked his office door and moved to the window. His office overlooked the crowded harbor. God, he hated it here. Jakarta was a godforsaken swath of dirt, its people at the mercy of a corrupt government.

Of course, that corruption was what allowed Viktor to operate with anonymity. His high-level military connections believed they would receive cutting-edge biotechnology in exchange for hosting and protecting him.

But how much longer could Viktor maintain the charade?

The barbarians were at the doors and windows. If he didn't come up with a solid resolution soon, everything would fall apart.

And it was all *her* fault. When he got his hands on Catalina Dion . . .

He started toward his desk, rubbing his hip. The throb was a reminder that he should have taken a pain tablet an hour ago. Something else that was *her* fault. His pelvis had been shattered in that car accident. His whole life had been shattered.

After swallowing the pill, Viktor opened a file on his computer. He reread the reports, looking for something new; something he'd overlooked.

The truth of the matter was the CIA had no clue where Catalina Dion was. No one did. Even Dante Johnson had seemed to buy the bullshit story that she was dead. Johnson's failure to make more than a few cursory inquiries had forced Viktor to take harsher action. Was it working?

Viktor had to get his hands on Catalina *now*. Everything he'd worked for, all his plans, teetered on finding her. He opened Johnson's dossier. What a supreme injustice to actually need Johnson's help to track down the bitch who had stolen his life's work.

The thought that Johnson was his last hope made him ill.

Closing the files, Viktor steepled his fingers beneath his chin. His gaze fell on the gilt-edged frame beside his telephone. Beneath the glass was the last photograph taken of his wife and son. Lera. Adrik.

Both were dead, rotting in the ground. And the people responsible . . . Dante Johnson and Catalina Dion . . . hadn't finished paying for their deaths.

The painkiller Viktor had taken finally kicked in, its trademark euphoria claiming him. He knew it wouldn't last long, but while it did . . .

He picked up the frame and traced the woman's smile with his finger.

Chapter 13

"Uzbekistan? I don't want to move there, Viktor! They say the air is so thick you can scarcely breathe. And if you won't think of my comfort, think of Adrik. He's so tiny yet."

"We will get a house in the country then."

"But I like the city. Why can't you seek a position in the West?"

Viktor sighed. He should have waited to tell her. "Not everyone in the West understands my work, Lera."

This brought a laugh to her lips. "I don't understand your work! But I do understand you have no small amount of power. Use it, my darling! Demand they build you a new facility someplace clean. And warm."

"Are you saying you want more sunshine? We could plan a trip—"

The ringing of his personal cell phone interrupted him. Viktor glanced at the display, then held up a hand. The call, while expected, wasn't urgent. However, it was important they talked today. "Give me one moment."

Ever obedient, Lera turned and began gathering their lunch containers. The slight slump of her shoulders was the only outward indication of her disappointment. She might complain for a moment after he hung up, but she never stayed mad. It was more like listening to a tiny bluebird squawk over a lost seed. A little bluebird that could so easily be made happy by another seed.

Perhaps he'd send her and Adrik to visit his aunt in Berlin. They could shop, see a ballet. Lera loved the ballet. In most ways, she was such an ideal wife. Young. Trusting. Generally cheerful. She asked no questions about his work, and her complaints about his long hours had dwindled to nothing since little Adrik's arrival. She was even starting to make noise about having a second child.

Yes, a perfect wife; a perfect son. And with his new deal, they were on the verge of having it all. If she still wanted sun then, he'd buy her a private island in the Caribbean.

He spoke into the phone, his attention on the lullaby Lera sang to their son. "I will call you back shortly. I am with someone."

"That may be too late."

Alarmed, Viktor turned his back to his wife. His voice dropped to a hiss. "Is this regarding our previous discussion?"

"Yes. Except the time schedule has changed drastically. We believe you now have less than twelve hours."

A herd of questions stampeded through his mind, but he knew better than to voice them. Not in front of Lera. And certainly not on a phone that wasn't secure.

"I see." The other party had already disconnected but he kept up the pretense in front of his wife, staring into space, weighing options. "Then perhaps we can meet tomorrow? Please call my secretary to make an appointment."

There had been rumors for weeks that the *Institut* was under surveillance. He'd taken appropriate measures, but . . .

"Come and kiss your son, Viktor. Adrik is getting fussy." Lera interrupted his thoughts. "And we will leave you to your work."

Pushing to his feet, Viktor straightened his jacket. "If you will give me a moment, I will drive home with you. Along the way we can talk about taking a holiday."

"You're taking the afternoon off?" His little bluebird smiled. "Should I shout it out to your employees? They'll think you've gone mad."

Immediately he frowned. "I'd prefer they thought I was simply driving you and Adrik home. If they believe I will return shortly, the productivity will remain high." Grabbing his briefcase, he set it on his desk. "Let me gather a few things and speak to my assistant."

"I'm going to change Adrik, then."

As soon as Lera and the baby swept out, Viktor slipped into the night manager's office that was adjacent to his. Not bothering with the overhead light, he turned on the computer and attached the external hard drive. His fingers flew over the computer keys, backing up the day's work to both hard drives. As soon as that finished, he disconnected the external one and slid it into his pocket.

Then he typed in a final command on the keyboard. This had to be perfect. He read back the string, made one correction, and then paused before hitting ENTER. The enormity of what he was doing hit him like a physical blow. Destroying years of research. Years of test data, irreplaceable studies.

You have copies of it all, he reminded himself. *Nothing will be lost.* And it was all borne of his genius to begin with. This was merely insurance that no one would profit from his work after he'd left!

Viktor hit the key, watched the virus program launch and then hibernate. It was time delayed. He shut off the monitor and hurried back to his own office, where he placed the external hard drive into his briefcase, right beside his personal notebook. *That* was the true Holy Grail. The stuff he deigned to let the others see was nothing compared to the brilliance spilled onto the pages of that notebook.

Lera bounded back through the door just then, Adrik whimpering in her arms. "You're still not finished? The baby needs his nap."

"On the contrary, I am finished. Come along."

On the way out, Viktor motioned to the pert blonde who served as his assistant. She smiled shyly at him, crossing and uncrossing her arms in a nervous gesture that raised and lowered her lovely breasts. He'd once overheard her whispered gushes to another employee and recognized that she'd had a crush. On him.

He'd miss her.

It was strange to think there had actually been a time at the end of Lera's pregnancy that he'd entertained the idea of seducing her. But then his son had been born. And instead of feeling tired, Lera was so eager to have more children she actually hounded him for sex now.

"Little Adrik isn't feeling well," Viktor explained. "I'm going to drive him and his mother home. If you need to reach me before I return, call my mobile phone."

Outside the building, he grasped Lera's arm and hurried to the car. Whether it was guilt over what he'd done, or something else, the urge to flee was suddenly quite strong.

"Slow down, please, Viktor! I will trip."

He eased up, but not by much.

When they reached Lera's Mercedes, he yanked open the passenger door.

"I should put Adrik in his seat in the back," she began.

"He is fretting right now. Perhaps if you hold him, he'll drift off to sleep."

"But my lap belt."

"Lera, please! We're only a short distance from the house."

He shut her door and climbed behind the wheel. He had a name for the feeling now: a distinct sensation that he was being watched. Had someone inside caught on to him already?

Two white vans were turning into the car lot as he was pulling out. Maybe it was nothing, but there had been something about the way the driver of the first had looked at him as he'd shot past that made Viktor nervous.

In his rearview mirror, he watched the second van's brake lights come on. The van immediately came shooting backward, wheels screaming as it shot out into the street again, just missing a red sedan.

Viktor punched the accelerator, swerving to avoid a bicyclist. "Hold on, Lera."

She looked at him as if he were crazy. "What's

wrong?" She grabbed the dash in front of her, bracing her arm. "Slow down, Viktor!"

Adrik was crying in earnest now, which distracted Lera momentarily as Viktor zigzagged through the streets, uncertain where to go. Who were the men in the vans? KGB, State Security Agents? Had the warning come too late? Was someone at the *Institut* already aware of his plan?

No! He'd been plenty cautious. Borderline fanatic. Which meant his pursuers could also be thugs. Kidnappers even. He mentally reviewed a list of his potential enemies. It was longer than he liked.

Whoever this was, he didn't want to lead them to his secluded estate and chance being trapped. And he couldn't risk going to the police as it was even possible that the men inside the van were the local authorities working on behest of the State.

"Viktor, I beg you—slow down!" Lera screamed, grabbing at his arm even as she tried to hold on to the baby. "You're going to kill us! Kill your son!"

Shoving her hand away, he glanced in the rearview mirror. Only one of the vans had followed, and it was gaining on them. Where had the other van gone? To cut them off?

Viktor ran a traffic light. The van followed, swerving wildly to avoid hitting another car as it passed through the intersection.

Lera had glanced over her shoulder, only now understanding that they were being chased. "Who are those men? And why are they wearing masks? A gun!"

She screamed at the same time the back window of the Mercedes exploded.

"Get down!" Viktor shouted.

He drove wildly, heading toward the downtown district. In spite of the chaos, his thoughts cleared. He knew exactly what to do. He'd go straight to the police after all.

In his mind, he imagined storming into the station, outraged and indignant. *Some idiots are chasing us. They terrified my wife and son. I was afraid they were trying to kidnap us. I have received threats.*

If necessary, he could twist the events to make himself appear a hero. He had, after all, taken steps to frame the incompetent night manager. Viktor could further save the day by producing a backup copy of the computer files, stored offsite of course.

The van closed in again, this time speeding up and bumping the back of the Mercedes. Lera and Adrik were both wailing and he needed to calm them.

"Just a few more blocks, Lera. And I swear we'll be safe."

Hitting the gas, Viktor cut down an alley. He clipped a large metal garbage bin as he plunged into the narrow space between the two run-down buildings. He knew where he was now. This shortcut would bring him out just a block from the police barracks.

Forced to divide his attention between the alley and the rearview mirror, he didn't see the man until he was almost on him. Somehow he managed to miss the pedestrian.

Still maxing out the throttle, Viktor sent the car hurtling toward the opening just ahead. They'd make it—as long as a delivery truck, or that other van—didn't turn in and block their escape.

He glanced in the rearview mirror again, surprised when the van appeared to have slowed some, almost as if it were breaking off the pursuit. Had they realized where he was heading?

"Ha! You cowards," he shouted and grinned over at his frightened wife and son. Hitting the mouth of the alley, he jerked the wheel hard to the right, the Mercedes bursting onto the street.

And into the path of another car. Lera screamed.

Swearing, Viktor swerved, but almost immediately realized that the car had gotten away from him. Lera was still screaming as the vehicle slammed into a large truck parked in the road. Something smashed into them from behind, causing the Mercedes to go airborne, flipping end over end before slamming to earth. His neck whiplashed, sending agony down his spine. His arm was broken, useless.

And then there was nothing. No more pain. No more screaming. No light.

Sometime later, he floated up from darkness. He blinked, eyes stinging. The pain returned, slowly at first, and then with more severity. He'd obviously passed out for a few seconds.

The sound of sirens grew more pronounced. Someone was trying to get his door open.

"Lera?"

It hurt to turn his head, but his wife, his son were so quiet now. He expected to see blood and prayed their injuries would not be too severe.

The front seat was empty. But the windshield had a gaping hole in the glass.

"Lera!"

Unable to move, he focused on the rearview mirror. Behind him, a crowd huddled around a lifeless form in the road.

A lifeless little bluebird wearing the same exact coat as Lera.

Chapter 14

Key West, Florida
July 7
(Present Day)

It took barely a half-week for Dante's place to look as if he'd been there a month. Pizza and Chinese carryout boxes overflowed the kitchen garbage can. Dirty plates and cups were stacked in the sink.

Travis had returned to Langley four days ago. Rocco had gone on to Gitmo for appearances' sake, but had returned to Key West late last night.

Dante stood in the center of the living room, explaining what he'd done while Rocco sucked down a cup of coffee and polished off a slice of cold pizza. Breakfast of champions.

"It looks like an office supply truck took a dump in here," Rocco observed between chews.

He wasn't too far off the mark. Dante had taken down the apartment's mismatched seascapes and covered most of the wall with paper. Photographs, maps, charts, time lines. Other reports and files covered the coffee table.

As promised, Travis had been e-mailing copies of Dante's old case files. After reading everything, Dante printed and highlighted key parts, then sorted and re-sorted the info by jobs, known associates, and personal data.

Because they'd worked together, most of Rocco's, Max's, and Harry's assignments were included as well.

"Damn, I'd forgotten about half of these, too," Rocco complained. "Please tell me the mind is the first thing to go. What's your overall assessment on disgruntled adversaries?"

"Excluding the Taliban—they hate the world—the most likely players are Minh Tran and Obert Svenson." Svenson was another slippery arms dealer they'd tried unsuccessfully to take down.

"My money's still on Tran," Rocco said. "Has Travis connected either of them to Cat?"

"She and Max worked the Svenson case with MI6. Nothing solid on Tran yet."

Rocco pointed to another list. "What about DeBono? And the Belarus job?"

"DeBono died last year in prison. Viktor Zadovsky never fully recovered from that wreck. He's still in Belarus, in a nursing home. His partner died when the Chechen rebels invaded the institute."

"Chechens. Now there's another nice bunch," Rocco muttered as he studied the pins stuck in the map. "Is there a geographic pattern to these cases?"

"None. The assignments seem random regardless of whether I sort them by person, locale, or date."

Rocco picked up a British security report stamped EYES

ONLY. "When I grow up, I want to be Travis. He's got more contacts than God." Setting his coffee mug aside, he flipped through the report. "How much you wanna bet T's one of those nameless rogues we hear about who run shadow government agencies behind our backs."

"He's not old and stodgy enough. But it would explain how he comes up with stuff." Dante was referring to the foreign files Travis had managed to access on Catalina Dion. As a contractor, she'd worked for other agencies as well as the CIA.

"Did you know that Cat had been doing this for so long?" Rocco asked.

Dante shook his head, started to say, *We fucked more than we talked.* But that sounded like braggadocio. Or sour grapes. Hell, rotten grapes. "From what I can tell, she turned pro thirteen years ago."

"She's got more aliases than I do. Do we know if Dion is even her real surname?"

"No. But all the big players had that same birth certificate and it appears authentic."

"Whoopee shit."

"Exactly. Travis ran down vitals, parents, etc., but there are no living relatives." The birth certificate in question showed that Catalina Maria Dion was born in Barcelona, Spain, thirty-three years ago.

Other documents had her age ranging between twenty-seven and thirty-five, a factor that in this business, wasn't unusual.

Dante was thirty-six, but over the years, he'd had IDs ranging a fifteen-year span. He'd also used multiple aliases; it had been a running joke between him and Cat that neither of them knew the other's real name.

Which at the time had been copacetic. It was an unwritten rule not to ask personal questions of people they worked with. It was also second nature to give away little. Or to simply adapt lies from their cover personas.

He'd done it plenty of times. In fantasy, he could make his life sound like it rivaled James Bond's. Cat's had sounded like Mata Hari Meets Bat Girl.

"She's definitely worked for all the major security agencies." Rocco read a list. "England, Israel, France."

"Almost every American ally. Travis is also checking out who she didn't work for. Right now, though, it appears she was in a position to cherry pick assignments. Everyone wanted her."

A person with Cat's skill set would be in constant demand. She was fluent in multiple languages and could mimic dialects perfectly. Combine that with her near perfect photographic memory, her mastery of disguise, and her explosives background, and she was any security agency's wet dream.

"So who did the initial background and clearances on her—however many years ago?" Rocco asked.

"She started with MI6, working directly under Remi St. James." Remi St. James was the infamous British spymaster who'd gone on to open a private security firm after his so-called retirement from MI6. "If St. James vetted her, she would have been considered golden. Untouchable." Translation: No background checks needed.

"Didn't St. James leave the biz for good after nine/eleven?"

"Actually he closed shop and vanished right around the same time I was captured," Dante said. "He's another literal dead end."

"Does Travis think he's been murdered, too?"

Nodding, Dante moved to another grouping of papers tacked up on the wall. "The odds aren't in his favor. See this list? It's Cat's known associates. The ones on the left are confirmed homicides." Max and Harry topped the list. In the last four months, two MI6 agents, and one Mossad operative had all died in deliberate bombings. "Travis got the preliminary lab reports on my boat. The explosive used was identical to what was used overseas. Semtex."

"New stuff?"

"Brand new. Whoever designed that bomb was advertising." The detection taggants that were now added to plastic explosive gave it a distinctive vapor signature. It was as identifiable as a fingerprint; not the type of mistake a pro would make.

He eyed the list of dead agents. Had any of these men caught a whiff of cologne before their brains were blown out?

Rocco pointed to the bottom. "Why are these names scratched off?"

"Their deaths have been attributed to verifiable causes. Those last two guys died in a raid on an Afghanistan stronghold."

Now Rocco's attention shifted to the four names on the right-hand side. "Alive: You and I. Gotcha. Remi St. James with a question mark. And who is Giselle Barclay?"

"You knew her as Topaz. Turns out she was our source on the Pakistan job. She was also St. James's lover, so she stayed behind the scenes. However, she was also a friend of Cat's. And Giselle disappeared around the same time St. James did."

"Find one, I bet you'll find them both. Any chance they're working with Cat?"

"Travis says no on St. James, or else MI6 would have a noticeable hard-on. They consider St. James a national hero." If St. James were indeed dead by Cat's hand, there would be holy hell to pay if the Brits caught her first. "Giselle's a wild card."

"Hold that thought. I need more caffeine." Rocco grabbed his cup and disappeared into the kitchen.

Alone, Dante focused on the most barren spot on the wall: the section containing personal data on Cat.

There were lots of pictures. The camera obviously loved her. He knew the short, blond hair he'd seen her with most frequently had been artificial. Yeah, she'd been meticulous about roots, but no one had that shade of white blond hair naturally.

He studied the various shots. Were any of them the *real* Catalina Dion? She was adept with wigs and makeup, frequently using facial prostheses to disguise her natural beauty.

Rocco returned with more pizza in hand. "Any reports of video exposés on the other agents?"

"None besides me."

Rocco squinted. "I don't get it. If she's trying to cover her tracks by eliminating anyone who might know personal details—why be so blatant with the cologne? The Semtex?"

"Beats the shit out of me, too. We're missing something."

"What did you learn about her fake demise?" Rocco asked.

"According to the death certificate, Margo Sheldon, a known alias of Cat's, drowned just outside of Paris, in the Seine. A year ago. Police received an anonymous call that a woman had jumped from a bridge. The body was identified by a woman claiming to be her sister, Bernice, who filed a missing person complaint the day before. The coroner noted track marks on the victim's arms and legs and her *sister* confirmed that Margo had a drug problem."

Rocco groaned. "It doesn't get more clichéd than that. Find a homeless addict with the correct physical resemblance, shoot her up, and stage an accident. Bet the body was cremated."

"Yup. And it gets better. The photographs and lab samples disappeared as well."

Dante's phone rang just then. Travis had supplied both men with tricked-out cell phones modified to deter detection.

"Rocco back?" Travis asked when Dante answered.

"Yeah, he's here."

"Good. Check your e-mail. I got a lead on Remi St. James."

Stepping over the coffee table, Dante moved to fire up his laptop. "Tell me it's not another body."

"It's not. Turns out St. James was diagnosed with lung cancer almost two years ago. Surgery and conventional chemo didn't help, so he opted to try an experimental treatment in Jamaica, which actually seemed successful. Until he was diagnosed with early Alzheimer's."

Jesus. "What a waste." Dante had never met Remi St. James, but was familiar with the man's reputation. "Is he still in Jamaica?"

"Negative. But the doctor who treated him there is affiliated with another experimental clinic in the Bahamas. For Alzheimer's."

"Can we confirm patient registrations?"

"I've struck out with all the alibis I know St. James has used. And most of the superwealthy clientele at the

Bahamas check in under aliases anyway. Lots of celebs. We'll need a visual."

Dante glanced at his watch. It was eleven o'clock. "I can be in Freeport this afternoon."

Under the guise of researching treatment options for his fictional mother, Dante was able to book an appointment at the Freeport clinic for the next morning. Rocco had opted to stay in Key West to review the new files Travis sent, but as Dante eyed the clinic's exterior, he wondered if he should have stayed in Key West. Places like this, no matter how nice, made him feel uncomfortable. "Experimental" brought to mind guinea pigs. Is that how they viewed patients here?

Nouveau Place looked more like an exclusive hotel than clinic. Private and exclusive, the walled compound exuded a quiet desperation. A confirmation that money didn't buy everything.

Dante arrived early for his 10 a.m. meeting with the clinic's new patient representative, Sally McDonald.

Sally greeted him warmly and offered a tour. "So how did you hear about us?"

"A friend of my mother's is being treated here." When Sally didn't ask for a name, Dante went on. "I've done some research, but wanted to see your facility personally before building up my family's hopes."

"That's understandable." Sally was an attractive brunette, whose tanned skin made her look older than forty-two. Still she was the picture of empathy. "How long since your mother's diagnosis?"

"Three weeks. Seems longer."

"It always does." She led the way, showing off the private gardens first. The neatly manicured plants had an artificial look, the blooms reminding Dante of flowers from a funeral spray. The few patients and staff that he saw were all female.

As they walked, they discussed Dante's mother's disease, created right off the Internet.

"The options we've been given aren't pleasant," Dante said.

"That's where treatment centers such as this come in."

Treatment. He stopped cold, as a picture floated across his mind. He'd been strapped to a table once . . . But where?

"We offer hope," Sally was saying. "In a landscape that's very bleak."

"Exactly." He took a deep breath, wondering how much of the conversation he'd blanked out.

Sally touched his hand briefly, the empathy once more resurfacing. "I understand how upsetting this must be for you. For all the strides medicine has made, there is much to be conquered. Let me show you one of our guest suites now."

Dante's hopes of checking out more patients were dashed by a hallway lined with closed doors.

After the tour, they ended up in Sally's office. He sat in one of the chairs in front of her desk, while she gathered a packet of information.

"Some of these forms may seem redundant," she said. "But we believe in being thorough. Our fee schedule is all-inclusive and based on the patient's level of self-care. Also, there's a list of the medical information we would need on your mother in order to do a preliminary evaluation. If you like, I'd be happy to review these with you."

She leaned slightly forward and gave him an *I'm available* smile.

"By all means." Dante tugged out the chair next to his, encouraging the woman's flirting.

She moved from behind her desk and slid in the offered seat. For the next thirty minutes, they discussed the forms and the clinic, while politely volleying personal questions.

He learned that Sally was divorced. She promised to show him the island when he returned.

"And last but not least, we have the releases," she said. "As you know, our treatments, while successful, are considered experimental. If someone in the family has been appointed guardian, they will need to sign these. Any questions?"

Lots of questions, he thought. "I believe you covered everything, though I'm sure my sister will think of something I forgot to ask." He forced a grin. "Actually, I'd like to take you to lunch. If you're available, that is."

Sally beamed. "I have to wait until my assistant returns. I could meet you someplace if you'd like."

"I don't mind hanging around. In fact, maybe you can help me with one other matter. I'd like to check on my mother's friend, but I'm embarrassed to admit I've forgotten his name." He made a show of checking his pockets before opening his briefcase. "Mom gave me some old photographs to share with him, but it looks like I've lost them, too. No! Here they are." He withdrew several pictures, then handed her the most recent shot of Remi St. James. "Knowing Mom, this isn't a current picture. She gets things mixed up."

"That's common." Sally's smile faded as soon as she looked at the photograph. "This looks like Mr. Barry."

"Yes!" Dante snapped his fingers, pretending not to notice her sudden reticence. "That sounds familiar. While you're waiting for your assistant, could I say hello, perhaps show Mr. Barry the other photos Mom sent?"

"I'm afraid that's not possible."

"Patient privacy, right? I'd never ask you to break a rule."

"In this case . . . well, it's not exactly a rule." Sally chose her words carefully. "Mr. Barry passed away."

Dante wanted to gnash his teeth. "When?"

"Just last week."

He'd get the exact date from her shortly. "I'm sorry. I hadn't heard. I suppose I should have contacted his family before coming here."

"Um, how well do you know Mr. Barry's family? Do you by chance have contact information for them?"

"Not with me," he said. "Is there something I could perhaps pass along when I get home?"

"No." It was evident Sally had an internal debate going on inside her head. Patient privacy would be one issue. The clinic's image another. You didn't sell medical services by advertising dead clients.

"From what I gathered, Mr. Barry's prognosis wasn't good to begin with. I'm sure the clinic did everything possible." Dante dropped his voice. "If you'd like, I could call my sister later; perhaps ask her to get a phone number from Mom's address book."

"Would you mind?"

"Not at all. I'll admit I'm a little surprised you don't

have it already. Unless . . . Oh, I get it. His family didn't know he was here, did they?"

Her eyes flared, but her voice remained businesslike. "They knew. One of them at least. Actually I should probably contact the authorities while you're here. They might be interested in whatever information you have."

There was only reason why the local authorities were involved: suspicious death.

"I doubt I can be of help. I, uh, sense we're both tiptoeing around here, trying to avoid asking each other for private information. Tell you what." He touched the top of her hand. "Let's agree this discussion is off the record."

Sally's eyes softened, and then she nodded. "Mr. Barry took his own life, but I must emphasize it was through no fault or negligence on the clinic's part. It's believed his daughter helped, both in supplying the drug and in distracting his private nurse."

His daughter. To Dante's knowledge, Remi St. James had no children.

"Mom mentioned his daughter. Said we'd played together as young children, though I don't recall it." Dante shuffled the remaining photos he still held. "In fact, this is supposed to be a photograph Mr. Barry sent my mom a few years back."

Sally cocked her head to one side as she looked at the photograph of Catalina Dion. "I'm not sure. The hair's different. But . . ." Using her fingers, she cropped off the blond hair, then nodded. "Yes, that's her. I only met her twice, but I recognize her eyes."

Cat's eyes. Dante blocked the memory of flashing green eyes.

"What's different about the hair?" he asked.

"When I met her, it was shoulder length and red. A tacky artificial orange-red. Like a wig."

"And when did you last see her?"

Sally glanced at the calendar on the wall. "The day her father died. July second."

Chapter 15

Freeport, Grand Bahamas
July 8
(Present Day)

Lunch with Sally yielded little new information regarding Remi St. James. According to her, *Mr. Barry* had been treated like an A-list celebrity.

"I wasn't even certain that was his real name," she admitted. "We do have patients who come and go under extreme privacy measures. Frequently, the administrative staff aren't even aware of their presence."

Over the course of an hour and a half, Dante learned that St. James had been a patient at the clinic for less than three months and that initially the treatment appeared to arrest and reverse the progression of his Alzheimer's.

"Unfortunately, about a month ago, he suffered a stroke," Sally said. "Which left him largely paralyzed and unable to continue with the treatment."

Dante read between the lines. Without the experimental

drugs, St. James faced the certainty that the Alzheimer's would return.

Jesus, did the people coming here realize they faced eternal treatments? And had anyone questioned the connection between the treatment and the stroke?

Focus on Cat. "You said his daughter only visited twice. When was the first time?"

"Right after his stroke. Come to think of it, that first time she was accompanied by an elderly gentleman in a wheelchair."

This piqued Dante's attention, and while Sally couldn't provide any other description, it did prove Cat had an accomplice. No doubt the wheelchair was a ruse.

"If Mr. Barry was paralyzed," Dante said. "How did he kill himself?"

"According to the coroner, he bit into a cyanide-type capsule. Technically, I suppose it was an assisted suicide."

Sally used the term as if it were a decision born of loving compassion. The Cat Dante recalled from the video had no such compassion.

"Could it have been something other than an assisted suicide? I mean his daughter had just visited."

Sally dismissed the notion with a wave of her hand. "No. Absolutely not. A nurse had been with him several hours after his daughter left. From what I understand, cyanide is fast acting. We do believe his daughter hid the capsule in his sheets, where he could access it with a slight turn of his head."

Dante grimaced at the thought of spending his days strapped to a bed, while slowly losing his mind. Yeah, cyanide would do the job.

"In her own way," Sally went on, "his daughter may

have thought she was helping him. He, um, let it be known how he felt in regards to his prognosis."

"Guess we'll never know." At least not until Dante located Cat.

Sally had driven her own car and had to rush off for an afternoon appointment, but before leaving she gave him her personal cell phone number with a sly wink. "Call anytime."

After settling the tab, Dante left the restaurant and made his way through the crowded Port Lucaya Marketplace. He'd suggested this spot for lunch both to support his image as a visitor and to get Sally as far removed from the office as possible. He wanted her guard lowered; he wanted to distance her from her business setting.

It had worked. Short of producing St. James's medical files—which the coroner had—she had answered his questions. And raised a few. Dante couldn't reconcile the two images of Cat. One as a dark angel, one as a cold-blooded murderess. Her presence here on July 2 also skewed the timeline of events, the logistics.

If Cat had indeed been in Freeport less than twelve hours before Dante's boat blew, she had to have help. And Dante now had a pretty good idea who that helper was.

He tugged out his cell phone and hit Travis Franks's number. While waiting for the number to ring, he pressed the phone to his ear, trying to block the snatches of conversation that floated his way in English, Italian, and French. A small child cried in the universal language of tears.

"I found St. James," he said when Travis answered.

"You don't sound too happy about it."

"Hold on." He ducked into an alcove, where it was quieter. Then he filled Travis in on what he'd learned.

"Damn shame he's gone," Travis said. "The man was a legend. Did you convince your contact to let you have a look at his records?"

"The clinic turned all his files over to the medical examiner. The ME's holding his body, pending a full investigation."

"I've got contacts down there," Travis said. "Maybe I can get prints to verify it was in fact St. James."

"I'm curious what his records have for personal data, too." While it was likely all fabricated, Dante knew better than to assume. It wasn't unusual for a big case to turn on the smallest, most unobtrusive slip.

"There's only one other person we can't account for now," Dante went on. "And that's St. James's former girlfriend, Giselle Barclay. She and Cat knew each other. The first time Cat visited St. James, she was accompanied by someone in a wheelchair. I suspect that may have been Giselle in disguise."

"Best friends forever," Travis said.

"No shit. Cat's final visit here was the same day my boat was destroyed. Even with a private plane on standby, she would have been hard-pressed to have gotten to Key West in time to procure and set the explosives."

"I'll start by getting the passenger manifests, both commercial and private, for July second."

"I can look over the lists, too." Dante didn't expect Cat to use one of her better-known aliases, but an obscure one might jump out.

"I'll also dig deeper on Barclay's and St. James's

relationship," Travis said. "When are you headed back to Key West?"

"Tonight."

"Call me tomorrow."

After disconnecting, Dante rejoined the crowd. As he headed toward the taxi queue out front he stepped sideways to accommodate a woman pushing a double stroller the size of a Mac truck. He accidently brushed shoulders with a woman headed in the opposite direction.

That's when he smelled it.

Cat's cologne.

Dante jerked as if physically struck. What the fuck?

He sniffed the air but the elusive scent had already dissipated in the balmy breeze. Turning on his heels, he quickly retraced his steps.

There! He caught the scent again.

It was a no-brainer that she'd tailed him, and that she now wanted him to follow her trail. Alert, he eyed the crowd, looking for the trap. This had SET UP written all over it.

"Come on, show yourself," he muttered.

Heading back toward the restaurant, he followed the maddening scent. It was stronger now. Consistent.

He concentrated on the knot of people dead ahead, zeroing in on one woman who was hurrying away. From him. She was the right height, right build. A scarf covered her hair. One of Cat's favorite tricks. In certain cultures/ locales, a nondescript scarf hid hair color and style, made the person less noticeable.

Moving in closer, Dante inhaled again, confirming that she was the source of the scent. She walked even faster now, her sixth sense undoubtedly kicking in and letting her know she was being followed.

That was the point of this whole charade, right? To lead him to a more private spot, where she probably had an ambush ready. He had to keep her out in the open.

No.

He had to catch her. *Now.*

Rage-tinged adrenaline roared in his ears as anticipation spiked. He was directly behind her. Sweet Jesus . . . this was it!

He grasped her upper arm firmly and spun her back toward him, simultaneously pulling her tightly into his embrace.

Touching her gave him a jolt. A blast of emotional overload. *God, I love this woman.*

At the thought, a lightning bolt of electricity seemed to spear his brain, disorienting him. This woman . . . this bitch had betrayed him.

He had her crushed fully against his chest now, her arms pinned. His hand slid up toward her neck.

"Darling!" He brushed his lips close to hers. "I've been looking all over for you."

The woman's shrill cry of outrage broke through the haze.

A hand grasped Dante from behind just as it registered. *This isn't Cat.* The woman he held was Asian and addressed him angrily in Japanese.

It wasn't . . . . *her.*

The grip on his shoulder tightened. "Let go of my wife!"

Dante complied immediately, moving backward, struggling to control and defuse. What the hell had just happened?

"I am very sorry!" Dante said.

The woman huddled behind her husband as Dante

continued his apology, aware that more than one person stared. "Boy, did I mess up! My wife is wearing a scarf just like that. And she has that same cologne."

"And where is this wife of yours?" The man looked unconvinced.

Dante twisted his head, taking in the crowd. "Beth was supposed to meet me here. If you'll wait, I'm sure she'll be along soon and you'll see for yourself how I made the mistake."

The man turned to speak with his wife, in what Dante assumed was an explanation. The woman nodded and shrugged once, before shaking her head.

"We do not wish to wait," the man said. "In the future you should be more cautious."

"I will. But wait. Would you mind asking your wife the name of the cologne she's wearing? Beth's been hinting that she's almost out and her birthday is next month. I'd like to pick some up, duty-free, as a surprise."

At first it seemed the man was going to refuse. Then he sighed and addressed his wife once again.

This time the woman smiled. "Ahhh." Opening her handbag, she withdrew a slip of paper and scribbled a note, which she passed to her husband with another flurry of Japanese.

Clearly put out, the man quickly translated his wife's writing to English before thrusting the paper at Dante. "She said it's a custom blend and very expensive. From Hong Kong. Here's the formula name and website, so you can order something similar."

Bowing in thanks, Dante watched them hurry away. He pocketed the note and immediately ducked inside the nearest shop. He pretended to look at a rack of souvenir shirts, forcing his hands to quit trembling.

What was wrong with him? The blind rage that had come over him had been instantaneous and mind-numbing. He had been ready to shake the woman violently when he'd thought she was Cat.

Yes, Dante had always had a temper, but he'd also always been able to control it. And yes, he wanted—hell, he lived for—the chance to even the score with Cat. But what he'd just felt, that strong desire—need—to snap her spine in half, had been nearly uncontrollable. He had to get a grip here.

Dante pulled out the scrap of paper and read the woman's note. He hadn't considered that the cologne was a private label, and yet it made perfect sense. Cat used to tease that few men could afford to cater to her fondness of designer clothes, expensive jewelry. The woman had champagne tastes.

He wanted to contact the perfumery ASAP, figure out a way to access their customer list. If by chance they kept it on computer . . .

Feeling calmer, Dante left the store. Tugging out his cell phone again, he punched in Rocco's phone number. He needed to bring his friend up to speed on Remi St. James, but he also wanted to see what kind of contacts Rocco had in Hong Kong.

For the first time since the explosion, he felt encouraged. He hadn't caught up to her yet, but he was getting closer. He could feel it.

Perhaps the cologne was a bigger clue than he realized.

Chapter 16

Key West, Florida
July 8
(Present Day)

Rocco shifted his laptop onto the coffee table in Dante's living room. Damn thing was scorching his legs.

DOWNLOADING . . . 35% COMPLETE flashed on and off. He closed his eyes, felt the fatigue of reading an LCD screen for too long.

Travis had been sending copies of Rocco's case files. He'd omitted the ones that duplicated what Dante already had, but still the number of cases they *hadn't* worked together surprised him.

Initially, he'd been printing them, but ran out of ink cartridges and didn't want to stop to run to the store. And so far, nothing major—or even minor—had surfaced. He hoped that would change with this next batch; the cases he'd worked while Dante had been believed dead.

Gone, he corrected. If Rocco lived ten thousand years, he'd still never forgive himself for not looking harder, faster, better. The thought of his friend being held and tortured all that time . . . It sickened Rocco to recall how many times he'd been in Southeast Asia during that same period.

Yeah, Dante wanted, and rightfully deserved, a full measure of vengeance, but damn it, Rocco burned for it, too. For his friend and for himself.

He cracked an eyelid, to check the screen. 55% COMPLETE.

"Shit!" A small warning flashed at the bottom. LOW BATTERY. How long had that sucker been on? He stood up, knocking a stack of files off the table. Where in the hell had he put the charger?

Spying a black cord poking from under a stack of papers across the room, he quickly retrieved it. But not without triggering a file avalanche.

Ignoring the mess, he plugged the laptop in. Five seconds to spare. Not bad. 75% COMPLETE. By the time he got another cup of coffee, it would be finished.

If Dante's place had looked like a disaster when he'd left yesterday, it now resembled a junkyard hit by an atomic bomb. And until they shredded and burned all these documents, he didn't dare check on a maid service either.

Searching the cabinets for garbage bags, Rocco grabbed several and started loading up the obvious *secure* trash—food wrappers, boxes, beer and soda bottles.

Two trips to the Dumpster later, the place did look better. Still not the Taj Mahal, but better. Now his friend needed garbage bags and ink cartridges. And coffee.

With the last cup of Joe in hand, he returned to his laptop. 95% COMPLETE. That last 5% always took the longest to download. Go figure.

He glanced at the time: 3 p.m. He would need to take off late that evening to avoid—for as long as possible—

the appearance that he and Dante were working together. And God knows he could sift through reports anywhere.

Changing screens, he checked e-mail. It was too soon to expect any information out of Hong Kong, not that he expected any miracles on that front.

After Dante had called from Freeport earlier this afternoon, Rocco had done a preliminary check on the perfumery. He recognized the address on the firm's website: one of the newest shopping districts in Hong Kong. Millionaire Mall. Exclusive.

He'd even called the place, under the guise of ordering perfume for his girlfriend. The proprietor spoke perfect English and, once started, chattered endlessly about his rare oils that spanned the globe from Russia to Rio, and how he had perfected a distillation process. Blah, blah, blah.

When it came to perfumes, Rocco only cared how the end product smelled on female flesh. Naked flesh. The really good stuff didn't need clothes to enhance it.

Twice Rocco steered the conversation back to the specific blend the woman in Freeport had worn. In the background he'd heard the faint click of computer keys, as if the man were checking his records. That they were computerized held promise from a hacking aspect.

"That fragrance has already been commissioned for four women. That's our maximum," the man apologized. "However, we can create something like it, yet different—better!—for you."

Four women. Was one an alias for Catalina Dion? Before hanging up, the man reminded Rocco that they cheerfully accepted all major credit cards. "Our initial consultation fee is five hundred dollars U.S."

Five hundred and no cologne yet?

Obviously, Cat hadn't changed. While Rocco had never gotten to know her well—he'd been pretty much consumed with his own personal disasters back in those days—what he recalled was a picture of class. The tasteful, understated kind purchased with Black Amex cards.

Had that taste for the good life proved too tempting? When Remi St. James closed shop, had Cat found it easier to make a living selling secrets? The money could be colossal depending on what you knew. And whom you knew. Catalina Dion had worked for many different agencies, including the late, great Remi St. James. She had to be a freakin' gold mine of knowledge.

But what had caused her to turn? Or had that been her plan from the start? Infiltrate the allied world's highest levels of security, earn accolades, earn trust, all while salting away secrets for a rainy day.

He shook his head. It didn't fit, but he'd learned long ago that logic rarely applied to anything outside of math and geometry.

He scanned his e-mails, unable to resist opening a couple bawdy jokes from one of his buddies in Afghanistan. In a wired world, where a joke could be worn thin after two bouts with a handful of Microsoft Outlook users, this guy always had fresh stuff.

Rocco's computer burped—sound effects courtesy of that same buddy—signaling the download had finished. Closing out e-mail, he opened the new files and began perusing folders. There was one job in particular he was searching for.

"Now where the fuck are you?"

The last file—figures—was it. He pulled the computer

back on his lap and began reading reports. Ever since Travis raised the possibility that the explosion could have been meant for both men, something had been bugging Rocco. Something that pertained to one specific job.

He paged down the report. On the surface, the case had appeared to be a random drug bust that went bad. Under the surface . . . different story.

Rocco had practically volunteered for that particular assignment when he'd learned the destination. Taiwan.

Having just bailed his then-fourteen-year-old nephew out of jail for the second time, for possession of heroin, Rocco had a Bunyan-sized axe to grind.

Determined to root out the drug's ultimate source, he'd patiently traced the heroin being sold near his nephew's neighborhood in Raleigh, North Carolina, first to Los Angeles, then to Taiwan's infamous Dragon's Blood Cartel.

Before going out on that mission, Rocco had memorized the bios and photographs of the key cartel couriers. Then he'd beaten the bushes of his network of snitches in the Southeast Asian straits.

His efforts seemed to pay off when he'd gotten word on one of the Dragon courier's secret routes. Rocco had kept that information to himself, knowing the accuracy of snitches was generally poor.

When he indeed spotted the courier, Rocco had pushed his way front and center, eager to wipe that smug look off the courier's face.

Jesus, how stupid can one man get?

In retrospect, the little inconsistencies he'd ignored that day loomed large. The courier had been on deck, easy to spot. When they'd intercepted the vessel, the cocky SOB hadn't even made a run for it. In fact, he'd raised his hands in mock defeat and offered to send over his boat's captain—the ultimate signal of surrender.

Or more accurately, delay.

A tiny speed boat had blasted out from behind the courier's boat, seemingly powered by automatic gunfire. Rocco had narrowly avoided catching a bullet. Even after hitting the deck, wood splinted around him. In the end, no one on his ship was injured, though the courier and his captain had both died.

Rocco had been saddled with the nickname "Dances with Bullets" afterward. His team had celebrated the courier's demise, joking about how the man had made their job easier by staying on his feet a bit too long after the attack began. But six months later, Rocco was bailing his nephew out of jail again.

Rocco scrubbed his face with his hands.

He'd been fucking played.

He'd let his personal agenda cloud his judgment. The courier had given in too easily. Rocco had told himself it was because arrest meant little. With the corrupt court system overseas, the courier would never see jail. And more, the loss of a boatload of heroin was nothing to the cartel. In fact, astute businessmen that they were, they knew to allow for the occasional loss of inventory.

He pinched the bridge of his nose, recalling the incident. The courier's supreme confidence should have tipped Rocco off. The bastard had *known*. The courier's intent had been to lure Rocco forward, never expecting his own shit to hit the Eternal Fan.

Had the shooter taken out the courier once he'd realized Rocco had survived? No loose ends. No loose tongues.

Okay, so someone had tried to kill Rocco that day. But

tying that incident to Catalina Dion was a stretch. She'd
need to have access to someone with a lot of connections
in Southeast Asia. Someone big. Like Minh Tran.

Minh Tran, who was also suspected in Dante's capture.

Jesus. How had he missed that? Rocco looked at the
report again, spotting the loose thread. His snitch. Jaleel . . .
the one who'd whispered the Dragon courier's route and
acted surprised as hell later.

Rocco needed to find Jaleel, but he wasn't about to put
out his usual feelers. No, this required finesse. The I'm-
gonna-fuck-you-up kind of finesse.

Opening a new browser window, he checked on flights,
then powered down his laptop.

It was after midnight when Dante finally arrived back
in Key West. Afternoon storms had delayed his flight out
of Freeport. He grabbed a few hours' sleep but jolted
awake when his phone rang at 6 a.m.

"Good morning, sunshine," Rocco said.

Dante groaned. Rocco wasn't a morning person, which
meant he'd probably been out all night and was just now
getting home.

"What's up?" Dante tugged on jeans and made his way
to the kitchen to start coffee.

"Getting that list of cologne clients was relatively easy.
As it turns out, the man's competitor already hacks his
files regularly."

"And?" Dante slammed the cabinet shut. Where the
fuck was—

"You're out of coffee. Printer ink and paper, too."

"Gee, thanks. Any more bad news?"

"Well, since you asked. The cologne's another dead end. Besides Keiko Chan, who must be the Japanese lady you accosted, the other customers are the wife and two daughters of the French ambassador."

"Shit. Figures." Dante had known it wouldn't be that easy . . . but still. He headed back to the bedroom to find a shirt and his truck keys.

"I'm checking a few other suppliers," Rocco went on. "The cologne biz is as cutthroat as any, so there are several companies who knock off the high-dollar custom stuff at half the price. Cat may have gotten hers from one of them. Don't hold your breath since con artists keep few records."

Dante looked around for his shoes. "Yeah, well, I've decided that trying to trace a woman by her cologne is as asinine as it gets. After spending five hours in a crowded airport, I started thinking every perfume I smelled was it."

Which had damn near driven him crazy. He'd ended up tranquilizing his senses with tequila. Too much tequila, judging by his headache.

"Any news from Travis?" Rocco asked.

"He's hoping to score with the Freeport medical examiner today. He's also trying to run down info on Giselle Barclay. Sounds like she's Cat's equal in the bitch department. Basically, it feels like I'm back at square one."

"You know, maybe you're barking up the wrong tree," Rocco said. "Maybe you need to try a different tack. A different approach."

"Different how? Help me out here, bro. I haven't even had a fucking cup of coffee yet."

"Think about your relationship with Cat. What was your favorite thing to do? Where did you go? What did you eat? What did you discuss while eating? You know . . . the good times."

Dante bristled. "Dude, she tried to kill me. The good times were . . . an act."

"If that's the case, then it would have been even harder to keep that act pure. We draw from our own experiences to fabricate covers. She had to let something slip. But you've got to step back to see it." Rocco's phone started beeping. "Shit! I've got another call. Later, man."

Disconnecting, Dante started for the door. Halfway there he paused. Rocco had a point. This also wasn't the first time someone had implied that he'd lost his objectivity when it came to Cat. Dr. Houston had suggested the same thing, even going so far as to encourage the use of self-hypnosis and biofeedback.

He wandered back toward the bedroom and pulled a small box out of the closet. Inside the box, untouched, were the relaxation CDs Dr. Houston had given him.

Back then, Dante was also being pressured by Dr. Winchette to explore his premonitions. Dante had basically refused to explore anything. Fuck anger management. At the time he'd relished his anger.

But now . . .

He picked up one CD. Would these help him shelve the anger long enough to remember the good times he'd had with Cat? Whether she'd been faking wasn't the point. *He'd* had strong feelings. *He'd* fallen in love.

Hell, he'd even considered marriage.

Now, though, Dante couldn't think of her without wanting to go ballistic. What had been so damn special about her?

Besides the sex . . .

Chapter 17

"So you had an unhappy childhood?" Dante picked up his wineglass, watching Cat over the rim. Hardly daring to believe she was finally here with him.

After months of dreaming about making love to this beauty and juggling impossible schedules, he'd been forced at the last minute to cancel their very first planned rendezvous. And then she'd backed out of the second one, dropping out of sight into another role.

He'd begun to wonder if he was cursed. Doomed to *wanting* without ever receiving.

Now, however, it appeared the third time was indeed a charm. The goddess of love had cut him some slack. He and Cat were together, on a romantic island, with a week to spend however they saw fit.

His choice: in bed.

"What makes you think I had an unpleasant childhood?" Cat replied.

He grinned. All through dinner, she'd mimicked him—answering questions with questions, telling him zero. Even her expression gave away nothing. Maybe amusement. The lady was good. She was also—thank you, Jesus—still interested in him. His worries that time and distance would snuff the sparks that had smoldered between them in Belarus evaporated.

Most of them anyway. He still had the occasional nightmare where he hadn't reached Cat in time. The missile attack on the laboratory, launched by Chechen rebels, had killed most of the staff. Getting Cat out alive and undetected hadn't been easy.

With that mission scrubbed, they'd both shipped out to other assignments; he within the Agency, her with *I could tell you, but then I'd have to kill you.*

As a contract agent, Cat moved around a lot. Or so he supposed. One of their agreements had been never to discuss work.

Steel drum–influenced Christmas Muzak played softly over the speakers scattered around the hotel's restaurant.

Cat's flight had been delayed getting in and she'd been famished. His suggestion that they eat before going up to their room hadn't been motivated by chivalry. Quite the opposite. If he'd been alone with her in a room with a bed, the only hunger he'd be feeding would be his libido. Hell, scratch the bed even. *Alone* would have been provocation enough.

At one point, back in Belarus, Dante had thought he'd go mad with wanting her. She'd indicated a similar need.

Now, though, delaying had become a game of who could hold out the longest.

Cat played dirty, too. During the first course, she had started playing footsie with his balls, giving him the wide-eyed *What?* stare.

Two could play that game.

In retaliation, he'd lingered over his entrée. Instead of rushing the meal so they could get naked and horizontal, he found himself savoring every bite. Anticipating. Then he'd ordered dessert. *Pre-dessert.* Cat was the only sugar he craved.

"Most people," he went on, "when asked about their favorite Christmas memory, yak about the year they got a new bike, or a BB gun. Maybe for you it was Barbie."

"Which one for you?"

"It damn sure wasn't Barbie."

She narrowed her eyes. "I'm betting the BB gun. Or did you get the old you'll-shoot-your-eye-out speech instead?"

"See? You're doing it again."

"What again? This?" Her foot stroked his crotch, dropping away before he could react.

She picked up her wine goblet, her bright red nails glinting as her fingers slid up to cup the glass. He wanted those hands cupping him, those fancy red nails stroking his—

He cleared his throat. "Your reluctance to give a straight answer leads me to believe that Christmas was a disappointing time for you."

Cat's laughter was enticing. If sound were tangible, he'd dart around the room plucking her laughs from midair; not wanting to share any part of her.

"I'm not biting, Dr. Freud," she said. "What you term 'reluctance' is simply me honoring our agreement not to discuss our pasts. Good, bad, or indifferent."

"Another nonanswer. Remi St. James taught you that, right?"

"Nor do I expect you to discuss your past. Your mentors." She leaned in, her voice a whisper. "Unless you really want to talk about that BB gun you got. But I'm guessing you've got other things on your mind, right?"

Her size six teased him again. Dante clenched his jaw. Where the hell was that waiter with dessert?

"Actually, it was a Winchester rifle. Thirty-ought-six," he said. "I was twelve and dying to go hunting with my uncle."

"Oh, I see. Shoot the poor deer's eye out instead?" Her frown seemed genuine.

It was Dante's turn to laugh. The woman was credited with more than one confirmed kill, yet talk of Bambi and thundersticks upset her.

Dessert arrived with a flurry. The chocolate cheesecake and a crème brûlée were *presented*. As their waiter poured coffee and simpered in Cat's direction, Dante slid his hand beneath the floor-length tablecloth.

This time, when her foot came up, he was ready. Cupping her heel, he rubbed her fully against his erection.

"Sir?" The waiter turned back to him. "Anything else?" *King-size bed, Cat naked.* "We're good." Dante scowled. *Just leave.*

Cat arched a brow at the waiter's retreating backside. "Wow. That look was more effective than waving a club."

"He's posturing for a good tip—which he'll earn by leaving us alone." Dante stroked her instep as he spoke, his thumb pressing up and in, massaging.

"That feels divine. Where'd you learn reflexology?" She let her eyes drift shut for a moment, which was almost a sin. If eyes were the mirror of the soul, Cat's reflected Heaven. God's soul.

"No questions about our past," he said. "Remember?"

"A pony."

"Excuse me?"

"My favorite Christmas present." She lowered her voice. "Damn you're good."

"We haven't even begun the *good*." He shifted his hand slightly, stroking more firmly. "This is tantric reflexology. If I rub there, you should start to feel excited. Stimulated." He brushed her foot against his erection again.

Cat arched her toes, prolonging contact. "Something feels excited."

"And if I exert pressure here." He pressed his fingers into the ball of her foot. "You should either have an orgasm . . . or wet your pants. Unfortunately, there's a fine line between the meridians to the Mons Venus and to the kidneys."

She started giggling. "There's also a fine line between rubbing and tickling." Tugging her foot back, she pushed her dessert plate aside, barely touched.

"Ready to blow this place?"

"I'm ready to blow something." She winked. "But you haven't finished your cake."

"I'll get something sweet upstairs." Dante pulled out his wallet and signaled to the waiter.

A few minutes later they strolled across the expansive lobby toward the bank of elevators. Dante had his arm draped loosely about Cat's shoulder, enjoyed the slight pressure of her hand at his waist.

"This place has only been open a few months and already it's getting rave reviews," he said.

She nodded, looking around. "I can see why."

"I understand they've got great—" He stopped, instantly alert.

Cat had paused so suddenly he'd almost tripped. He scanned the group of people straight ahead who'd just exited one of the elevator cars. Had one of them caught her attention?

She took a step backward, her gaze softening. That's when Dante realized she was staring at one of the large oil paintings set up on ornate gilt easels throughout the lobby. Relief melted his tension.

"A perpetual art show," the concierge had informed Dante at check-in. As befitting the Christmas season, the current works were churches.

"You know this place?" He pointed to the canvas.

She shook her head. "I have a friend who collects sacred art. She would like this piece."

Dante steered her toward the front desk. "Let's find out who the artist is then."

She stopped him—tugging him back to her side. "There will be time for that later. You didn't get dessert yet, remember?"

The look she gave him sent his pulse to the moon. Then south. To the pole. It took an effort not to run to the elevator.

Once inside, she asked, "What floor?" Twice.

It took an effort to think. "Twelve," he said. "Our room number is 1223. Today's date."

As soon as the doors shut, Cat slid closer. He met her and

took over. His mouth found hers as he pressed her against the wall. She opened, their tongues dueling, teasing.

His hands cupped her face as he ravished her lips. So sweet . . . Her hand grasped his cock, rubbing the solid length of it. He accepted her invitation and ground his crotch against her, pinning her in place.

The bell sounded.

They practically jumped apart, both breathing hard.

Dante looked at the digital numbers—relieved to see the number 12 illuminated. He'd nearly lost control—had forgotten where they were.

Grateful their room was only a short distance down the hall, he dug out the key card. He let Cat step inside the room first. Then he paused to lock and secure the door.

She didn't move away when he turned back, and with a little noise, she flew into his arms. Once again her hands went to his cock, stroking it briefly before going to work on his belt. He liked her priorities: skip clothes, go straight for the crotch.

Dante decided to dazzle her by acting like a gentleman. He'd remove her shirt first, slow and easy. But as he moved to unfasten her blouse he ripped one of the buttons off. Shit. He moved to the next button and fumbled it too, all thumbs, all dick. Damn it, he used to be a master at this.

"I'll buy you a new one," he whispered against her mouth. Then he tore the fabric apart.

She made a breathy noise of approval and stepped backward. She had on a sexy red bra, the low cups thrusting her generous breasts up in a tantalizing display. Her necklace, up till now concealed beneath her shirt, made him smile.

His fingers skimmed the firm swells of flesh, catching the green *locket* dangling between her breasts.

"Mistletoe?"

"'Tis the season," she murmured.

That he managed to unfasten her front-hook bra without destroying it was a fucking miracle. Spreading the cups wide, he leaned away and just stared.

He'd long fantasized what Cat would look like naked. She exceeded his fantasy. Her breasts were full and round, with dusky nipples that pearled beneath his palms. And the tiny, exotic, *more, more* noises she made in response to his touch were gonna kill him.

She unzipped his fly, then began shoving his pants down with one hand, while her other hand worked its way inside his briefs. He jerked as her fingers closed over the swollen head of his cock and lightly squeezed. No, *that* was gonna kill him.

"Oh, Sweet Jesus, I want this." Her voice was husky.

"You read minds, too?"

She squeezed again.

He grinned again.

"Do you have a rubber handy?" she whispered.

"In my pocket."

She stepped away as he attempted to drag his pants back up, nearly tripping in the process. He looked up to find that Cat had removed her skirt and shoes. She stood totally naked except for that bit of mistletoe.

She was so damn beautiful. So damn perfect. And shit . . . his mouth was hanging open. Great. He probably looked like one of those cartoon characters just before their eyeballs fell to the floor.

"Here let me," she said, tugging the foil package from his hand.

Earth to Dante. He ripped his shirt open and dropped it. Then he toed off his shoes and kicked out of his pants.

Now Cat stared, her beautiful green eyes caressing his chest, dropping lower, lower . . . then widening.

"Um. Wow. You're really . . . nice. Nice and, um, big."

"We'll go slowly. Easy." Jesus, she really was kinda tiny . . . except for her rack.

"The hell you say." She palmed the condom. "And you're sure this will fit."

"Positive." He watched, enthralled, as she grasped the shaft of his cock, holding it steady while slowly, too slowly, unrolling the condom, stroking him as she went. First time *that* had ever made him want to come.

"Finished?" Now his voice sounded cartoonish.

"We haven't even started."

"I can fix that." He grasped her shoulders, urging her close for another kiss. She pressed her whole body to his, scorching his flesh with hers.

In his dreams, they'd made love for hours. Funny thing, dreams . . .

"I'm about to explode," he warned. "I won't last."

"Me either. The first time is always awkward anyway." She panted as she spoke. "So what say we just slam-dunk it, get this one out of the way. And move on to round two."

"Okay. And after that, I want to marry and live happily ever after."

"You trying to break the mood here?" she joked back.

Dante lifted her as she spoke, bracing her against the wall. She wrapped her legs around his waist and made a slight noise as he positioned his cock between her legs. She was wet and hot and ready.

He was beyond ready, yet still he hesitated. Wanting to

remember it all. Every feeling. Every sensation. She was right; they hadn't even started. And already he never wanted it to end.

She squirmed, pushing her breasts into his face. "Please, please!"

His mouth closed over one tip. He teased her nipple with his teeth as he pushed partway in and paused, savoring that delicious hesitation, the tightness of her body that held him back for a fraction of a second before melting around him like a warm, sweet rain. Her velvety softness hugged him, sheathed him. Welcomed him. He slid in farther, deeper.

"You were wrong," he whispered. "This isn't awkward." He pressed all the way in. Then slowly drew back. "It's fucking divine."

Cat shuddered, whimpered. "Harder." She rolled her hips. "This slow stuff . . . will destroy me."

He began pumping harder, faster, and was rewarded with her nails scratching his shoulders, clawing his back as she strained to meet each thrust. "Better?"

"Yes, oh, yes." She let out a satisfied hiss and then stiffened. "Yes, there!"

There pushed Dante over the edge. With a growl, he started grinding into her, thrusting, pounding, filling . . . being filled.

And as a powerful climax ripped through both of them, he knew he'd never, ever, get enough of this woman.

Chapter 18

Rio de Janeiro, Brazil
July 9
(Present Day)

"You owe me two thousand, U.S.," the man, a forger, whispered in Portuguese. He smiled, displaying rotting teeth that matched his breath.

Cat bowed her head, hiding her anger. In a different life, she would have taken him down before the last word left his mouth. Perhaps with a lightning-fast karate chop to his larynx. Not enough to cause permanent damage, yet painful enough to send the message that she wasn't a woman to be fucked with.

Of course, in a different life, the documents she needed would have been handled in-house. She wouldn't be dealing with a local lowlife. Hell, for that matter, she wouldn't be hiding, running, always on guard.

Still she longed to teach him a lesson. They were the only patrons in the small bookstore.

She trembled with the effort to keep her hands fisted

at her sides. "We agreed on seventeen hundred. U.S."
You ass.

The man shrugged, and then tugged a book from the
shelf above his head. "If it's a problem, we can negotiate
the balance."

His innuendo of sex-in-exchange had her reimagining
the blow. She'd hand him his testicles. Then walk. The
small dagger strapped to her thigh grew heavy, reminding
her of its presence. Too bad that wasn't an option either.

She had expected these passports two days ago, not
that she could have actually left then. Not with Sister
Dores ill.

"I can't imagine that your work is worth . . . extra," she
said.

He handed her the book. "See for yourself."

The book naturally fell open near the middle where
two passports were wedged. One for her, one for Marco.

Assuring they were still alone in the shop, she examined the documents. They were not the best, though this
man wouldn't be aware that she knew the difference.

She was accustomed to perfection, had a collection of
high-quality forgeries stashed in her hiding spot. The
problem was all but one bore known aliases. Using them
would be like shooting off a signal gun.

Aside from being too crisp—she'd smudge and wrinkle
them up later—the passports appeared good enough to get
them out of South America. She had a second, better, set
saved for later, when they reached their final destination.

She would have preferred to have several sets, but this was
the best she could do on short notice and with limited funds.

"You have the corresponding birth certificates?" she
asked.

The man withdrew an envelope from his pocket and hesitated, as if thinking about asking for even more.

Again she struggled with the temptation to teach him a lesson. But this wasn't the place. And she damn sure didn't have time.

While she didn't like being shaken down, she had been prepared for it. It was part and parcel of dealing with the sleazy street networks. Even the more reliable ones were shysters.

"Um . . . The doctor said I should wait until the blood tests come back before . . ." She gave him a worried look, then shrugged. "I mean HIV can't turn to AIDS that fast, can it?"

The man leaned back, as if not wanting her to breathe on him now. "How much money do you have?"

She made a pained face. "Eighteen hundred. But you wouldn't take it all, would you?"

"Yes, and then we'll call it even." The man held out his hand. "Besides, when you find your husband, you'll get more."

She had told him she was searching for a wayward husband who'd gone off seeking better work in Colombia. His smirk just then said he didn't believe she'd find him.

With an anguished sigh, only partly fake, she withdrew her cash and completed the trade.

Cat made certain that the certificates matched the passports before putting them away. The forger fanned the hundred-dollar bills and swiped a counterfeit detection pen across them. Still no honor among thieves.

Exiting the store, she walked four blocks before doubling back two. She was in a hurry, but she couldn't take chances. Not now.

Confident she wasn't being followed, she boarded a crowded bus. With frequent stops, it was just as fast to walk. But today taking the bus was about conserving energy. She had slept little the past three nights.

The virus sweeping through the city had hit the orphanage hard. All the babies, including Marco, were sick now. They cried during the night, miserable with vomiting and diarrhea, as Cat moved from crib to crib, soothing and changing diapers. The younger nun, Sister Lolita, had also been sick, and the day after Cat returned, Sister Dores had come down with it as well.

Cat had secretly worried the seventy-seven-year-old nun wouldn't recover. To lose her . . . A lump formed in Cat's throat. Sister Dores was the closest thing to a mother Cat had ever known.

Abandoned at age three on the mean streets of Rio, she had been taken into the orphanage by Sister Dores. And she'd stayed long past the age that most children left. When Cat turned sixteen, the nun had even helped her obtain a fake passport to pursue a modeling career in Mexico City.

Though that opportunity hadn't turned out—good God she'd been naïve back then—she'd stayed in Mexico, getting work at an illegal fireworks factory and discovering her natural affinity for gunpowder.

Sister Dores once again intervened, helping Cat get a missionary-sponsored scholarship to a small business college in England. But life as an administrative assistant wasn't in the cards.

She'd gone to London, where she'd eventually met Giselle Barclay, and then Remi St. James. Meeting Remi had been her first life-changing experience. He'd taught her how to use and enhance her prodigious memory skills. And so much more. God, she missed him. Giselle, too. All the people she'd loved.

Including Dante? She had a memory of dark hair, dark eyes, and strong arms.

No . . . she was still angry at him.

It does no good to stay angry with the dead.

Dante. Max. Both had died. She blinked away tears, refusing to grieve. She'd once acted rashly in grief and look what it had cost her . . .

The bus jerked to a stop, forcing Cat's thoughts back to the present. Climbing off, she zigzagged through the streets and alleys toward the deserted convent two blocks from the orphanage. Like many older buildings in this area, the convent had been damaged by fire, but as still-consecrated property, it had avoided the latest wave of reconstruction.

After assuring she was alone, Cat turned down the walkway beside the wall and entered the building's basement. Sister Dores had shown her this secret chamber, used long ago by nuns helping runaway slaves. *Lying in order to save another's life isn't a sin.* Sister Dores had been the last of her order to live in the old convent.

Inside, Cat lit a candle and let herself into the small room hidden behind the brick facade behind the old furnace. Once inside, she began lifting the floorboards and tucked away the new passports. That was it. She now had everything packed and ready to go. As soon as Marco was well enough to travel, they could leave.

She'd postponed their departure long enough. In fact, this morning she had even debated skipping work, though it meant forfeiting the week's wages that Ernesto owed her.

But after paying more for her passports, she reconsidered. The stash of money she had would have to last them awhile, so every cent counted.

She left the convent and hurried away. She would work today and then go in just long enough tomorrow to collect her pay. Then—providing Sister Dores and Marco were both better—she and her son would disappear.

She wrapped a bandanna around her head as she walked. When she drew close to the alley leading to *Pouca Flor,* she slumped her shoulders, assuming her *Luzia* persona before ducking into the brothel's basement where laundry was done.

"I wish I could stay home in bed when I am sick!" Theresa, one of the other maids, chided her. "But if I don't work, my children will not eat."

Cat tied on an apron. Theresa had five children and another on the way. How did women go through the pain of childbirth over and over? Once had nearly killed Cat.

"I will work through lunch," Cat said. "And you can take an extra break when you-know-who isn't around. Is he pissed that I'm late?" Moot question, she realized. Ernesto, the brothel's owner, was always in a bad mood. The only time she'd seen him smile was when he was counting his money.

"Actually he hasn't been down here. Half of his girls are sick and he's making them work anyway. I swear he would sell his own mother if the price was right."

Cat shrugged without comment. As much as she hated the exploitation, the prostitutes made more money. If she could have peddled her body without showing her face . . .

Grabbing the basket of wet sheets Theresa had just washed, Cat carted them to one of the ancient dryers.

The laundry here never ended. Neither did the floor scrubbing. She and the other maids cleaned up after men who cared little about the women they fucked and even less about the mess they left behind. Yet they expected a spotless room and clean sheets.

Ernesto was especially picky about the front parlor, where men paid big bucks for cheap whiskey while the available prostitutes paraded by, each trying to outproposition the other. Some of the things Cat had heard the women offer to do sickened her. Maybe she wouldn't make such a great prostitute after all.

From the hall, they heard their boss swearing.

"Uh-oh, I spoke too soon," Theresa said.

"Theresa! Luzia! Get buckets and come quickly. The toilets upstairs aren't working."

Cat bit back a groan, wishing she hadn't come in. But now that she was here, she wouldn't leave the other woman alone to face such a mess.

Once Ernesto left, Theresa was very vocal about her boss's request. "I don't know how you do this without complaining." Theresa shook her head. "I would go crazy holding it in."

Been there, done that.

Cat straightened. "I try to keep in mind that it can always get worse."

Much worse.

Two hours later, Cat returned to the laundry room with the latest batch of dirty sheets she'd collected upstairs. Theresa shoved more towels into the dryer, but had trouble straightening her back.

Cat moved to relieve her. "I'll get that. Take a break."

"Marsala just came in, so that will help us catch up." Theresa moved to sit down. "She said all her sister's children are sick, too. Oh, and a child came by asking for you. Said that Sister Dores promised you'd give her a candy."

Cat froze. "What child?"

"One of those urchins the nuns feed."

While the orphanage housed only infants, Sister Dores continued to hand out bread and a kind word to the older children who lived by their wits on the streets.

"What did the child say?"

Theresa lifted her shoulders. "She kept asking for candy, said the nun promised. I shooed her away. If Ernesto caught her begging— Where are you going?"

Cat had stripped off her apron. If Sister Dores had sent someone here, it meant there was a problem.

Marco! Had her son gotten worse?

Or had the unthinkable happened? Had someone come looking for Cat? She swayed, felt as if she'd been punched.

"I'll be right back," Cat said. "I just need to find the child, to see if the nuns need something."

"The way you worry about those nuns—you should have been one," Theresa called after her.

Outside, Cat hurried away from the brothel. Ever cautious, she took a different route to the orphanage.

When she arrived, she circled the crumbling building, looking for signs of anything out of the ordinary. Saint Maria's had once been a beautiful old church, but a fire a year ago destroyed one wing. The roof of the main building collapsed nine months ago, rendering the church unusable. Many parishioners had started going to Saint

Bernadette's once it became apparent there was no money for repairs.

Because the orphanage was housed in a separate building, it had remained operating, but Sister Dores had long predicted that the facility would be closed or consolidated.

The nun had been right.

That a rowdy group of children played in the road was a good sign. These street-wizened denizens had a sixth sense about danger. They would have hidden if a newcomer or stranger were about.

Satisfied, Cat approached the back stairs, bounding up the wooden steps without sound, a skill she'd honed years ago and that still served her well.

She let herself in the unlocked door and hurried toward the nursery. Both Sister Dores and Sister Lolita held crying babies. Zetta, another volunteer, was changing another infant.

"Where is he?" Cat's eyes swept the room, not finding her son.

Sister Dores laid the infant she held in a crib, then hurried to Cat's side. "Marco is at the hospital. He is okay, but his fever rose so high this morning he started having convulsions."

Cat felt her knees weaken. "Is he is still there?"

"Yes, they want to keep him overnight. He's badly dehydrated and if his fever spikes again . . ."

"I will go to him." She turned to leave and misstepped.

Sister Dores caught her arm. "You don't look well."

"I just turned too fast." *And I'm worried to death about*

my son. She couldn't say that in front of the others. "None of us have had much sleep lately."

"And some of us have had a little more sleep than you," Sister Dores said. "You've been up all night, taking care of sick babies and working long hours."

"I'll rest when I get to the hospital."

"More likely you'll collapse."

"I'll be fine."

Cat took off and ran all the way to the hospital, forcing herself to calm down before going in.

At the children's ward, she approached the nurses' desk. The large room behind the desk echoed with children's cries. She scanned the cribs.

"May I help you?" a nurse asked.

"I work at the orphanage," Cat said. "Sister Dores is concerned about the boy, Marco, she brought in earlier. He's . . . new, and she doesn't want him to feel abandoned. She would like me to sit with him if that's okay."

The nurse nodded, pointed. "Bed seven on the left."

Marco was lying in the crib, whimpering as he sucked his thumb. Tears welled in Cat's eyes as she approached.

His eyes opened then and a smile of recognition lit his face. Her beautiful, beautiful boy. He started whimpering again.

"Shhhh," she whispered. She dropped down to his level and stuck her arms through the slats to keep him still. He latched on to her thumb and started to cry. "It's all right, little one. I'm here."

Stroking his head, she started to sing softly. After a moment, he quieted then yawned. His eyes drifted shut and still Cat sang. In sleep, his grip on her thumb tightened, as if to never let go.

Dante . . .

They looked so much alike, sometimes it hurt.

It hurt.

It hurt.

And that pain brought back all the memories she wanted to forget.

Chapter 19

Ambergris Caye, Belize
June 30
(Twenty-Four Months Ago)

He'd left a message at the front desk. *Something came up.* She hadn't read beyond the first line.

It wasn't the first time Dante had stood her up. It was the ninth. How apropos. Last inning. She was pissed off that she'd kept score.

Sore loser? Damn straight.

She thought about calling her friend Giselle. Except she'd find little sympathy there. Last time they talked, Giselle had given her the old "you can't trust a gorgeous man, they all think with their dicks" lecture.

Check. Dante *was* gorgeous. He had that straight black hair, which always needed a trim, and always fell over those deep brown eyes. *Big* deep brown eyes, she corrected. The kind of eyes that compelled a woman to obey. Worse, he was tall and well built. Well hung. And though she'd never tell Giselle, she liked it when he thought with his dick.

And therein lay the problem.

She'd arrived at the resort a day early, hoping time alone at her favorite place—the beach—would help her find courage.

She tossed the bag of massage oils she'd just purchased into a trash receptacle as she made her way in the rain toward their—her!—private cabana. She'd planned to stage a seduction. Something special to make amends for her short temper of late.

Except how did one seduce a no-show?

Handwriting's on the wall, girl.

Yeah, the floor and ceiling, too.

She paused outside the cabana's entry, dreading what awaited her. Slipping inside, she peeked into the bathroom. The pregnancy test kit she'd bought yesterday sat unopened on the counter. Suddenly she saw it for what it was. A relationship test.

Part of her had hoped Dante would make it to the room before she got back from shopping. He'd see the kit and figure it out. At that point he could have walked—or at least thought over what to say.

She hadn't expected joyous overtures. He'd made it clear from the beginning that he never wanted kids.

"People in our line of work . . . it's not fair to the kid. Every time I walk out that door, there's a damned good chance I'm not coming back. And if I piss off the wrong people and they come after—"

She knew the spiel. Had agreed with it one hundred percent.

Until three weeks ago. She was never late. And her boobs were tender, her moods anything but. She'd perfected the art of denial. She couldn't be pregnant. Period. They'd never *ever* had unprotected sex. Double period. Hell, Dante had even been phobic about using condoms she'd purchased.

Then she'd done a little no-fucking-way research on the Internet. One site posted a two percent breakage rate for condoms. Two out of one hundred. She should have been pregnant twice after their last vacation. Further reading had been flat-out depressing. Incorrect usage—which included rushing, ripping packages with teeth/nails—bumped the failure rate to fifteen percent. And the tests conducted by Consumer Reports comparing brands . . .

She felt guilty for all the times she'd given other women the *yeah-right* eye roll. *Oh, sure, it was an accident.* And so help her, if Dante accused her of entrapment, she'd—

What? Get mad? Cry? Two more arts she'd perfected of late.

Her biggest mistake had been letting herself fantasize about settling down with Dante, to raise a perfect little family. Like on TV. God knows she had no real life experience to draw on. She had gone from life on the streets to life in an orphanage. What did she know about child rearing? Families?

That didn't stop her from dreaming the impossible dream. But it was a long drop off cloud nine.

She picked up the test kit. Set it down. She couldn't be pregnant. Maybe it was the flu. A virus. Stress even. Except . . . none of those things swelled your breasts.

She sighed. There was nothing for it. Closing the bathroom door, she opened the box.

Her cell phone rang. She jumped, dropping the stick as she raced out of the bathroom. Where, oh, where had she left her goddamn phone? On the floor. Of course.

She answered with a breathless "Hello."

"You sound out of breath." It was Dante. The soft hitch that always hit her abdomen at the sound of his voice was even stronger now. The baby?

He chuckled, his voice low, husky. "Am I, um, disturbing something?"

That was her cue to tell him she was masturbating, thinking of him . . .

"No, actually I just got back from a walk," she said. Not really a lie. "Where are you?"

"Nowhere fun."

Disappointment resettled on her shoulders like a buzzard interrupted. They never said where they were, but this time she had secretly hoped he'd say, *"Surprise! I'm in the lobby."*

She moved to the window and looked out at the tropical downpour. "Well, you're missing beautiful weather here. Sunny. Hot."

"Rub it in."

"Any chance you'll get away later in the week?"

"No. In fact, I may be out of touch for a while."

A while could mean a week or months. "Can you be a little more specific?"

"No."

Just no. Not, *no, I'm sorry*. Just no.

Damn it, she was tired of this. Of not knowing where he went, or when he'd be back. Or where she stood in the bigger scheme of his life.

Oh, like he knows where you always go, and when you're coming back. And how life seems gray when you're not with him.

"Okay, then," she said. "I'll let you go."

"Wait. You sound upset. I know this was short notice. And I promise I'll make it up."

"This was supposed to be a makeup for the last time. Or was it the time before that?" She wished she could do sarcasm without sounding whiney.

"What do you want me to say? You know—"

"Yeah." She cut him off, not wanting to hear all the things that reminded her of how unimportant she was in his life. "I know."

Background noise, voices, filtered through on his end of the phone. He wasn't alone. Jesus, they couldn't even have a decent argument.

His voice dropped. "Look, I've got to go. Will you be available when I get back?"

Available? She bit her lip to keep from screeching. That's all it was to him. Sex.

"If I'm not, I'm sure you'll find someone else who is," she snapped.

"You want dependable, get a Volvo." He sighed. "Look, if this is about what we've discussed before . . ." Another sigh. "I'm not white-picket-fence material, Cat."

She recalled the conversation. She'd brought up the subject of commitment, had thought maybe they'd had something special enough to label. Something beyond yes-oh-sweet-lord-fuck-me-now-please.

Memories of all their fun times together shimmered. She'd been tickled to learn he played a mean game of handball. She'd left him in the dirt at a motocross track and then had to fight to beat him to the finish line. He'd taken her sailing—her first time ever—and had run her bikini up with the sail. She'd made certain his snow white ass had gotten just as sunburned as hers.

Everything they did seemed so good, so right.

And after all they'd done, they couldn't even discuss commitment? She'd called him a chicken.

He'd parried by declaring himself committed to his work, his country.

But no man could serve two masters. Or mistresses.

And who should be called chicken now? *Bawk, bawk, bawk. Tell him.*

"If that's what you need," Dante went on. "I understand."

You don't understand shit. She struggled to hold her tongue, but lost. "Fuck the Volvo. All I need is you."

Muffled sounds came across the connection—he had his hand across the phone while talking to someone else. He hadn't even heard what she said. Tears stung her eyes.

"Look," he came back on, voice harried. "I've got to go. Can we rain check this?"

The test kit in the bathroom . . . She couldn't rain check a baby.

"No. We can't. This is good-bye, Dante. For good."

Chapter 20

Key West, Florida
July 9
(Present Day)

Dante's eyes snapped open.

His experiment had worked. But at a price. He felt emotionally battered. Fractured. His memories of Cat held no middle ground; they had all been extremes.

Hate. Avenge.

Joy. Ecstasy. Hope.

Despair. Loss.

Fuck! He wanted to weep *and* laugh, to kill *and* to protect. It was tearing him in two, destroying him bit by bit.

He sucked in air, seeking control. He still had a fierce hard-on, painful. His cock throbbed, demanding attention, release. It would be so easy to jack off, but he refused to give her another victory.

He sat up, ignoring the slight dizziness as he lurched toward the bathroom. The shower. The water was cold, stinging his skin. But instead of easing his hard-on, the needles of spray stimulated. The sensation intensified, his skin tightening, his balls aching, closing in.

Nothing . . . mattered . . . except . . .

Fuck. Fuck her. *Fucking her.* Jesus, if she were here right now . . .

"Oh, baby, let me take care of that. Shhh," Cat whispered as she dropped to her knees, tugged open his pants.

His cock sprang forth, a heat-seeking missile. Armed, ready. His legs shook with the effort to keep it under control, to hold back.

"I know what you need." More whispers before her mouth closed over his need, her lips stretching to take him in.

Deeper . . . yes. Suck it . . . yes. Harder . . . yes.

She knew. She always knew. At times like this, she sensed his desperation and offered ease, comfort. Made his world right once again.

Deeper . . . yes. Harder . . . yes. His hands speared though her hair. His cock disappeared in and out, glistening wet, her pace now frantic.

She was in control. He was at her mercy.

No more.

Dante opened his eyes, took a deep breath.

He was sitting in the shower, the water no longer running. That he still had a hard-on made him feel fractionally better. He'd won that round.

Climbing to his feet, he didn't bother drying off. He threw on a pair of sweats, his sneakers, and took off for a run.

He returned an hour later, exhausted and pissed. But *good* pissed. The run had cleared the fog. He took a real shower then made his way to the kitchen. He opened the refrigerator, let the cold air revive him. He opened the cabinet, closed it. No coffee fairy. Damn.

He turned back to the fridge. According to the digital clock on the microwave, it wasn't quite 10 a.m, but in the immortal words of Jimmy Buffet, "It's five o'clock somewhere."

He grabbed a beer and slipped outside to the small patio. Plunking down into the lone lawn chair, he took a long swig, finally ready to examine what had popped out of the Pandora's box that was his mind.

This was exactly why he'd refused to explore hypnosis further in the hospital. The memories he *wanted* to recall—those lost times in prison—remained fuzzy, beyond his reach. Whereas the people and times he wanted to forget—mainly Cat—blew into his mind anytime he lowered his guard.

Be objective. Right.

How about . . . just being honest. He'd loved Cat, had even thought of leaving the Agency, to settle down, to start a family. That he'd never told her that was a small consolation. Rocco thought he was insane, but he understood. So had Max. Harry had been fatalistic. *"I don't get what's so damn special about the broad? Is the sex that damn phenomenal?"*

At the time, Dante had ignored Harry's lone voice of cynicism. But maybe Harry had been the only one who was right. Maybe Dante had been blinded.

Or *blindsided.*

The videos—her betrayal. It always came back to that.

Well, so much for being honest with himself. He leaned his head back and let the sea breeze soothe him.

As his mind calmed, a single detail from his time with Cat surfaced.

The painting. In the hotel lobby.

It had been a church. Nothing spectacular, as he recalled. In fact, compared to some of the others in that same display, it seemed fairly plain. But Cat had been mesmerized. The artist's style had struck a deep chord with her.

The look on her face had haunted him. There had been . . . longing. Remembrance.

Shit. He set his beer aside. It wasn't the painting's style that hit her. It was the subject. *The church.*

And what he'd watched flicker across her face had been homesickness. Dante had seen that same poignant mix of pain and elation flash across a soldier's face every time a letter from home found its way across the Middle East to the fields of war.

That church was a clue to Cat's past. Maybe not the key, but at least a piece of the puzzle. He tried to focus on the painting's details. Who the hell had the artist been?

They'd never returned to check.

He pushed out of the lawn chair. Back inside his apartment, he turned on his laptop. A Google search on church paintings came back with eleven gazillion hits. A total waste of 2.1 seconds.

Next he looked up the resort they'd stayed at and browsed the lobby photographs. Nothing. So he called the place.

"The art shows change quarterly," the desk clerk told him.

"This would have been two years ago last December," Dante said.

December twenty-third. Room 1223.

"I'm sorry, sir, I don't have access to that information," she began.

"How about the concierge? He seemed to know a lot about the shows."

"Hold, please."

A few minutes later the concierge answered.

Dante identified himself as a previous guest. "That first Christmas the hotel opened, they had artwork displayed in the lobby."

"Ah, yes. 'Churches of the World.' It was my personal favorite."

Dante scribbled a note. "There was a certain painting I'd like to find for my anniversary. Perhaps you could help me find the artist's name?"

"Actually, he was a local at the time. Paul Patterson. I believe he's since moved back to Connecticut."

After thanking the man, Dante did a second search using the artist's name. Paul Patterson, artist, didn't have nearly the web presence of Paul Patterson, Mega-Realtor.

And while two galleries had one painting each, neither were of churches. The bio was old, stating that Paul and his wife, Pearl, lived in the Caribbean.

Logging on to a different database, Dante ran the names again and scored a phone listing and address in Waterbury, Connecticut.

He dialed and *voila!*, Pearl Patterson answered.

"This is Dan Hogan. I'm trying to reach Paul Patterson," Dante said. "I'm interested in a painting that I saw in Anguilla two years ago."

He knew by the way Pearl caught her breath what her next words would be.

"My husband died ten months ago. Emphysema. He so

hated when I nagged him about smoking." She sighed with a sad resignation. "There is a local dealer who has some of his works. I'm sorry, which one did you say?"

"These were churches—" Dante looked at his notes. "'Churches of the World.' The one I'm looking for was white and had bright red flowers."

"Oh, I think I recall that one. Paul was obsessed with God after being diagnosed. That was his last project, in fact. But I don't believe any of those are available."

"Do you by chance know where the churches he chose were located?"

"Me? No. But if you'll leave your number, I'll check with my daughter. She kept most of her father's sketch books and notes when I moved into assisted living. I brought very little here."

Dante thanked the woman and hung up, disappointed, but not surprised. Untraceable cologne. A vague painting. So much for contemplating his navel.

No sooner had he closed his phone than it rang again. It was Travis Franks.

"Tell me something good." Dante went in search of his beer. He had to go to the store today.

"I e-mailed you copies of Remi St. James's medical files. I ran everything on the forms, and as expected, it's all fabricated."

"I'm batting a hundred today. Any luck getting the passenger lists in and out of Freeport?

"I got 'em, but no hits against Cat's known aliases. So far everyone that went in and out within that time period appears legit. She could have used one name in, a different one out."

"Or left by boat. Or even went to another island and flew out."

"I'll expand the search. In the meantime, I'll forward the passenger manifests I have. Scan the names, see if anything pops up for you."

After disconnecting, Dante felt more frustrated than ever. He checked e-mail and paged through the medical records on Remi St. James. The man had dropped a small fortune on his treatment. Which if St. James was as rich as was rumored, he could have well afforded. Travis was already attempting to trace St. James's bank accounts, but Dante doubted Cat would have been stupid enough to access those accounts and leave a paper trail.

Then again . . .

Next he looked over passenger lists until his eyes hurt. At noon he stopped and stretched. Maybe he'd go out and get some real food. Stop by and see Iris and Truman, before coming back and going through it all over again. There had to be something here.

In the end, Dante went to the grocery store first, then picked up a bucket of fried chicken—Iris's favorite—and took it to the marina.

Iris greeted him with a hug and then peeked inside one of the bags he'd set on the galley's tiny table. "My stomach and your mind must have a telepathic link."

"That explains a lot," Dante grumbled.

"And look who's here." Iris pointed to the couch.

D-dog was stretched out on a small mountain of pillows. His cone and most of the bandages were gone, but his hind quarter was still splinted. The dog raised his head, growled, and resettled himself.

"I'd hoped his near-death experience would change his attitude," Dante said.

"It has! Why, he's sweeter than ever, aren't you, Darling-dog?" The mutt returned Iris's adoring look. "I just sprang him this morning. 'Course, Truman's already carping about feeling tied down with a dog. Like we go anywhere!"

"Don't listen to her," Truman joked as he entered and shook Dante's hand. "I thought that was your truck outside."

Over the next hour, he talked fishing with Truman and listened to Iris's view on election politics. "Send me to Washington for a week, and I'll fix those rascally bastards," she said.

Dante was still chuckling when he left. As he climbed in his truck, his cell phone rang. P. PATTERSON showed on the caller ID.

"You won't believe this!" Pearl's voice was triumphant. "I went to look in that old cabinet of Paul's that I kept and there was a file labeled CHURCHES. He kept the photographs of all the ones he painted. I'm so pleased to have discovered these! Now, I think I've found the one you mentioned. A white church with baskets of red hibiscus? The back of that picture says 'Saint Maria's.'"

Dante was trying to find a working pen in his truck. Damn heat had baked the ink. "Do you know where it's located?" He'd guess there were hundreds of churches with that name. Maybe thousands.

"I can't read Paul's scrawl. R—E—O. Rio, perhaps? You know, that would make sense. He spent a couple weeks in Brazil, before returning to paint these."

"Rio de Janeiro." A city famous for welcoming and

hiding fugitives. "You've been most helpful, Mrs. Patterson."

Racing back to his apartment, Dante did a search on the church. Bingo. There was even a photograph of Saint Maria's in Rio de Janeiro. He squinted at it. Imagined red flowers.

Yeah, that was it. One of the entries stated that the church had burned and was scheduled to be razed. He wrote down the address.

Okay, he'd found the church—but what did it mean? Had Cat spent time in Rio at some point? The more he thought about it, the more he realized it was the one place he'd never heard her mention. Interesting.

Was it true she had wanted the painting for a friend? Any chance that friend lived in Rio? Any chance that friend was Giselle Barclay?

"Crap shoot, crap shoot, crap shoot." But as long as he was chasing wild hares anyway . . .

Dante called Travis. "I've got a long shot. Based on nothing more solid than an old memory. Is there a way to cross-reference the names on the Freeport list against flights in and out of Rio de Janeiro over that same period? And include Giselle Barclay's known aliases."

"You don't ask for much, do you?" Travis exhaled. "Let me consult my oracle and get back to you."

Chapter 21

Bangkok, Thailand
July 11
(Present Day)

Rocco sat in a dim corner of the bar's outside patio. In another part of town, *al fresco*, Thai style, would be considered premium seating. He'd have been overlooking a mink-and-pearls crowd.

Here, depending on the prevailing wind, *al fresco* required a strong constitution. And the only fur in sight was on the rats that scurried past.

The docks weren't far away and tonight the smell of fish and pollution battled with the mélange of garbage from the alleyway behind him.

The inside of the place wasn't much better. At least outside the breeze could shift. And here he had four different escape routes immediately available with no worries of being trapped in a building with one exit.

He'd been in town two long and frustrating days. And wouldn't you know the rush of travel and jetlag had caught up—just as he was getting ready to leave again. Returning to Thailand was an even bigger risk these days, considering both sides of the Pacific had tabooed the journey.

Didn't stop him, but to avoid taunting fate, Rocco limited his stays to forty-eight hours or less. In and out. Wham, bam.

A slight twitch in the air alerted him to the fact he had company. Someone was behind the fence that lined the side of the patio. Rocco checked the switchblade tucked inside his sleeve, then he picked up his scotch and pretended to take a drink.

A man vaulted over the fence with a ninja-like ease and landed right in front of the point of Rocco's knife.

"Easy, my friend." Diego Marques raised his hands in mock surrender.

Rocco sat back down. "One of these days you're going pull that stunt and find yourself sushied."

Grinning, Diego took the seat opposite. "I have great faith in both of us. Your control is impeccable, but my speed . . ."

The blade retracted with a *slish*. "Cut the shit; the smell's bad enough as it is." Rocco slid an envelope across the table.

"All business tonight, eh?" Diego peeked inside and made an appreciative grimace. "That will buy a lot of Girl Scout cookies. But . . ." He pushed the envelope toward the center of the table. "We're doing this all backwards. Why?"

In past dealings, Rocco would request a service, and if Diego was interested, he'd name his price. They *always* haggled. Diego was good, but his opinion of his value was as inflated as his ego.

"I'm on a deadline," Rocco said. "And I know what I usually end up paying for an address."

"That's three times the norm. You looking for triplets?"

"One man. But he is—or was—employed by a mutual *friend*."

"You're suggesting my loyalty is for sale?" Diego examined the empty glass sitting on the table, then picked up the bottle of scotch and loosened the lid. He sniffed the contents before pouring himself a drink. "Okay, I give up. Who is this person?"

"Jaleel." The snitch who'd told Rocco about the cartel's drug route.

With a dramatic sigh, Diego shoved the money all the way back. "I understand his last job didn't go so hot. Diving with sharks. No cage. Bait and blood sacks tied to his weight belt."

Well, that explained why Jaleel couldn't be found. "Pissed off Minh Tran one too many times?"

"Tran offered me a very sweet deal to locate the man, so I don't think he was the one who bagged Jaleel."

"Any idea who Jaleel was freelancing for then?"

"Not yet. But for a price," Diego's eyes shifted back to the envelope. "I can assure that you'll learn first."

"I'll think about it." Yes, Rocco wanted to know, but he wasn't paying big bucks to get details on something that he'd hear about eventually through the back alley grapevines.

And dead, Jaleel was, well, even more worthless than he'd been alive. Shit. This whole damn trip had turned out to be a waste. Another of his snitches who'd promised the latest and greatest on SugarCane production had vanished as well. Guess it was sign.

"Gotta run." Rocco checked his watch as he scooped up the envelope. He shipped out in two hours. "Feel free to stay and enjoy the ambience."

"Not so fast." Diego raised his glass. Like Rocco, he'd never actually drank. Not in a dump like this. "I have something else that might be of interest."

"About?"

"That prison guard you were looking for a few months back? Skihawtra?"

Skihawtra. It took Rocco a minute to recall Ping's surname. "You found him?"

"Not yet. But someone else is searching for him, too."

"Who?"

Diego shrugged. "I'm still working on it. My contact in customs said Skihawtra's passport was flagged by one of the head honchos."

While corruption was openly accepted here, it did have a pecking order. And a hierarchy. Governmental head honchos didn't come cheap and didn't work for just anyone.

"I want to know who's asking," Rocco said. "But that's not worth this." He held up the envelope. "As you said, this is three times the norm."

"There's more." Diego had on his Cheshire Cat smile. "Someone's also asking about the man who escorted the American prisoner out of that Bangkok jail."

Rocco debated briefly about extending his trip a few more days. Except he'd just promised to meet Dante again. And staying in Thailand beyond the forty-eight-hour limit he'd negotiated with the goddess of Fate was just plain reckless. He'd have to plan another trip.

Rocco surrendered the cash. "You know which name I want first, right?"

"Word to the wise." Diego grew uncharacteristically serious. "Be cautious with your travels. There's talk of a special election here, so the ruling party is looking for sacrificial lambs. Any leniency they hand out will be reserved for potential voters. Whereas harsh sentences handed out to foreigners will be lauded."

Luc melted back into the shadows. "I'll be in touch," he heard the large American say.

That same man now walked toward a car.

So you're the American searching for my father. Why? A half-dozen reasons crossed Luc's mind. He hoped that after he met with his uncle tonight, all those questions would be answered.

Then Luc would decide whether or not to tell the American where his father was buried. Right now, though, Luc wasn't even certain himself.

Just before reaching his car, the American casually dropped something into a trash can. Luc recognized the muffled clattering.

The man had just ditched his knife. He'd likely bought it upon arriving, which meant he must be leaving again. Luc was tempted to follow, but the American now knew that someone had asked about him. Which meant he'd be more vigilant.

Once the American pulled away, Luc relaxed and refocused on Diego Marques.

Diego was considered a folk hero in Luc's world. Diego was the model of success other criminals aspired to. He worked for himself and didn't have to deal with the unending protocols that were the bane of the various crime cartels.

Unlike Luc, Diego had found a specialty that provided a lucrative living. An encyclopedia of international information, Diego was extremely picky about who he worked with, too. Simply being able to afford him wasn't enough. He required references. Credentials.

Luc had been correct in surmising that Diego was one of the few who could have arranged to smuggle an injured American prisoner out of the country. Then Luc had checked around some more and confirmed Diego had indeed been in the area four months ago. Slowly the pieces were starting to come together.

As Luc watched, Diego pulled out his cell phone. No ring, vibrate only. The man listened, said "Thanks," and disconnected.

A minute later, a sports car driven by a gorgeous blonde pulled up. As Diego approached, she climbed out from behind the wheel, showing off long legs, a tiny skirt, and an even tinier top. She spread her legs slightly, leaning back against the car. Diego brushed one hand across her bare midriff, the other claiming a very large breast. The woman moaned as if having an orgasm. They broke apart, climbed in the car, and disappeared into the night.

Yeah, Luc wanted to be just like Diego Marques.

He remained in the shadows another few minutes, then eased across the alley to the garbage can. The trash he had to fish through was disgusting, but the switchblade more than made up for it.

A quality piece with a fine balance, it was wrapped in a handkerchief used to wipe prints. Pity to buy something this nice and have to discard it. But on the other hand, who wanted to get stuck in a knife fight with a cheap piece of shit?

Luc ejected the six-inch blade and sliced the air. He'd watched the American pull this knife on Diego. Since few would dare pull such a stunt, it said much about the American's skill. The fact that Diego hadn't retaliated indicated the two were friends. Was the American one of Diego's counterparts?

Flipping the blade up into the air, Luc caught it by the tip. Then he pocketed the closed knife and took off. Depending on what he learned from his uncle, it wasn't inconceivable that Luc might be scheduling his own meeting with Diego.

Or even the American.

Moving so light-footed that even the normally nervous alley rats didn't squeak and run, Luc ran a false trail, doubling back to assure no one followed.

Just like Diego had when he'd followed him here. Except Luc had tailed Diego from the rooftops.

And while Luc didn't have anywhere near the number of enemies Diego was rumored to have, there was a certain party he needed to avoid. Not that they were smart enough to catch Luc.

After navigating a few more streets on foot, Luc again took to the roof to survey the area. Here and there, the darkness was broken by an occasional light. But his uncle hadn't shown up yet.

Would he come? Luc pulled out the notes he'd received. None of them told the whole story. Luc had snooped around a bit on his own, but for every question answered, ten more popped up.

Luc hadn't seen his uncle—anyone in his family—in

more than ten years. He'd run away at age thirteen. And
the things he'd done since . . . That he felt nervous about
this reunion surprised him. He'd thought his heart had
turned to stone long ago.

A month ago Luc had received word his uncle searched
for him. Knowing it likely meant his father had died and
that his mother needed him, Luc had made the long trek
to this parents' home.

Finding their simple thatch hut *gone* had unnerved
him. The house had been burned, the ruins removed. As
if someone had tried to erase their very existence. Guilt
had besieged Luc as he worried that his enemies had discovered his real name and found his parents. If this had
been because of him . . .

Staying hidden, Luc had then made his way to his
uncle's house, but it, too, was destroyed. Wary of openly
approaching the tiny village near his parents' home, Luc
waited until one of the old men, a friend of his father's,
went off alone to fish.

The man had seemed horrified to see Luc. "I was told
you were dead." Then the man told Luc about how his
father, Ping, had gone to work at a prison. "This will be
hard to hear, but he was shot while helping a prisoner
escape. The prisoner died, too."

Apparently, Luc's mother had left in shame to go live
with a sister far away. It was assumed Luc's uncle had accompanied her. That their houses both mysteriously
burned down one night was believed to be an omen by
the overly superstitious townspeople. The prison in the
jungle had swirled with dark evil. An evil that had cor-
rupted Ping.

"You should leave," the old man advised. "And tell no one we spoke of this."

Luc then made his way to his mother's sister. But his auntie hadn't seen Luc's mother in years. And she knew nothing of Ping's death.

Returning to the jungle, Luc quietly searched for the prison. He found that it, too, was gone; burned and razed just as his parents' home had been. And what little he gathered from the local grapevines added to his confusion. Had the prisoner indeed escaped? Had the prisoner been a Westerner? And what about the American who'd been asking questions about the prison?

Finally, Luc had received a note from his uncle confirming that both his parents were dead. Murdered, but no details were given. That his uncle was now in hiding and needed help to leave the area confirmed that his uncle was indeed involved somehow. No surprise. When he lived at home, Luc recalled the two brothers always hatching crazy schemes. But had this one cost his parents' lives?

In the darkness below Luc heard a sound. A shadow moved. His uncle.

Luc checked the other end of the alley before shimmying through an exhaust pipe in the roof that led to a little-used supply room of a now-closed business.

Opening the door, Luc motioned the man inside.

"Uncle! Come in quickly."

Clearly not expecting the door to have opened thus, his uncle drew in a sharp breath and clutched at his chest. "Luc!"

"Shh." Motioning his uncle to be silent, Luc pulled the man inside and shut the door before turning on a small lamp.

The ache in the pit of his stomach sharpened as his eyes took in his uncle. The years had not been kind to the older man. Drinking and dissipation were partly to blame, but the mantle of horror and grief his uncle carried was demanding a heavy toll.

"How you have grown! You were a boy when I last saw you. Now you're a man. Your father . . ." His uncle began to weep, hiding his face.

"Come over here." Luc led the man to a chair in the far corner, then returned to listen at the door, giving the older man a chance to compose his thoughts.

And Luc a chance to steel himself.

After a moment, Luc returned to his uncle's side. The older man's eyes lit up when Luc handed him a slim flask.

"You always were my favorite nephew."

"Your only nephew. I have food, too." Luc passed his uncle a small loaf of bread, filled with cheese.

While his uncle ate, Luc told him what he'd learned about his father after going back to the jungle.

"It's all lies! And you must promise me to never go back there!" his uncle said between bites. "It is bad enough they're searching for me."

"Who is searching?"

"The guards from the prison. They don't want anyone to question what went on there. They killed your father!"

"Tell me about my mother first," Luc said.

His uncle nodded, understanding Luc's hesitancy to discuss his father. "Your mother was summoned to the prison, to claim you father's body."

"She went alone?"

"I wasn't there when this happened, you see. I had gone searching for you at your father's behest."

Luc frowned. "Finish about my mother."

"One of the orderlies told me he saw your mother go into a room with a guard. She was weeping. He waited around, to help her, but she never came out. Then later two body bags were removed from that room." His uncle paused. "He knew by the size one was female."

Turning away, Luc punched the wall, swearing to avenge his mother. "They will pay!"

"When I returned and found our homes destroyed, I knew there was trouble," his uncle went on. "Then a neighbor said the prison guards had asked about me. You, too. I told a neighbor you had died years ago but that Ping had never told his wife. If you've gone back since . . ."

"I only saw one man. And I lied about where I lived. Now tell me everything you know," Luc said. "They say my father was shot while helping a prisoner. But what really happened?"

"Your father was helping a prisoner, Luc, but not like they say. The warden had personally enlisted your father's assistance for this. He was getting paid extra, you see. But then the American—"

"The prisoner was American?"

"Yes. The prisoner offered your father a blood chit in exchange for his help."

Luc couldn't hold back a groan. He could well imagine his father's reaction. A fucking blood chit. As a child, Luc had watched his father and uncle get drunk numerous times. One or the other would start retelling the tales their drunken uncle had told them of magical blood chits. Stupid men believed stupid tales.

"If my father was offered those two choices," Luc said,

"I know he would have chosen the chit. So did the warden learn of his double-cross?"

"I don't know." His uncle took a sip from the flask again. "I warned Ping not to be greedy, to be happy with the chit. But he went back to see the warden and was never seen again."

"Greedy? How about dim-witted?" Luc struggled to keep his voice low. "Let me guess the rest. You were his partner in all this, and because the prisoner did escape, they are now searching for you, too. I always thought you were smarter than my father."

Looking offended, his uncle pushed to his feet. "You shouldn't speak ill of the dead! Especially when you don't know the full story. I will leave."

"No. Please sit, Uncle. And finish telling your story."

An awkward silence fell between them. "My only involvement was in trying to locate you. Along with the chit, your father was promised passage to America, for all of us. He wanted you to come. He . . . he regretted that he'd made you leave, and in his own way, yes, perhaps a stupid way, he thought this could make it up."

His uncle dug into his pocket, and pulled out a sheaf of papers. On top, wrapped in plastic, was a small square of paper. He tapped the plastic. "This is your father's legacy to you."

"This?" Luc picked up the small scrap of paper. "This cost both my parents' their lives? Do you even know what this writing says?" While Luc could speak English, he couldn't read it.

"Blood chit." His uncle pointed to the letters. "Call Travis Franks. Case number 495-29-1111DJ. The rest is a phone number. And those other papers are notes your father made about things he saw at the prison."

Luc stared at the pathetic pages that had cost two lives, his vision blurring.

His uncle squeezed Luc's hand. "Your father would want you to have this. He said that even if the prisoner didn't escape, there would be a reward. He said they'd pay for his knowledge."

His father's knowledge. Gee, that would equate to enough to buy a cup of tea.

"We are almost out of time." Luc handed his uncle an envelope. "This passport will get you into Australia. Inside is the name of a man who helps Chinese dissidents fleeing communism. We all look alike to them; so use it to your advantage." Luc reached in his pocket and withdrew a roll of bills. That this wasn't his money would only get him in deeper trouble. "U.S. dollars. Keep them until you are in Australia."

Once again his uncle started weeping. "Ping . . . your father would be so proud of you."

No. He wouldn't. But Luc nodded anyway. "I suppose I could have come home first. We must leave now, Uncle."

At the door his uncle hugged him. Both understood they'd never see each other again. The feeling of aloneness that briefly filled Luc was swept aside by a desire for retaliation. For both of his parents.

"Tell me what happened to the prison?" Luc asked. "No one seems to know where it came from or where it went."

"I beg you, Luc, do not seek them out! Your father saw many horrible things there. You should leave with me!"

Luc shook his head. "My parents were killed by these butchers, so I understand what they are capable of. But their deeds shouldn't go unpunished. And I'm the only one who can avenge my parents."

His uncle looked up at the ceiling for a long moment. Then he exhaled heavily. "I know one man who worked at the prison for just a short time when it first opened. He got sick and moved away. Tell him I sent you, or else he'll refuse to talk."

Chapter 22

Rio de Janeiro, Brazil
July 12
(Present Day)

Dante had been in South America less than twelve hours. His first impression hadn't wavered: Rio de Janeiro was the ultimate hiding spot.

The city offered roughly four hundred fifty square miles of surface area. He refused to think in terms of cubic miles, which would mean including the surrounding hills that were plastered with *favela*-style shanties, stacked one upon another.

Over six million people called the city home, a population that more than doubled when the larger metropolitan area was included.

Needle in a haystack didn't come close. Yet, damn if Dante could stay away. His gut screamed that she was here . . . somewhere.

When Travis Franks had searched passenger flights between Freeport and Rio de Janeiro, they'd hit pay dirt. A woman, *Luzia Gomez*, had left Freeport, July 2, the same day that Remi St. James's so-called daughter made her final, fatal visit. Her flight to Rio connected in Mexico City. Further crosschecking revealed she had made a similar trip a month earlier, which coincided with the timeframe of St. James's daughter's first visit to the clinic.

If Luzia Gomez was indeed Catalina Dion, then Cat couldn't have been in Key West when his boat blew. But that didn't mean she wasn't guilty.

The fact that Giselle Barclay hadn't been seen in a year further suggested the two women were a team. With Giselle's help, the two women could have split up, Giselle going to take care of Dante, while Cat took care of St. James.

It made sense in a weird *Thelma & Louise* way. Killing each other's lover lessened potential glitches that could arise from having been personally involved with the victim.

It would have been easy enough for Giselle to leave the right clues: the cologne and telltale broken heart. Hell, maybe Cat's disguise while visiting St. James mimicked Giselle. If St. James was impaired, he'd have been easy to fool.

Right now, Dante's biggest challenge was finding the *correct* Luzia Gomez. Travis had come up with a list of fourteen Brazilian passport holders living in Rio with that same name. Of the six passport photos he'd managed to get, none were helpful. And given Cat's abilities for altering her looks . . .

Rather than do nothing while Travis continued culling resources, Dante—already in disguise himself—had started checking the passport addresses.

Two of them caught his attention because of their

relative proximity to Saint Maria's, the church in Paul Patterson's painting. It was as good a place as any to start.

The fact that the locations were in a *favela* didn't deter him. While he could better imagine Cat holed up in one of Rio's glittering mansions, a mansion drew attention.

He'd decided to look for the church first. Unlike some of the other shanty towns, this smaller *favela* boasted a new and growing commercial district that catered to Rio's booming sex trade.

Any concerns Dante had about his disguise, which included dreadlocks and a mustache, vanished. The streets were crowded with foot traffic, but the mostly male tourists largely ignored each other. Broad daylight was prime time here, as the streets were safer.

As Dante walked away from the crowds, he took in the ruined buildings lining the deserted south side. He'd been told that the majority of residents had been run off by the rash of fires that were conveniently freeing up large tracts of land along the main road.

Even Saint Maria's had fallen victim to the torch. The ruling crime lords wouldn't want the faithful returning here every Sunday. Better to cut the cord, or burn it, and force the church to follow its flock to greener pastures.

He slowed as he passed the church, recalling details from the painting. What little remained of the building's broken skeleton was rapidly succumbing to the surrounding blight. Only the front steps and covered portico remained somewhat intact. A portion of the back supposedly housed a soup kitchen and small orphanage, but those were closing, too.

Considered more mission to the poor than church, Saint Maria's didn't keep records of parishioners either.

And since there wasn't a lighted marquee out front bearing the message I'M HERE!—he was wasting time. There hadn't been a solid connection between Cat and the church in the painting, other than the fact it suggested Rio as a place to look.

Dante moved on to the first address on his list a few blocks beyond the church. Because street signs were nonexistent here, he consulted his map.

"Figures," he muttered as he stared at an empty field. How many addresses would yield the same?

Leaving the main road, he headed east one block, then turned left, already knowing what he'd find. The buildings on this street had been gutted by fire as well. Strike two.

As he turned away, an older man hobbled out through one of the doorways of a roofless ruin. He approached Dante with an open hand extended.

Dante's Portuguese was nonexistent, but he knew some Spanish. Digging out a small bill, he motioned the man closer.

"I'm looking for a friend." He held up a photograph of Cat.

The old man wrinkled his nose and shook his head as he grabbed for the money and missed, nearly falling over. Dante steadied the man's arm, realized he was drunk. At eleven o'clock in the morning.

"Her name is Luzia Gomez."

"Luzia?" The old man belched and nodded, before launching into a nearly unintelligible string of Portuguese.

Dante caught one word. *"Flor?"* he repeated.

The old man bobbed his head. *"Pouca flor."*

Little flower? Dante played with the translation in his head. Flower shop?

"Luzia works at a flower shop?" he asked in Spanish.

"Sí." The old man rubbed his fingers indicating money.

"First show me *Pouca flor*." Dante held up his map.

The man turned the map around, seeming to have a hard time focusing.

Dante pointed to one spot, for a reference. "Saint Maria's."

Nodding, the man pointed to the main road. *"Luzia. Pouca flor."*

Leaving the old man with several bills, Dante retraced his path. If there really was a Luzia Gomez working at this flower shop, he didn't expect her to be Cat. Most likely none of the people on his list would be, but at least he could eliminate them. At least it was action.

Back on the main road, he headed north again, to the red light district. The streets were busier here. Large brothels dominated both sides of the road. The newer ones had balconies lining the upper floors. Scantily dressed women bent low across the railings, teasing and taunting.

As Dante passed one of the older buildings, he stopped short. POUCA FLOR, the sign read. Little Flower.

The hawker on the front steps hadn't missed Dante's delay. The man swooped in, cajoling him in multiple languages to come inside and sample the wares. "Buy a drink! Watch the women! We have the best!"

A whorehouse. Had the old man been trying to tell him that Luzia Gomez was a prostitute? A memory of Cat stripping as she sat on an old iron-framed bed flitted through Dante's mind.

Climbing the steps, he went inside.

* * *

Cat dripped with sweat. This felt like the hundredth basket of wet sheets she'd lugged to the dryers.

And still Theresa had a small mountain waiting to be washed. It never ended.

"Two more days," she whispered to herself. Two more days and she'd never see the *Pouca Flor* and its filthy laundry again.

Marco had been released from the hospital yesterday. Cat worried it was premature. "He's still weak," she had told Sister Dores.

The nun had disagreed. "Little ones bounce back quickly. You'll see. In two or three days you won't have known he was even sick."

Cat wasn't so sure, which added to the funny feeling in her stomach. Now that it was definite she and Marco were leaving, every insecurity she had about being a mother, about caring for her son, haunted her. Could she do it without Sister Dores's help?

Marco had only been four months old when they'd arrived on the orphanage's steps. Cat hadn't known where else to go . . . and Sister Dores, God bless her, had taken them in, never asking the first question.

Cat swiped her face on one of the sheets before tossing it in the dryer. The wetness felt icy against her skin. *Please no fever,* she prayed. The last thing she needed was to get sick. *I just need sleep.*

"Just two more days," she muttered again.

"Luzia! Theresa!" Ernesto's voice echoed in the cavernous basement.

Cat motioned for Theresa to stay put. The pregnant woman's ankles were so swollen she could barely walk and she'd been holding her side all day. The chances of her going full-term with this pregnancy didn't seem good. Cat hurried to the staircase leading up from the basement.

"Get up here with a mop and floor polish!" Ernesto glared down from above. "The bar sink sprang a leak, and if it ruins my new wood floors, there will be hell to pay." Still cursing, he stomped off.

"I'll go." Theresa was already waddling toward the supply closet.

"No, I'll get it."

"You made the last three runs."

And soon I won't be here to cover for you. Cat swallowed against the hitch in her throat. Of everyone who worked here, Theresa was the only one she'd consider a friend and not even a close one at that.

Shaking her head, Cat shooed the other woman back. "Go empty the front dryers for me, and we'll both take a break when I get back."

The brothel's bar was crowded.

As a first-timer, requesting no specific prostitute, Dante was seated in a small booth. He caught a glance of himself in the mirror. He looked like a reggae clone of the four other men wearing dreads. He'd adapted a slight Caribbean accent to alter his voice. Like most in the bar, he kept his sunglasses on.

He looked around, pretending to concentrate on the women. He needed to watch for subtle clues. If Cat was here, she'd be in disguise, too. He kept his expectations low. The chances of finding her here weren't good. Hell, nothing came this easy.

The brothel's setup wasn't original. Customers sat at tables and booths as an unending parade of prostitutes trolled by in bright, gaudy costumes. The air of competitiveness was tangible as the women paused beside a table, extolling their particular forte. Words and dialect didn't matter. The women communicated with a sign language that a blind man could read.

The bottle of beer Dante ordered was delivered by a woman who wore multiple piercings on her tongue and inside her cheeks. He paid his tab, watching as she tucked the bills into her tight-fitting, Fort Knox–size bra.

He had already weighed what to do if Cat, or Giselle even, actually turned out to be one of the prostitutes who approached. Giving in to instinct and grabbing her by the neck was out. But so was waiting to follow her later.

He'd bet the prostitutes lived here, stuck like indentured servants, paying most of their earnings back to the owner for room and board. The women might not go out for days.

He would need to get her alone.

A tall prostitute approached. Dante let his eyes drift up and down, as if considering her wares. That a part of him felt repulsed, angry even, at the idea of Cat offering herself like this came out of nowhere. He squashed the feeling by recalling scenes from the video. Yes, she could do this. With a fucking smile on her face.

The man and woman at the next table struck a deal. They stood in unison and headed for the elaborate staircase that led up to the second and third floors.

Dante's gaze drifted upward. Was Cat upstairs now, servicing someone? His grip tightened on his beer bottle and he forced his attention elsewhere.

A cleaning woman came in from a back room, her shoulders hunched as she carried a bucket toward the bar. Dropping to her knees, she started mopping a section of floor, oblivious to the crowd.

A whisper of awareness brushed the base of Dante's spine. Immediately he straightened, glancing around slowly. His senses had gone haywire again, sounds louder, colors brighter. *Watch. Listen.*

A woman descended the staircase. Too short. His eyes darted toward the women at the bar. Who or what had tripped his perception?

His gaze shifted past the cleaning woman, back to the staircase. Damn it! There it was again.

The cleaning woman straightened. She had her back to the room, but turned sideways to wring out a rag. For a moment her posture unbent. Dante caught a brief glimpse of her profile before she shook her head, allowing her dark shoulder-length hair to once again shield her face as she scrubbed.

He nearly came out of his seat.

Sweet Jesus . . .

It. Was. Her.

Catalina Dion had a picture-perfect profile. He watched the woman scrub. Cat also had an unmistakable grace, a mesmerizing flow to her arms, her shoulders. God, it really was her.

He forced himself to look away, not wanting her to become aware that he stared. Elation and rage pumped through his veins. He waved off the prostitute before him.

A man in a suit, his long hair clubbed back in a ponytail, approached Dante's table with the swagger of ownership.

The man spoke first in Portuguese, then switched

easily to Spanish. "You are not yet seeing what you like, *señor*? I assure you, my girls are the finest of the fine." He dropped his voice to a whisper. "At *Pouca Flor*, every need, any desire, is negotiable."

The inference was plain. For a price, the owner would pander to anything. Excellent.

"Actually, this might sound a bit strange," Dante began.

The man leaned forward, greed lighting his eyes. "No. Please, go on."

"That cleaning woman . . . I, uh, have a certain fantasy."

"Luzia?" The man's amused disbelief vanished as he watched Dante tug a roll of bills from his pocket.

Dante was careful not to react to the owner's confirmation of the name. *Luzia Gomez*. Dante glanced over his shoulder. The woman had finished scrubbing and hurried toward a rear door.

"My fantasy includes being bathed, scrubbed actually. But . . ." Dante dropped his voice. "Sometimes beautiful women are too intimidating and I can't get it, uh . . ."

The man gave an oily smile and nodded. "*Sí*. It happens to all of us."

Dante forced an expression of relief. "She is available, right?"

"*Everything* here is available. But that one is rather . . . shy. However, I'm sure a man of your skill could charm her."

"I'm a little shy myself. She sounds perfect for what I want." Peeling off several hundreds, Dante gave the man an uncertain look. "This will cover it?"

"A room with a bath is extra." The man waggled two fingers. "It will be a few minutes before she is . . . ready. Let me show you to a room."

At the topmost floor, the man unlocked the door. "A small hint, *señor*: If you are already in a tub, she can't refuse your request for help, now can she?"

Dante nodded. "And if she does, I'll simply have to convince her to play along."

Chapter 23

Rio de Janeiro, Brazil
July 12
(Present Day)

Cat dumped the bucket of water, then lowered herself to the floor next to Theresa.

The supply closet, a tiny room with stone walls, was always a few degrees cooler than the poorly vented laundry room. Compared to the coolness of the barroom, however, it felt like an oven and Cat had found herself wanting to dawdle upstairs.

I must be getting sick. She hated the atmosphere in the bar. Desperation and degradation were twin ghosts, haunting the prostitutes and all who entered.

And yet if she ever had to . . .

"I set the dryers for an extra five minutes." The other woman kicked off her shoes. "God knows we deserve it. We've been working twice as hard since Marsala quit again."

Eyes closed, Cat simply nodded. Ernesto was nobody's fool. If he could get two women to do the job of three . . .

The door pushed open unexpectedly, startling the women. Cat leaped to her feet, effectively blocking the view while grabbing the door before it could hit Theresa as she struggled to get up.

Ernesto scowled at her. "There you are! I've been looking for you!"

"I'm helping Theresa get another box of detergent from the top shelf," Cat lied. If Ernesto caught them taking a break, he'd cut their pay.

"Let Theresa finish in here. I have a special job for you. Come with me."

Cat mentally rolled her eyes. *Special* meant something like a drunken customer had puked in one of the pricier rooms and he wanted it cleaned, pronto. Could she really take two more days of this?

She followed Ernesto toward the staircase. To her surprise, he stopped at the shelf beside the door and pointed to the stacks of clean towels. A fresh bar of soap and a back brush had been set next to them.

"I have a very important client staying in room 307. Take these supplies up and let yourself in." He handed her a passkey reluctantly—as if it were the key to his safe. "Return my key the moment you're done."

"Of course."

"He might require a little assistance," Ernesto went on. "He is getting ready for Bettina and wants to look his best."

A little assistance meant the customer was likely too old and feeble to remove his own clothes and shoes. Certain men should be banned from Viagra.

"Room 307," she repeated as she pocketed the key.

This also wasn't the first time Ernesto had pretended his establishment was classy enough to offer room service. Mr. Viagra probably had deep pockets that Ernesto was determined to empty. Maybe, just maybe, she'd score a tip first.

Ernesto waved a hand toward her hair. "And for God's sake, straighten up a bit first. Get the dirt off your cheeks so you don't give the wrong impression. And hurry. He's waiting."

It was tempting to flip her middle finger to his retreating back. Except in two more days, she could do it to his face. *After* she collected her pay.

Theresa waddled up behind her. "Here, I'll go. You deserve a break more than I do."

"If I didn't have to return the stupid passkey, I'd let you." Cat sighed. "But we both know he'd be pissed if I gave it to you."

"And neither of us needs that. I'll get to work then." Theresa shuffled back toward the pile of laundry.

Cat paused long enough to wash her face—only because the cool wetness felt good—but left her hair straggling. Even if she'd had the energy to do more, she wouldn't. The last thing she wanted was to look attractive or neat here. Maybe in another lifetime stuff like that would matter again.

On the first floor, she slipped out the back and took the fire escape stairs to the third-floor hall window. If he could, Ernesto would have invisible cleaning staff, to avoid customers seeing a single face that wasn't heavily made up and ready for purchase.

Two more days.

Outside room 307, Cat paused. Shifting the towels

to one arm, she knocked. "Housekeeping," she called out in Portuguese.

When no one answered after her second attempt, she unlocked the door and slowly pushed it partway open. If the old man was already hooked up with Bettina, she didn't want to see.

The room was empty, the drapes drawn. She could hear water running in the tub and noticed the bathroom door was ajar.

"Hello?" she called out louder.

Obviously Mr. Viagra couldn't hear above the splashing. Which was fine. She'd set the towels and supplies right outside the bathroom and leave.

As she hurried into the room, a slight movement to the side caught her attention.

The door swung shut. A large man, wearing sunglasses, and sporting dreadlocks beneath a knit cap had been standing behind it. Angrier at her own carelessness than scared, Cat bobbed her head and started babbling in a frightened tone, uncertain whether this jerk even understood Portuguese.

"Excuse, excuse! I'll go see what is keeping your woman."

The man reached for the towels. She held them out as she moved past, eager to leave.

His hands closed over her wrists as the towels fell to the floor. Cat's response was instinctive. She thrust her arms apart and twisted her hands to break free. This wasn't the first time a customer had stepped over the line, but it would damn sure be the last. Fuck Ernesto and his the-customer-is-always-right motto.

The man countered her move, as if anticipating it.

Then he yanked her arms up and over her head before spinning her around and snapping her back against his chest.

"I've been waiting for you." The scorn in his *Jamaica-mon* voice barely registered as his breath brushed her ear, the back of her neck. That she couldn't see his face gave her chills; she hated anyone coming up behind her.

She tried a different tactic to break free, but he crossed her arms tightly in front of her, his hands cuffing her wrists and keeping her hands pegged uselessly. The man knew how to use his height and strength against a woman and she'd bet he was the abusive type.

Fury rose. As soon as she was free, she'd kick his damn—

"Cat got your tongue, Catalina?"

She stopped struggling. The man's voice had changed, his English perfect now. Perfectly recognizable. *Dante Johnson.*

It couldn't be. He was . . . dead.

But the height, the build . . .

He lifted her effortlessly and turned her sideways until she faced the dresser. As he leered over her shoulder she studied his reflection in the mirror. Though she couldn't see his eyes behind the dark glasses, she saw his chin, saw the hollows beneath his cheeks. His mouth. The features were unmistakably *her son's.*

She sagged forward as shock disrupted her system. Her heart slowed, the air suddenly too thick to enter her lungs. She tried to speak, but her mind couldn't supply words, answers. Logic failed. Emotions flooded her system, drowning her in pain, anger, confusion.

This was a man she'd never thought to see again. A man she'd once loved like no other.

The man who worked for the very agency that had sold her out to Viktor Zadovsky.

The man she'd gladly betrayed to save herself. *The videos.*

The events of a year ago slammed into her. She'd killed a man. She had stolen secrets. Giselle had died.

"Dante." The name left her lips in a hiss.

His beautiful mouth, the one that once made her melt, curved up in a chilling smile. "I've dreamed of seeing that look on your face."

Her brain jerked back online. "I thought you were—"

"Dead?" He made a harsh *tsk* noise. "Thanks for the confirmation. I wasn't sure if that bomb was serious or just a threat."

Bomb? She had no idea what he meant. Which was likely part of his plan to keep her disoriented. Hell, for all she knew, she was being recorded; he could be setting her up again.

"How did you find me?"

He smiled and winked. "We'll get to all those questions soon enough."

The innuendo was plain. There were probably others rushing up the staircase ready to take her into custody. She knew the drill. She'd be taken somewhere and questioned. And—

Marco.

Did Dante know? Was he here to take her son away, too? *Never.*

Feigning defeat, Cat hung her head. "Promise you won't let them hurt me."

Dante spun her back around to face him so fast her neck whiplashed. "It's not *them* you need to fear."

He tethered both her wrists in one large hand, before peeling off his sunglasses.

She stared. How could she have forgotten his eyes, so dark they were almost black? Bottomless. And frightening in their intensity, their hatred.

"I promise to show you the same sympathy I was shown," he whispered.

Cat closed her eyes and swooned, her head rolling to the side as her knees buckled.

The sudden shift of her weight forced Dante to counter. He took a step back and tried to re-grasp her wrists with both hands.

The moment he moved, she exploded into action. Her knee shot up, ramming straight and hard into his groin. As he spasmed in agony, she jerked one wrist free and grabbed the small dagger from her thigh.

Slicing the sharp blade across the top of his hand won her total freedom.

Still doubled over, Dante moved between her and the door. "You'll pay for that."

She stabbed the air between them and shifted backward. "No. I've paid enough. You won't get another thing from me."

Turning, she leaped for the window, tucking her head as she smashed through the glass.

Shards sliced her arms. Pain didn't register until she crashed onto the uneven roof below. A nail caught her thigh, ripping her skin.

Rolling to her feet, she jumped down onto the trash pile in the alley and sprang forward in a full run. Not slowing, she glanced over one shoulder.

Damn it! He was climbing out the window!

She redoubled her speed and turned at the intersecting street. Just as quickly, she ducked into another intersection and down a narrow walkway between two buildings before cutting across to a different alley.

Though no one was behind her now, Cat didn't let up.

Dante would be on the ground now, eating up her head start. By this time he'd have alerted his colleagues, too.

They would fan out. Ask questions. Hunt her down. And if they caught her . . .

Fear exploded in her brain. If they caught her, she'd be separated from Marco again.

That had happened once. During that horrible time when she and Giselle were trapped by Victor Zadovsky.

And God help her, she'd die before going through that again.

Chapter 24

Reims, France
May 3
(Fourteen Months Ago)

"Cat! Wake up." Giselle was shaking her.

Cat sat up with a cry of awareness. She was in Giselle's subcompact. They were on their way to meet—

She glanced at the dashboard clock. 7:30 p.m. "Are we there?"

"Almost," Giselle said. "You were dreaming."

Cat blinked away tears. She'd dreamt of Dante again. Of the horrible fire, of his body burned beyond recognition.

Please don't let that be true.

Cat had spent the last eleven months in a self-imposed exile in Canada, nursing a resentment that had grown as rapidly as her belly. Hiding from everyone who knew her, who knew Dante, not wanting people to report, "Wow, is she ever preggars! Huge!"

Dropping out of sight, going radio silent, had also allowed her pride to cling to the fantasy that Dante was pining away, miserable without her.

God, if she'd only known . . .

And then her son had been born.

In a moment of postpartum idiocy, she'd named him Dante Johnson Samuels, forced to use the surname of her then-current alias. She'd nicknamed the baby DJ, hoping to avoid the constant reminder of the man who'd broken her heart. But her son looked more like his father every day. And Cat realized there was no loving one without loving the other.

Enter Plan B: Regain prebaby body and set up a meeting with Dante.

Except . . . then she'd learned Dante had been killed in action, nearly seven months ago. Even before her son was born. Her friend Max was dead, too. She'd been desperate for details. Specifics.

The official report gave scant details and had been modified twice. Maybe it was denial, though Cat thought it was all too pat. She wanted the truth; felt entitled to it. But where to start? She'd been out of the loop, and most of her feelers had been uprooted when Remi shuttered his business.

Cat had contacted Giselle—who'd only recently emerged from her own exile following her breakup with Remi St. James.

Giselle confirmed the date of when Dante supposedly died: September 20, but beyond that the story got squidgy. Three operatives and an interpreter killed by mortar in Cambodia—changed to three operatives sold out by the interpreter, killed by an explosion in Laos.

Digging deeper, Giselle, bless her, found an even more interesting morsel: two operatives dead, one alive. Burma.

One alive.

Cat had clung to that, certain there had to be a rescue in the works. If the CIA knew there was a chance that their operatives were alive, they likely had a covert liberation in process. Except Giselle's source insisted no one knew—although he had undeniable proof. He promised a photograph for fifty thousand Euros now, with another fifty thousand due when the photograph was verified as legitimate. He'd also refused to work with anyone but Giselle—though thankfully, Giselle had convinced the man to let Cat come along.

The two women had met in Paris yesterday, to finalize their plan. All Cat could think about was *one alive.* It had to be Dante.

"We'll pull over in a minute," Giselle said now. "In case you need to pee before we get there." Giselle had to call ten minutes before their meeting at the small inn, outside Reims.

"I'd like to call and check on the baby, too."

"Ack!" Giselle pretended to gag herself. "We've been gone two flipping hours. Are you afraid he's taken up smoking and drinking already? He's fine! In fact, you should probably leave him with a sitter more often."

"Don't remind me!" Cat would have to look for work even sooner after tapping her savings for the fifty thousand. Which was nothing if it gave the unequivocal proof, which was what Giselle's source had promised.

One alive.

"You should hire a male nanny." Giselle arched a perfect eyebrow. "Or a male au pair. Trade for services."

"I can't even joke about that right now. It's hard enough to leave DJ for one evening."

"You'd think we'd left him with Gypsies. Doesn't *Le Soleil Béni's* coveted five-star rating mean anything to you?"

When Cat had shown up in Paris with baby in tow, Giselle had insisted on leaving him with a professional sitter provided through her hotel. To save money, Cat had booked a cheaper room elsewhere, but a five-star sitter would eat up that savings quickly.

"I guess this all sounds pretty silly to you," Cat said.

They had pulled over and Giselle shut off the engine and opened her car door. "Actually, I'm jealous. You at least have a part of the man you loved. I have nothing but bitterness and a lot of questions."

Questions that I could answer, Cat thought as she made her way to the lavatory.

Damn you, Remi, for putting me in this spot. Remi St. James had been diagnosed with lung cancer several months ago. He'd told no one—except, of course, the ever-faithful Alfred. Public image was everything to Remi. Yes, he was vain, but as a national hero, he was allowed to be.

In typical Remi fashion, he'd announced he was closing shop to travel the world. Few believed that story, however. The more frequently whispered consensus was that Remi St. James had gone deep undercover on a job that entailed no less than saving the entire solar system.

Remi responded with a sly wink. Before leaving, he handed out nice bonuses—which Cat had welcomed since she was planning her own maternity disappearance at that time.

But Giselle . . . had deserved better. *Here's a gold*

watch and a bonus for fine service. Men could be such heartless imbeciles.

Remi had made it worse, by later confiding in Cat about his illness and making her promise to tell no one. Remi was certain he'd recover, confident he'd make it up to Giselle after he was cured.

Maybe when Cat got back to Paris tonight, she'd call Alfred, see if *he* could talk Remi into relenting. Giselle looked . . . fragile. And love was so precious. It was terrible that Remi and Giselle weren't together.

What Cat wouldn't give to see Dante again . . .

Giselle was on her cell phone when Cat returned to the car. "Yes, I'm certain we weren't followed." Giselle looked at Cat, rolled her eyes. "Very good." She disconnected the call and cranked the engine. "He sounds scared to death. Afraid we might sell him out to the CIA or something."

"We're still meeting at the inn?" Cat asked.

"Yes. He said a public spot would make him feel safer." Giselle made a face. "We should have made *him* drive to Paris and meet us atop the Eiffel Tower. We could have gone totally *film noir*—freaked him out."

Cat smiled. For a moment, she'd sounded like the old Giselle, the bold, sometimes reckless Giselle that had befriended a shy Catalina in London.

The car slowed as Giselle made a turn. After a half-mile, Cat watched for the sign. She checked the time, calculated they should be back in Paris before midnight.

Cat pointed to a sign. "There." *Oiseau Bleu.* She translated the name in her head. Bluebird Inn.

They drove past, checking it out before returning. There were no cars on the road and only one vehicle at the small inn. Cat's heart thudded and she realized she'd been praying under her breath.

One alive.

Let it be Dante, please God.

Giselle pulled into the narrow drive and parked beside the green Renault. Cat grabbed her backpack and climbed out. They had agreed to leave the money locked in the car until they saw what the man had. If it was as good as he'd promised, Cat would get the money while Giselle grilled the man further.

"Slow down." Giselle grabbed her arm so they could walk together. "You don't want him to see how eager you are."

"Part of me is afraid—" Cat bit her lip. *Afraid Dante was dead or that he would never love her.*

But even if he hated her, she still wanted him to be alive.

Alive, there was hope.

They stepped up to the small covered entry. Giselle reached for the door's handle. "That's strange. It's locked. Let's go—"

Her sentence ended with a scream. Cat turned and then she, too, was screaming, falling, convulsing on the ground beside Giselle.

Taser registered in Cat's mind.

When the agony subsided, she struggled to roll away, but her limbs wouldn't move. Then she was jolted again, pinned to the ground by more spasms of jerking pain.

"That's enough, Karl."

There was something familiar about the voice, the accent, but Cat's ears were ringing. She turned her head to retch and felt her arms being tugged behind her and secured with handcuffs.

As she was hauled to her feet, she tried to count how many there were. Two? Three? A man stood behind her, another behind Giselle.

A stinging slap nearly knocked Cat back down.

"I said, look at me!" That voice . . . it couldn't be.

Cat looked up, prayed she was wrong.

She wasn't.

Viktor Zadovsky smiled. "Let's see if I can help jar your memory of our last time together," he said.

Then he slapped her again.

Chapter 25

Rio de Janeiro, Brazil
July 12
(Present Day)

Dante leaped off the roof, skinning his knuckles as he shoved upright and took off sprinting.

Cat had already reached the end of the alley. Turning right. she disappeared from sight.

"No!" He pushed harder. Pain shot up from his groin. He ignored it. Christ! He deserved it for being so fucking stupid. For being taken down by a couple of the oldest tricks in the book.

That he'd recognized the first ploy, a fake faint, didn't matter. He should have been expecting it. Instead he'd allowed the red-hot heat of anger to fog his judgment. He'd compromised his grip on her the moment he'd switched to one hand. Wanting to look straight in her eyes had cost him everything.

She'd slung her weight just enough to tip the balance, forcing him to compensate. And in that one nanosecond of movement, she'd nailed him in the balls. Strike one. The sheer agony of that moment had trapped him between passing out and puking.   •

His crowning moment of total idiocy quickly played out. That he hadn't checked Cat for a weapon first thing was one hundred percent unforgivable. Strike two.

Dante careened around the corner and into the crowded street. Pushing against the sedate flow of foot traffic coming toward the brothels gained him more than one irritated look.

Fuck, fuck, fuck! Where had Cat gone?

He slowed, taking in what now looked like wall-to-wall bodies, approaching in waves. Shit! He continued heading forward, scanning faces as he went.

At five-six, Cat would be shorter than most of these men. Her dark hair—dark! not blond—had been loose to her shoulders. He scanned the crowd farther ahead. If she was up there, she was blending in too well.

He paused at the first intersection. A narrow alley ran crossways but appeared empty in both directions.

The futility of searching on foot became glaringly obvious. Every half block there was another alley or street. She could have cut down any of these and gone God knows where from there.

He acknowledged his final fatal mistake. Underestimating his opponent was strike three. Cat was formidable. She knew the rules of evasion as well as he did. Maybe better, considering the thrashing he'd just been handed.

She also had a home field advantage that might prove unbeatable. The countless unmarked streets and walkways that wove randomly through the *favelas* frequently led to dead ends or traps. Going in alone was foolhardy. He'd already met his dumb shit quota for the day, thanks.

Turning back, he approached the brothel he'd just passed. The man at the door smiled and waved him in.

Dante shook his head. "Did you see a woman run past here a minute ago?" he asked in Spanish. "Dark hair, this tall." He held his hand at shoulder height.

The man's smile increased. "We have lots of dark-haired women that size. With nice big titties." The man held his hands out in front of his own chest.

Others who were standing around started laughing.

"She would have been running that way."

The man shrugged, his eyes flitting to the blood on Dante's hand. "I hear nothing, see nothing . . . except of course, for our beautiful women. They will make you forget about the one that got away. Go inside, see for yourself." The man's voice dropped. "Or move on!"

Dante forced an apology he didn't mean and took off, not wanting to call more attention to himself. He continued down the street, away from the brothels. The ache in his testicles had dulled, allowing the sting of defeat to register. He flexed his hand, grateful she hadn't cut deep enough to slice tendons.

He bought a bottle of water from a man pushing a cart. "Did you see a woman—"

The man blinked and cut him off with a rattle of Portuguese that Dante couldn't follow. He did, however, understand the headshake. No.

After using the water to wash the worst of the blood from his hand, Dante tugged out his cell phone and dialed the person he should have called first.

Travis Franks's voice mail picked up on the first ring.

"Dan Dipshit Hogan here. Hit the jackpot, but already blew it. Call me." Dante closed his phone.

The crowd thinned out as he drew close to the city proper. The streets of the business district just ahead were choked with cars and busses. If Cat had made it this far . . .

Disappointment drove a stake in his chest. It was hard to believe that a mere—what?—ten minutes ago he'd had Catalina Dion in his arms.

Cat in his arms. The head rush he'd felt washed back over him.

To say she had been blown away was the mother of all understatements. Once she'd recognized him, shock, surprise, denial had widened her eyes. Color had drained from her face, as if she'd seen a ghost. *Him.* She'd thought he was dead, blown to bits along with his sailboat. She'd thought her identity and her hiding spot were safe.

Terror had kicked in then. He'd watched a flash of guilt cross her brow, then—boom!—she'd gotten pissed.

And Dante had almost caved. Most women wore their anger like horror masks. Cat's beauty transformed it; on her it beguiled. Hell, he could remember teasing, trying to make her mad—

His phone rang.

"Yeah," he snapped.

"Dipshit."

Dante gave Travis a fast update. "She could be anywhere by now."

"We need to monitor the airport, though she'll be expecting that," Travis said. "How soon before Rocco gets there?"

"Tomorrow morning."

"Damn. I've come up with a couple Rio addresses that match one of Giselle Barclay's old aliases. I'll text them to your phone shortly. I'll also lift a few rocks, see if I can scare up some local muscle till Rocco gets his ass down there. In the meantime, go back to your hotel and cool off."

Dante hung up. The thought of going to his room smacked of hiding.

Instead he headed back to *Pouca Flor*. Dozens of questions reverberated in his mind. He needed to find out where Cat lived, what places she frequented. Who were her friends? Giselle remained unaccounted for, though hopefully one of the addresses Travis had would pay off. He wondered if Giselle, too, worked at the brothel. If so, she'd likely already fled. However, if Giselle worked elsewhere, and if Dante could find her first . . .

The owner of *Pouca Flor* was out on the front porch, speaking to one of the hawkers. Judging by his red face and hand gestures, he wasn't happy.

Dante walked straight toward him. "Hey!"

The owner stopped talking and put his hands on his hips, switching from Portuguese to Spanish. "You owe me for a broken window!"

"You mean the one your cleaning lady broke?" He held up his bleeding knuckles. "Right after she pulled a knife on me and stole all my money? What kind of place are you running here?"

As others stopped to listen, the owner's anger morphed to a syrupy sympathy.

He put a hand on Dante's shoulder and lowered his voice. "Please come back inside, *señor*, where we can discuss this like gentlemen and find a mutually agreeable resolution."

Chapter 26

Jakarta, Indonesia
July 12
(Present Day)

In spite of the hour—2 a.m.—Viktor grabbed the ring-ing cell phone from his nightstand. He hadn't been asleep yet anyway, his mind too active on all the wrong subjects. Where were these lively synapses when he needed them during the day?

The caller ID displayed OUT OF AREA. He didn't answer. If it was a call he was expecting, they would leave a message.

His eyelids felt heavy, but wouldn't stay shut. Nights were still the worst. The wispy dreams of Lera were se-ductive. But always they ended in a shattering of glass.

Lera. Adrik.

Tossing away his covers, Victor climbed out of bed and headed to the bathroom. Again. Fucking prostate. He caught his reflection in the bathroom mirror. A sleep-deprived zombie.

He had medications for the insomnia, but the toll they

took on him the following day—fuzzy thinking, sluggish responses—wasn't worth it.

And one way or another, he'd catch up on rest soon enough. The only question was whether it would be via a sweet dream-filled slumber, or the more permanent bullet-in-the-back-of-the-head-type sleep.

The disappointing reports he'd received today on the latest batch of tests confirmed that he was out of time. Out of options. People were beginning to suspect sleight of hand. There was a limit to the number of rabbits he could pull out of the same old hat.

He flushed the commode, envisioning his career—his dreams—swirling down the sewer. If he didn't get results soon, he'd have to consider plan B: killing off all his enemies. No simple task, or else it would have been plan A.

Back in the bedroom, he picked up the phone and retrieved the voice mail message.

From Grigori: "I have news. Need instructions on how to proceed."

Viktor listened to the message twice and found it impossible to contain the swell of hope. Grigori sounded excited. Had a clue been found on Catalina Dion's whereabouts?

He dialed Grigori's number. "Tell me your news." Victor's voice sounded overly loud to his own ears.

"He did it. She's been spotted."

Overwhelmed, Viktor sat down with a rush, half afraid he'd misheard. "Where?" he demanded.

"In the slums of Rio de Janeiro. Doesn't that just figure?"

Brazil. Of course. While the term "slum" was a misnomer, he didn't correct Grigori. A picture of the endless shanties formed in Viktor's mind. With twenty-five percent of Rio's population residing in the endlessly honeycombed *favelas*, it was a perfect place to hide.

In fact, they'd looked there before, but it was like searching for one raindrop in the ocean.

"Does he have her in custody?" Viktor asked.

"No. He trailed her to a brothel, but she must have spotted him and fled. He's searching for her again, but I knew you'd want to know."

He'd found her at a whorehouse? Poetic justice.

Energized, Viktor stood and moved to his desk, where he began piling papers into his briefcase. "Since we need to get to her first, I am relieved she got away."

If she disappeared into some secret CIA spider hole, it would be harder, though not impossible, to get to her before she struck a deal with them using *his* data. "How many people are with him?"

"He arrived alone."

If true, that wouldn't last long. Reinforcements were likely en route. "We're on our way. I'll bring Karl and Alexander. Continue doing what you've done: stay on him. The equipment is functioning properly?"

"When I'm able to use it, yes."

"He'll be upset she got away, which will sharpen his instincts. He'll increase his efforts. But so will she. And she must not escape!"

"Don't worry. I want her as much as you," Grigori said. "Maybe more."

Yes, Viktor had made certain of that. "You've done excellent work, comrade. Just don't let what she did to your brother interfere with our plan. You will get her when I am through."

"I look forward to it."

"From here on I want to know his every move. And, Grigori, when he finds her again, remember: he's expendable. But she is *not*. I need her alive."

Viktor disconnected. He dialed Karl and quickly relayed Grigori's news. "Make arrangements for travel. I'll be ready to leave within the hour."

"Do you think it's wise for you to go?"

"We'll use our usual precautions. And we'll be back before anyone knows I've left."

Karl disagreed. "Alexander and I can handle it. And I have resources in Rio, if backup is needed."

"I have too much riding on this, Karl! I want to be present when she's captured."

Viktor disconnected, not quite as excited after talking with Karl. The man had gotten too used to making decisions on Viktor's behalf. No more! Yes, there were risks in leaving his safe haven but they were minimal. That *Mr. Peabody* and Company were hibernating worked in his favor.

And Karl had no idea how grim the situation had grown. If Viktor didn't get a solution soon, all his fraud would be uncovered. And at that point, Viktor would be better off dead.

Because there would be no place on earth that would be safe.

Chapter 27

Rio de Janeiro, Brazil
July 12
(Present Day)

Cat raced down alley after alley, zigzagging away from the brothel. Away from any place she typically went, avoiding anyone who might recognize her.

Her first priority was distance; next was finding a safe place to hide. Just long enough to think, plan, regroup. But where to go? Right now every place seemed dangerous. Better to stay on the run.

About a mile and a half from the brothel, she slowed as she approached a shopping district. The alley widened behind a bakery. The smell of sweets combined with her overexertion and ended up nauseating her.

She paused long enough to get sick, beside a trash bin. Then she helped herself to one of the bakery's white aprons that hung on a clothesline. Ripping the sleeves from her shirt and wrapping the apron twice around would help confound someone searching for her by description.

She used the torn scraps of shirt to wipe the blood off her arms and legs, relieved to find that the cuts she'd gathered were superficial. Now that she'd slowed, the numbing effect of adrenaline wore off. She ached all over from crashing onto the roof. She tested her left wrist, grateful it wasn't broken.

At the end of the alley, she turned south and waded straight into the busy street market. At the first vendor she found, she bought a wide-brimmed straw hat. Piling her hair beneath provided a minor disguise. But not enough.

A bus pulled up near the corner. She darted on just before it left. She watched as they pulled away but no one appeared to give her or the bus a second thought. The relief she felt was momentary.

Though she felt confident she'd lost anyone who might have followed from the brothel, she knew that Dante and friends would have fanned out. How many people was she up against?

She had been stunned to find no one posted behind the brothel. The Rio Police would have posted three-quarters of their force at the back. Once a suspect hit an alleyway, it was game over. Suspect 1, Police 0. The *favela* never gave up her own.

And therein lay a clue.

The fact that no Brazilian law enforcement had been present—the Federal Police would never allow the CIA to work solo inside the state—indicated a clandestine operation, an extraction. Dante probably didn't have more than one or two other operatives with him. They'd sneak in, grab her—sedate her, if necessary—and slip her out of the country.

The scary part was, *To where?* Had they already struck another deal with Viktor Zadovsky?

After eight blocks, Cat climbed off the bus, carrying an abandoned newspaper tucked beneath her arm. She didn't want to get too far away. Yet. She wouldn't leave Rio without her son.

Regret that she hadn't left Brazil already dogged her steps. Alfred had warned her, but she hadn't acted fast enough. *Alfred.* Jesus . . . was that how Dante had found her? Because she'd helped Remi? Would she face charges in connection with Remi's suicide? If that was true, then perhaps Marco's identity was still secure.

The sidewalks had opened into a small business district. She moved briskly along, studying the skyline. Then she doubled back and entered a nondescript four-story building. Signs advertising OFFICES FOR RENT were posted on the doors. The lobby was deserted except for an elderly man who'd just hung up the pay phone. As he moved toward the exit, she studied the directory of private offices, mostly legal and medical.

The elevator began humming in descent. Moving away, Cat pushed open the heavy metal door and entered the stairwell. At the very top, she found a maintenance door. Jimmying the lock with her dagger, she eased onto the flat terraced roof. Startled pigeons flew off.

Staying low, she moved to an enclosed corner behind a row of large electrical boxes. From here she had two escape routes: the building next door was a mere jump away, plus there was a wrought iron fire escape down the side.

Fighting tears, she sank to the ground and closed her eyes. Her limbs trembled violently as she forced herself to breathe slowly.

Seeing Dante alive was a bigger shock than her mind could handle. More than her heart could take, too. The urge to wrap him in her arms and rejoice had been strong. To touch, to feel, to know he was real.

But those feelings had just as quickly been strangled by the venom she saw in his eyes. He had seen the video. Of that there was no doubt. That was probably the *bomb* he spoke of. *Bombshell.*

She rubbed her forehead, recalling exactly how damning the video had been.

Viktor had obviously made good on his threat to provide a copy to the CIA. Had the video forced the Agency to scrub the high-level mission Dante had been on? That was the only explanation for staging the deaths of three top operatives that Cat could come up with. The CIA would pretend they're dead, mourn, grieve, swear vengeance . . . then send them into deep, deep undercover assignments, something fate-of-the-free-world big.

If that were the case, then Giselle's persistent questions about Dante's death may have been perceived as a threat. Had the CIA sold them out to Zadovsky to quickly silence their queries?

And if Dante was alive, did it mean her friend Max—probably ex-friend now—was too?

Digging through the minefield that was the past made Cat's head hurt even worse. And solved nothing. She forced her focus back to the present. The here, the now, the oh-shit.

That she'd gotten away was a temporary win in a battle that had much bigger stakes.

For her it was Marco.

If Viktor Zadovsky ever learned about her son . . .

No. She'd taken extreme measures to keep Marco hidden.

And as painful as it was to contemplate, she might have to leave those measures in place, leave Marco at the orphanage for now. At least until she felt they could flee safely.

Right now, she was being hunted. If Dante captured her with her son, he'd know the truth. Would he even try to seek custody for a child he'd never wanted?

People like us can't have families.

Which one of us would be a worse parent?

She swallowed against the ache in her throat. She needed to warn Sister Dores. Once Dante started backtracking, there was a good chance he'd learn she had a connection to the orphanage.

She weighed the risks of using the pay phone down in the lobby. The chances of the church phone being tapped were slim. If Dante had known she was at the orphanage, it would have made better sense to nab her on her way to or from work. Confronting her at the brothel had been risky.

She emptied her pockets. What little money she had on her wouldn't last long. The prepaid card she carried for pay phones had been purchased at a random newsstand months ago. Thousands of those cards were sold daily for cash. They were untraceable. Still, she'd discard it after using it.

Peering over the edge of the roof, she studied the crowds and traffic below. Once she made a phone call from here, she'd need to find another place to hide until nightfall, when she could move around more freely.

Creeping downstairs, she was relieved to find the lobby empty. She dialed the church office, prayed one of the nuns would answer quickly.

Instead, Zetta, the other volunteer, answered.

Cat cut off the woman's overly cheerful explanation of how quickly she was packing up the last of the church office in preparation for moving. "I need to speak with Sister Dores right away."

"She is cooking. Can I give her a message?"

"Hang up and tell her to come to the office. I will call back in a few minutes." Cat disconnected without waiting for a reply.

Ducking back into the stairwell, she counted seconds, then called the orphanage a second time. Her hands were shaking again and she almost cried out when Sister Dores answered, sounding as normal and harried as ever.

"I can't talk long; this is urgent," Cat said. "Someone might be listening. Are the children okay and has anyone been there looking for me?" She didn't want mention her son's name.

The nun spoke slowly. "They are all fine. Uh, the sick ones are all eating again." Since Marco had been the only sick child not eating, Cat knew that Sister Dores understood her unspoken question. "And no one's been here," the nun went on. "Can you tell me what is wrong?"

"Someone very bad is searching for me, so I have to leave. I will be in touch, but remember our agreement." *Seven days.* If the nun didn't hear from Cat within a week, she was to assume the worst.

"I understand."

"Give the children my love." *Give Marco my love.* Cat's voice started to break. "I'll be in touch."

"We'll light a candle for your safe return."

A tear streaked down Cat's cheek. She dashed it away. That meant Sister Dores would hang a white handkerchief in the front window to indicate it was safe—or in this case, that no one had come by. A red kerchief would signal danger.

It was a system they'd created back when Cat and Marco had first arrived at the orphanage. After all that Cat had suffered at Viktor's hand, she'd been extremely paranoid. Scared to leave, scared to stay. Unable to forget the atrocities.

The kerchief in the window had helped exorcise those fears.

Fears that had now returned.

Chapter 28

Berlin, Germany
June 2
(Thirteen Months Ago)

Cat put the makeup on extra heavy.

Yesterday Viktor had been furious because her bruises had shown up on the video. Giselle had paid dearly for it. The week before he'd been upset her roots had darkened, had ordered her to color her hair. "You must look impeccable!" Viktor had commanded.

Cat no longer questioned how her friend could endure it. While Viktor never drugged Giselle *before* she was tortured, what he gave afterward blocked her pain. It also blocked the memory of what had gone before, so each time Giselle faced her horrors anew. She couldn't remember that it always ended when she passed out. She couldn't remember why she was being punished.

And though Cat dutifully explained every time that Giselle's torment was part of Cat's punishment—Viktor wanted no information from either of them—each session began with Giselle's awful cries of "But what have I done?"

And when Giselle screamed out that she'd tell Viktor anything if only they'd stop . . . Cat held her breath, afraid her friend would mention the tiny two-month-old infant that they'd left in Paris.

Dear God! What had happened to her son?

How much longer could this madness go on?

Behind her a whip cracked. Cat jumped and stepped back from the delicate eighteenth-century mirrored vanity. The house they were in, what little she'd seen of it, was large and filled with similar expensive antiques.

To torment her with his confidence that they'd never escape, Viktor freely explained they were at his late aunt's home outside Berlin. Judging from the occasional snippets she overheard in German from a television somewhere in the house, Cat believed this was true.

Cat turned now to face Viktor. His cell phone rang and he answered, business as usual. He knew Cat wouldn't scream or cry out again when he was on the phone.

Giselle had already been strung up in the far corner of the spacious bedroom. She dangled naked, on tiptoes, her arms pulled straight up and secured by the rope that hung from the ceiling. Giselle was gagged, but her eyes darted around wild and frightened. *But what have I done?*

Viktor was seated in a leather chair beside Giselle. He kept the phone pressed to one ear, while spooning sugar into his tea. "Yes, yes, it's going better than expected. Your little show of faith"—he glanced at Cat—"has convinced me. One of my associates will be in touch to consummate our final agreement."

Viktor met Cat's gaze as he ended the call. "Those

stupid bastards have no idea what they've done. They hand you over like a sacred lamb. As if anything could ever make up for the loss of my wife and son. I will make laughing stocks of them with these videos."

Cat had been told from day one of her captivity—Viktor enjoyed counting off days—that he blamed her for everything that had gone wrong in Belarus.

He knew there had been other agents involved, but Cat had infiltrated his inner sanctum: his lab. Her face was the face of deception. He even seemed convinced that the Chechen Rebels who'd attacked the *Institut* had done so at the CIA's behest. And since she'd worked for the CIA back then, she bore the onus of their guilt.

Cat had slowly come to realize that with Dante and the others actually dead, the CIA had sold her and Giselle out, to make amends with Zadovsky, who was now an all-powerful free agent.

Any guilt she might have felt over what she was being forced to do had long since fled. Some days she even relished the thought that these videos would indeed end up in the hands of the CIA's worst enemies.

Two men entered the bedroom.

Karl Romanov, Viktor's bodyguard and butt monkey, stepped around the video camera mounted on a tripod as he moved to stand beside Giselle. The other man, whom she knew only as Jeter, stood in the open doorway, eyeing Cat.

"I thought an audience might inspire you," Viktor said. "Take your place."

Cat walked across the icy cold room and perched on the edge of the bed. She'd been given the red lace outfit to wear again. A long-line corset bra, frilly garters, and seamed nylons with matching red stilettos that killed her feet. Literally.

There were razor blades imbedded inside her shoes. And if Cat winced as she walked, Giselle was whipped.

"I hope you remember what you did wrong yesterday." Viktor lit a cigarette. "Your friend could use a reprieve."

At Viktor's nod, Karl activated the camera. Cat forced herself to smile in Jeter's direction. Though he was off camera, it would appear that she was hell-bent on coaxing someone into her bed. That she was determined to woo him with her body, and failing that, to start spilling secrets of how she'd brought other operatives to their knees by fucking their bodies and minds.

Cat's failure to come across convincingly yesterday had resulted in her friend's punishment. *Oh, Giselle! I will not fail you again.*

Cat had quickly learned that what she said mattered little as long as she got the names and places right. Viktor knew which jobs she'd worked and with whom, but apparently not the specific details since he didn't correct her fabrications. Not that she was giving up much since the people she spoke of were now dead.

They filmed for only twenty minutes. Once Cat was completely naked—except for her shoes—and had promised to tell her lover more, soon, Viktor stopped filming. For Cat, it was both too long and not long enough.

When Viktor offered mocking applause, signaling the end, Giselle reacted with a Pavlovian whimper. Giselle knew what came next, what her part was. Looking at Viktor, Giselle begged with her eyes to be released.

Viktor withdrew a capped syringe from his pocket. "You want this, my pet?"

Jeter moved in and handcuffed Cat's wrists behind her. Then he grabbed the hair on the back of her head and forced her to watch Viktor's sick little show.

Giselle stared at the syringe, her body writhing. Behind the gag, she made animalistic noises.

"Show Karl how bad you want it," Viktor said.

Barely able to move, Giselle twisted, trying to get Karl's attention. He ignored her. Her noises grew louder until Karl backhanded her. Then Giselle bounced on her toes, her noises even more desperate.

Karl slapped her again. Across the face, the breasts. And Giselle bounced furiously, wanting more, more, more.

"I think that's enough," Viktor said finally.

Karl removed the gag and untied Giselle's hands. She was free . . . but all she did was stare at the syringe Viktor held.

"Now show me how bad you want this," Viktor said.

Giselle dropped to her knees at Viktor's feet and pushed his legs apart. She attacked his trousers, groping to free his flaccid penis.

And then she was sucking, making those awful animal noises again, her blond hair covering Viktor's lap. Viktor patted her head, and ignoring both women, he casually asked Karl if the day's mail had arrived.

A few minutes later Viktor lifted Giselle's hair and looked down at his still soft penis going in and out of her mouth.

"*Tsk*. You must not want it as badly as I thought," Viktor said. "Perhaps later."

"No, no, no, no." Giselle redoubled her efforts, sucking harder, moaning, crying, and clawing at Viktor's pants.

Cat detected Jeter's low smirk as he tightened the grip

on her hair, shaking her ever so slightly though not enough to get Viktor's attention.

Jeter knew, they all knew, that Viktor wouldn't get aroused until he looked at Cat. And the longer Viktor ignored Cat, the more frantic Giselle's efforts became.

Finally, Viktor met Cat's gaze and smiled. "See how nicely this goes when you do what you're supposed to?"

Cat tried to nod, but Jeter's grip was too tight.

Giselle was making different noises now as Viktor's penis began to enlarge. She knew that precious syringe was almost hers.

"You can get her ready for me," Viktor said to Jeter.

The grip on Cat's hair released and she was jerked to her feet. Then Jeter turned her back to the bed and bent her forward, facedown in the mattress. The razor blades chewed into her feet again.

Behind her, she heard Jeter lower his zipper. He pinched her buttock, silently daring her to react. "Now tell Viktor how bad you want him."

Chapter 29

Rio de Janeiro, Brazil
July 12
(Present Day)

Cat eased into her hiding spot at the convent. It was risky coming here in broad daylight, mere hours after being discovered. But her newly hatched plan depended on her moving fast.

Using bottled water, she bathed and changed into better clothes. She counted her stash of money. Part of her regretted what she was going to have to spend to pull this off. Another part was grateful she had the money available. If all went as planned—*no ifs*, it had to work—there'd still be enough for her and Marco to flee, to begin anew.

The temptation to go by the orphanage grew with each heartbeat. To see Marco just once more . . .

No.

She ticked off the reasons in her mind. It was likely the orphanage was being watched. Coming here was hazardous enough. And she had yet to make good her escape.

But the truth . . . the real reason she couldn't go see her son was that she knew she wouldn't be able to leave him.

She wiped away tears and started separating her cash. She divvied it up among the multiple hidden folds of her backpack, along with her other IDs.

Then she repacked her clothes, including the two wigs she'd need to match her passports. Anything she couldn't carry on her back had to stay behind.

Feeling queasy, she wiped the beads of perspiration from her forehead. Damn it, she couldn't get sick right now. She had a plan to execute. A plan she prayed wasn't totally insane.

Instead of hiding from Dante, she was going to lure him away. There was a flight leaving for Mexico City in three hours and she planned to be on it, ticketed as Luzia Gomez. If he hadn't already done so, Dante would eventually monitor the airlines.

He wouldn't have her arrested at Rio Airport, where she'd be taken into Brazilian custody and could fight extradition. Even if she lost, time in a foreign jail would give her an opportunity to strike a deal with her captors. Or better yet . . . to escape.

There was a risk he'd have someone waiting in Mexico City. But even if she was arrested there, at least she would have drawn Dante away from Rio. Away from Marco.

No *ifs*, she told herself again. After she landed in Mexico City, she'd book a flight to Amsterdam, but someone else would be on that flight, carrying her *Luzia* identification. Then using a brand new passport, she'd make her way back here, collect Marco and his passports, before vanishing.

Could she do this?

Once upon a time she'd been one of the best. She

had been trained by a master: Remi. And she'd loved a
master: Dante.

Dante was now her opponent and this was the final
episode.

Damn it, she *could* do this. She was a pro. She would
win.

A cool steeliness took over.

"Let the games begin."

Dante returned to his hotel thoroughly disgusted with
himself. It was almost six o'clock. More than six hours
had passed since Cat had bolted. That was one hellacious
head start.

That the airports were being watched would matter
only if Cat used a known alias.

If she used a different name, if she left Rio by car, or
train, or boat—she could be anywhere. Her head start
would grow exponentially with each minute, each mile.

But he also couldn't eliminate the possibility that she
was still right here in the city. Right under his nose. If she
had burrowed into one of Rio's hundreds of *favelas*, he'd
never find her.

Favelas had a strong social code. Communities were
tight knit, protecting their own while rejecting outsiders.
Most had their own system of justice and even protection,
courtesy of whichever crime cartel controlled the area.

Even the brothel owner, Ernesto, who seemed willing
to do anything for money, refused to violate *favela* sanc-
tity, claiming to keep no records on employees, or expendable day workers, as he called them. Ernesto's

reticence likely had more to do with his fear of reprisal than loyalty to the community.

Since Dante wasn't in Rio in any official capacity, there was a limit to how far he could push his irate-customer jag. Ernesto had tried to cajole him with a substitute prostitute. Failing that, the slimy bastard had offered another cleaning lady. A pregnant cleaning lady. Ernesto's final gesture had been to return half of Dante's money before basically throwing him out.

After that, Dante had tried to locate the squatter who'd first tipped him off about Luzia, but the man was gone. And the few other people he'd approached in the area had regarded him suspiciously and said nothing.

The rest of the afternoon had been spent hitting brick walls. The addresses Travis had forwarded on Giselle's alias turned up dry. He'd even ditched his disguise and returned to *Pouca Flor,* mingling with the crowds outside as he tried to keep an eye on the brothel in case Cat came back to the scene of the crime. But he couldn't watch both the front and the back.

Now his hotel room closed in. He finished the meal he'd ordered from room service and checked e-mail. Rocco had forwarded his itinerary but couldn't get there fast enough.

Dante decided to return to the brothel's neighborhood. Maybe by now the old drunk had returned to his place in the ruins.

But just as he was leaving, Travis called. Dante slipped back inside his room, hoping that Travis had found a local connection.

"Luzia Gomez boarded a flight out of Rio less than thirty minutes ago," Travis said. "Cash ticket, purchased last minute."

Shit. Dante fired up his laptop. "Destination?"

"Mexico City. ETA eighty-thirty a.m. local time, with a three-hour layover in Buenos Aires."

Dante did a quick calculation. That was sixteen hours from now. A private charter was the only way he could possibly make it to Mexico City before Cat. And even that was pushing it. Besides, there was no guarantee she'd continue on from Buenos Aires. Beating her to Argentina at this point would be impossible.

"If I take off for Mexico City, can you have Buenos Aires watched in case she bolts from there?" Dante asked.

"I'll work it. But there's another problem you need to be aware of," Travis said. "MI6 has picked up on our interest. I don't have specifics, but they've gone from raised antenna to full hard-on. I know these phones are still secure, but consider everything else potentially problematic for now."

"And if British intelligence is on this, then the Israelis won't be far behind," Dante said. If MI6 or the Mossad got to Cat first he'd never get to question her.

"It limits what I can do through the usual channels without tipping my hand." Travis was pissed. "As soon as you get this job wrapped, I've got another waiting in the wings."

Dante hung up without commenting on Travis's assumption that he'd continue working for the Agency. In Dante's book, everything hinged on finding Cat. And knowing that others searched for her as well sharpened his obsession.

Logging on to e-mail again, Dante reread Rocco's itinerary. Rocco had picked up a flight to Rio from L.A. with a *change of planes in Mexico City.* Yes! Dante dialed his friend's cell phone, which went directly to voice mail.

"Major changes here. Stay in Mexico City. I'll meet you there."

He looked up a few more things online, then he started calling private jet services, purposely avoiding the one the Agency favored. If MI6 and the Mossad had an ear to the ground, he had to tread lightly.

Chapter 30

Buenos Aires, Argentina
July 12
(Present Day)

Cat's layover in Buenos Aires stretched her nerves to spun glass.

That she hadn't been nabbed at Rio Airport had encouraged her. That courage had faltered when she'd deplaned here. She fully expected to be arrested and had already decided to cling to her alias, not to waver in her assertion that she was a Brazilian national.

Argentina's government would hand her over to Brazil before they surrendered her to the United States. But if Argentina knew it was the CIA who wanted her, Brazil could kiss her good-bye.

When no one appeared to give her a second thought, a new worry bloomed. Did Dante know she'd left Rio yet? The thought of him discovering her connection to the orphanage wasn't as scary now that Sister Dores had been warned. The nun would never give her away. Marco's name couldn't be traced to Cat . . . unless Dante actually saw the child. There was no denying Marco's Y chromosome donor.

Inside the terminal, Cat ate a sandwich, but got sick shortly thereafter. Nerves, she told herself. She purchased an antinausea medication and ibuprofen, hoping the combination stayed in her stomach as she moved to a different gate.

The sensation that she was being watched grew with each step she took. She studied the crowd, suspicious of a tall red headed woman wearing Dolce & Gabbana. Until the woman boarded a flight to London.

As the departure time for Mexico City drew close, Cat once again felt sick. Waiting until the last call to board, she approached the stewardess. No one rushed forward or shouted out an order to "freeze!"

Memorizing faces as she moved down the plane's aisle, Cat found a teenaged girl in her window seat. The girl tugged out her earphones long enough to ask, "Do you mind switching?"

Too tired to argue, Cat stowed her backpack under the seat in front of her. Then she offered a quick prayer of gratitude. She knew the anxiety would build anew as they approached Mexico City. The next few hours would be her best chance for sleep.

Still, she didn't close her eyes until she felt the plane pull away from the terminal. God, she felt awful and—

The plane slowed and a male voice came across the speakers. "This is the captain. We have encountered a mechanical problem and have to return to the terminal. Please remain in your seats. We will not be disembarking and hope to get back under way shortly."

He's lying. Cat gripped the armrests.

"Oh, crap," the girl beside her said. "My boyfriend is waiting for me in Mexico City."

Cat released her seat belt. The plane jerked to a stop again. She tried to peer around the sulking girl, to see out the window. It was dark outside, but in the glare of the terminal's bright lights she saw the walkway shift forward. If they weren't disembarking, why extend steps to the passenger door?

She started to rise, to head toward the bathroom. But four men, dressed in black SWAT gear, rushed into the front of the plane. Two of the men carried compact submachine guns. The passengers gasped in unison.

"Airport security!" the man in charge barked.

It was over. Cat's heart sank. She tried to formulate her response, but thoughts of her son intruded. Marco! Would she ever see him again?

The man was showing a piece of paper to the stewardess. The woman shrugged. Cat knew it was her photograph, probably not a recent one.

Two of the men had started down the aisle slowly. They paused at each row and scanned every face. As terrifying as it must have seemed for the other passengers, Cat refused to make it easy for them. To resist arrest would be foolish, but why volunteer?

A cell phone rang. The man up front answered.

Cat strained to read his lips. The men conducting the search were now two rows away. When they stepped forward, Cat looked up, prepared to meet their gaze.

"Paulo! Curtis!" The man clipped his cell phone back onto his belt and tipped his head toward the door.

Immediately, the men closest to Cat turned and rushed

off the plane. All the passengers started talking at once. Several demanded an explanation from the captain.

Cat was stunned, uncertain of what trick they were playing.

"What is happening?" the girl asked.

"I'm not certain," said Cat.

The stewardess had been speaking with one passenger, but moved away to answer the cabin phone. The noise dropped as everyone tried to eavesdrop. Then a whispered explanation spread from row to row.

The man across the aisle from Cat leaned toward her. "They thought some international terrorist was on this flight," he repeated. "But they called back the wrong plane."

The wrong plane . . . Sweet Jesus! She was okay. Marco was okay.

The captain came on with an apology, making a joke. But no one laughed, especially when they learned all outbound traffic had been temporarily halted.

Three hours later, Cat was still clenching the armrests as the plane finally ascended into the night sky.

Cat was getting sicker by the hour. No more telling herself it was stress, nerves. She'd bullied her psyche into blind obedience one too many times. The hypervigilance of the past year suddenly seemed to catch up.

Once the plane left Argentina, her body started shutting down. Chills blanketed her. The antinausea medicine seemed to work, but so far the ibuprofen wasn't helping her fever or aches.

She remembered how ill the two nuns had been. Was

this what poor little Marco had felt like when he was sick? God, she missed him even as she was grateful he wasn't with her right now.

Sister Dores's admonition to think of Marco first was never far from Cat's mind. Was this existence fair to her son?

No, it wasn't. It wasn't fair for either of them. But damn if Cat could ever bring herself to willingly give him up. There had to be another way. A safe place. Somewhere . . . Someplace . . .

She nearly jumped out of her skin when the plane touched down in Mexico City, unaware that she'd fallen asleep.

Her primary concern, that someone would be waiting to grab her inside the terminal, mushroomed. But with fear came the gift of adrenaline.

Another hour was all she needed. She had to book a ticket to Amsterdam. For her plan to have the best chance at success, Dante needed to think Luzia Gomez had headed to Europe.

Cat would take a cab to the closest bus station and find a willing runaway to take her flight. And right after that Cat would find a cheap room, lock herself in, and let this sickness run its course.

The plane had stopped, and everyone started moving. Cat stood, swayed, and grabbed the seat in front of her until the dizziness passed.

Please, just a little longer.

Walking took energy. Thinking took effort. That the wig she wore felt hot and heavy didn't help. Struggling to keep up with the crowd as they jostled down the jetway, Cat fell in behind an older, heavyset man who struggled with carrying two bags.

"Here. I'll help you." Forcing a smile through gritted teeth, Cat took one of his suitcases and linked her arm through his. "You lead the way."

The man called her a Good Samaritan and then started talking about his upcoming visit with a grandson. They walked as a couple into the terminal.

Cat scanned the crowd. The passengers milling around, waiting to board this flight as it continued on, looked unhappy. The unexpected delay in Argentina had caused an international ripple.

A severe wave of nausea hit Cat as they moved into the main terminal walkway. She spotted the restroom sign and stopped. Tugging her arm free, she gave the man back his bag.

"This is as far as I'm going," she said.

The man squeezed her fingers, asking for her name as he thanked her again. Pretending not to hear, Cat rushed into the ladies' room and barricaded herself in a corner stall.

Thanks to Travis's *help*, Dante had arrived in Mexico City four hours before Cat's flight arrived. He wasn't sure how Travis had managed to delay the flight in Buenos Aires, but Dante used the extra time to plan.

Rocco had arrived six hours before Dante and had already made the initial arrangements, tapping into local underground sources to secure the items they needed.

"The rest we'll play by ear once we have her," Rocco said.

"Provided she is on the plane."

Staying off the radar sometimes meant flying blind. While *Luzia Gomez* had reboarded in Buenos Aires, Dante wouldn't believe it was Cat until he'd visually confirmed it for himself.

Hell, at this point he wasn't certain Cat had even boarded in Rio. She could have given her tickets and passport away and remained in Rio. Or booked a flight elsewhere under another name. He recalled the cologne, the telltale sign. The thought that she was boldly taunting him again shortened his fuse.

"If she's not here, we'll just keep hunting," said Rocco. "The fact she's on the run is good. She'll screw up and we'll nail her."

"We just have to make damn sure we get her before anyone else."

"I'd like five minutes alone with whoever's broadcasting our business."

"I'd settle for two," Dante said.

"I'm betting that whoever it is contributed heavily to your smear campaign," Rocco went on. "Think about it. The circumstances of your return would have been a great opportunity to offload and defuse suspicions."

Now, as the flight from Buenos Aires pulled into the gate, Rocco and Dante split up.

Dante stood off to the side, hidden in a crowd. He watched the passengers stream forward and focused on the first knot of people, methodically scanning each and every face.

"Excúseme, por favor." A man pushed in front of Dante, blocking his view. Dante shifted left, but so did the man.

Shoving to the right, Dante regained a clear view but

now he'd lost track. Shit! He glanced down the corridor at the retreating bodies then back to the passengers still coming forth.

Damn it, Cat, where are you?

He felt his concentration heighten, like it had at the brothel when his hypersensitivity had literally pinged in her presence. *That only happens when I think of Cat.* Could he replicate that phenomenon now?

He pictured her with dagger in hand, when she'd cut him, when she'd escaped. Sure enough, something inside his head seemed to spark. Then his senses burst to life, shimmering outside his body like an aura.

Oh, yeah. *She was here.* He could feel it.

Following his instincts, he hurried after the people he'd just missed. The drumbeats in his head grew louder. *Ba-bam, ba-bam.* He started focusing on the women, felt a tug in his brain.

The sensation grew stronger when he focused on one woman with short gray hair. A wig. *Bingo.*

She had been walking beside an older man, but now stopped.

For a second, Dante thought she was headed back toward him. Instead she abruptly dashed into the ladies' room.

Had she known she was being followed?

Dante's phone vibrated.

"You got her?" asked Rocco.

"She's in the restroom. Get over here."

The realization that he'd found Cat again sank in. He'd blown it last time. Now he was ready.

She'd be armed—somehow—and she'd change her disguise. But he was prepared for all her tricks. All he needed was twenty seconds.

Dante took up a position outside the restroom. He made eye contact with Rocco and marked the time. He'd give it two minutes, tops. Then he'd go in after her.

Cat peeled off the wig. Beneath it her hair was soaked. The sudden contrast of cooler air was delicious.

Feeling revived, she left the stall. Within seconds she felt lightheaded again. Lurching forward, she caught herself on the sink. Twisting the faucet, she scooped water into her mouth. Then she splashed it on her face and her wrists.

The restroom grew eerily quiet. Cat became aware that people stared at her. A glance at her reflection revealed why. She had no color, her eyes overly bright. And she was shaking. Sweating profusely. She had another flashback of Giselle . . .

Jesus. These women thought Cat was a junkie. Maybe desperate for a fix. Concerned someone might report her to security, she grabbed her backpack and moved to leave.

A line had formed, but the women clustered near the door gave her a wide berth. Where two seconds ago Cat had been freezing, she now felt too warm. The stuffy air made her feel claustrophobic.

Eager to be free of the close quarters, Cat shifted sideways and squeezed out of the restroom.

She turned sharply into the corridor and ran straight into a man. Balance lost, she wove sideways as her backpack slid off her shoulder. The man's hand shot forward, steadying her. Grateful he'd prevented her from falling, she mumbled an apology.

"Excuse me." She bent to retrieve her pack.

Too late she felt something brush her neck. There was

a prick, a sting. She straightened, clamping her hand to her neck as she rounded on the man.

"Dante."

Slinging her bag in front of her took more effort than it should have. Her legs wobbled as her knees began to soften. "What did you . . ."

Her tongue tingled, going numb. Mute. She met his eyes and knew. He'd drugged her.

Oh, Jesus, no!

"Here, darling, let me help you." He'd caught her bag and hefted it to his shoulder. "Still feeling bad?"

She knew his words were for the benefit of anyone watching, listening. He pulled her close, brushing his mouth close to her cheek, her ear. To anyone observing, Dante probably looked like a caring lover.

"I'm going to do everything they did—and worse—to you, Cat," he whispered.

His words made no sense, yet the malice that they were spoken with made her fear him. *The drug.*

He nodded at someone behind her.

She blinked. *Must fight.*

"Just sit down, honey, and we'll get you out of here fast."

Dante's hand was on her shoulder, pushing her down, but she didn't fall far. It registered that she was in a wheelchair. They were moving. Too fast.

"Stop!" she shouted. "Let me go!"

Except she wasn't really shouting. The drug had her trapped in that dark, awful void of nightmares and fears.

Fight, damn it! Don't give up!

The very words Cat had screamed at Giselle had come back to haunt her.

Chapter 31

Berlin, Germany
July 4
(Twelve Months Ago)

Giselle was dying. Cat had watched her friend slowly deteriorate over the last weeks, but her rate of decline had increased dramatically in the three days since Viktor had left them in Jeter's care.

Viktor treated them like animals. They were kept naked and wore collars. Lately, he'd kept them caged in his private lab, a mere arm's length away. Some breakthrough in an experiment had him so involved in his work that he'd quit making videos—much to Jeter's dismay.

As Cat recalled from Belarus, Viktor rarely slept, rarely left his desk. Unfortunately, his cruelty hadn't abated as his work increased. Cat had begged him to punish her instead, which only made it harder on Giselle.

"Your job is to watch her suffer," Viktor had said. "To know that you caused every bit and can do nothing to stop it—for the rest of your life."

With Viktor in the lab constantly, their torment had grown even more frequent. Particularly, Giselle's, who'd been forced to stand in as a literal lab rat more than once. The long-standing rumors of Viktor's knowledge and interest in mind-controlling substances were true, as he demonstrated with Giselle.

"Her addiction interferes with certain results," Viktor had complained to Cat. "But once the formulation is perfected, you'll see firsthand the full effect."

Cat realized that was one more reason why she was never drugged. She would be Victor's next guinea pig and he wanted her pure.

Provided she was still alive when Viktor returned.

Jeter clearly enjoyed being in charge of them. But where Viktor was calculating in his torture—always careful not to push it too far—Jeter was reckless. *Too far* was his goal. He got off on cruelty.

Jeter struck harder and more frequently. He denied them food. He also withheld Giselle's shots too long, getting his kicks out of watching her beg, watching her do anything he asked . . . only to deny her again and again.

He'd even handcuffed Cat to a lab table and raped her while telling Giselle that she had to do better, that she wasn't satisfying Jeter nearly as much as Cat was . . . and therefore, Cat might be rewarded with Giselle's fix. Poor Giselle.

Cat checked the time. Jeter had actually left them alone this evening, making Cat pray that Viktor was returning.

In the last few hours, Giselle's withdrawal symptoms had grown severe. Unable to stand, she lay in her cage, covered in her own vomit, crying, "But what did I do?"

Cat's attempts to soothe her friend seemed to go unheard, leaving her to feel even more helpless and alone.

Her secret worry for her son haunted her as well. What had the hotel done when Giselle and Cat hadn't returned? Had her son been turned over to the authorities as abandoned?

Her son had been barely two months old when Cat had left him in Paris. He had just begun to smile, laugh. Now he was four months old. Cat had been gone for half of his life. Had he forgotten her?

"Please . . . help . . . me," Giselle whispered.

"I'm here, Giselle."

Cat quieted as the key grated in the door. *Please be Viktor.*

Jeter pushed the door open and immediately made a face at the smell. "Jesus! What have you done in here?"

"She is sick," Cat said.

"That's obvious!" He held his hand over his nose and mouth as he retreated toward the door. "You'll have to clean it up before morning, you know."

Did that mean Viktor would return tomorrow?

Not wanting Jeter to leave yet, Cat grasped the bars of her cage and hung her head in defeat, the way Giselle did. "Please can we have food? We're both so weak." She raised her eyes. "I'm so hungry; I'll do anything . . . anything for food."

The look on Jeter's face changed from surprise to eagerness. Cat was always obedient, but she never acted cowed. Now she realized that in submission lay power. Jeter liked to dominate the weak.

He moved closer, lowered his voice. "Food? What would you do for some fine Belgium chocolate?"

Cat let tears come to her eyes. She opened her mouth slightly, touched her tongue to her lip. "I'd do . . ." She swallowed, tried not to gag. "What would you like me to do?"

Jeter's eyes darkened as he reached in his pocket and withdrew a pair of handcuffs. He signaled her to raise her wrists. Cat obeyed, grateful he cuffed them in front of her.

When he unlocked her cage, Cat hesitated, looking at him warily, as if frightened of what he might do or ask.

Jeter's smile widened. "I will take you to the kitchen and show you all my food." He tugged on the handcuff chain, leading her out of the lab.

Cat hadn't seen the main living areas of the house. That it looked normal was bizarre. Mary Poppins would have felt at home here.

Jeter pulled her across the kitchen and into a food pantry. Heavy, oversized pots and pans filled the lower shelves. The upper rows were lined with grocery items and food staples.

Cat pretended to tremble, her eyes darting back and forth as she leaned closer to the shelf. "Oh, peaches. I love peaches."

Jeter positioned himself in the doorway between the kitchen and the pantry. He grabbed a square tin, shook it. "Chocolate. Remember?" He spread his legs, assuming *the stance*.

Cat knew what Giselle was conditioned to do. She slowly dropped to her knees. "Yes, anything."

With shaking hands, she reached for his fly. As soon as Cat freed his engorged penis, Jeter shoved the tin back on the shelf and braced his hands against the doorjamb. "You will not stop until I say."

Cat stroked his shaft slowly with her cuffed hands, flicking her thumbs across the sensitive spot just below the head. He groaned with pleasure and thrust his pelvis forward. Cat opened her mouth. Jeter exhaled and thrust again.

Then he screamed.

Cat wrenched the handcuff chain tightly around his penis, hoping to sever it. Jeter punched her in the jaw, still howling with pain. Cat fell backward, against the shelves, but immediately jumped back to her feet.

She plowed headfirst into Jeter's stomach. Hampered by his pants wrapped at his ankles, he slammed backward, hitting the floor. Cat landed on top of him. She raised her hands and bashed his temple repeatedly with the heavy can she'd snatched off the shelf.

Jeter's grip released. She rolled free and knelt over his unconscious body, feeling sick.

Not now.

She searched his pockets, withdrew the heavy ring of keys. Unlocking herself first, she dragged Jeter toward the refrigerator and cuffed one arm to the door.

She was free. *Giselle. Her son.*

Cat flew to the door on the opposite wall. The alarm panel blinked: INACTIVE. Jeter had been so fucking certain of his power over Giselle he'd grown complacent. Careless.

She yanked the door open and spotted two cars in the garage. She found the Audi fob on the key ring and hit it. The car alarm chirped off.

Thank you, God, thank you! Cat ran back down to the lab.

"Giselle! Giselle! I'm going to get us out of here!"

It took a moment to find the right key, but at last Cat flung the cage open. She pulled on her friend's arm.

Giselle groaned. "Leave me."

"Never! Giselle, please try and get up." But Giselle

wouldn't move. Cat tried to provoke her friend into action. "Fight damn it! Don't give up!"

"I'll do anything . . . please . . ."

Cat moved to Viktor's desk and began shoving keys into the locked drawers. The prefilled syringes were in the last drawer she opened.

Cat grabbed one. "Look, Giselle! Look what I found!"

"Oh!" Giselle grew animated and pushed up, her eyes fixed on the syringe.

"Come on, sweetheart. And I will give it to you."

By the time Cat got her into the backseat of the Audi, Giselle was sobbing and begging.

"Forgive me, my friend." Finding a vein was difficult, but Cat managed to give the injection.

Giselle's relief was immediate. "Ahhh." She slid sideways in the seat. Cat closed the car door.

Knowing Giselle was settled for the moment allowed Cat to think, plan. They were both naked. They needed clothes. Food, water. They didn't dare stop once they left. Even going to the police was risky. Viktor had friends in horribly high places and Cat wouldn't risk capture again.

Back inside, she hurried to one of the bedrooms, grabbed the first clothes she found. Jeter's. She slid on pants and a shirt, grabbed extras and a blanket for Giselle.

Giselle. Cat paused, realizing her friend would need more of the drug, too. Returning to the lab, Cat opened and closed the desk drawers searching for that stash of syringes.

She grabbed a handful and started to turn away. Then she spotted the locked file box that held Viktor's notebooks. His laptop. All his precious secrets that he treated with more reverence than human life. She should destroy them. Their loss would bother him far more than Cat's escape.

No. The disappearance of Viktor's notebooks would assure Cat's and Giselle's continued freedom.

She looked around the lab, spied a cardboard box of supplies. Dumping the contents, she loaded the locked file box then scooped all the papers from the top of his desk, too. God, she hoped Viktor would be furious to find his lab a mess! His papers and his *pets* both gone!

As she went to pick up the box, her eyes landed on the handheld device that Jeter had used to track Giselle. Jesus! How could she have forgotten? She and Giselle were both tagged, and if Viktor had another device . . . She searched the supply cabinet, grabbing scalpels, forceps, and probes.

Cat lugged the heavy box to the car, dumped it on the front seat. Now she was nervous, suddenly frantic to get away. Her hands shook as she started the car. She punched the buttons near the visor until one opened the garage door.

Her son. They had to get to Paris fast. No! Not fast.

If they were stopped in a stolen car—a car that likely had a tracking device as well . . . Overwhelmed, Cat started to cry then just as quickly dashed away her tears.

There was only one place they could go now. Only one person who would help both her and Giselle.

Remi St. James.

Chapter 32

Uncertain Location
Uncertain Date
(Present Time)

Cat came awake, gasping for air. The nightmare . . . Giselle. Marco.

God, where was she? The darkness surrounding her was unfamiliar and fed her worst fears. Did Viktor Zadovsky have her again? Where was her son?

Must find Marco.

Panicked, she tried to move, couldn't. Her arms were bound. Her legs, too. Struggling set off wracking spasms in her back muscles and resuscitated a host of other aches and pains. Had she been beaten?

Stop.

Breathe.

Assess.

Remi's long-ago lesson came to mind. Cat inhaled, tentatively at first, in and out, through the nose. The pain in her back soon subsided, but didn't go away. She tallied her bones.

Nothing broken. Good. She blinked, continuing her physical assessment. Her eyelids felt like they'd been stuffed with sand. Swallowing was difficult; her tongue swollen and dry. Her jaw ached like she'd been KO'd, but again, nothing broken.

A myriad of other sensations registered now. She was naked. Something covered her, a lightweight blanket perhaps. Had her captor discovered she no longer feared rape?

Another memory shimmered. A plane. She'd been sick on the plane. Then again in the airport. In Mexico.

It all spiraled back. *Dante.*

He'd been there, waiting. She'd been careless and he'd nabbed her as she exited the restroom. There had been a sting, a burning in her neck. He'd drugged her.

And then what? Her recollections beyond that point were sketchy; the sequence uncertain. She remembered retching. Her head being held over a toilet. Dante had been yelling, shaking her. *Talk to me, Cat. Answer me, damn you!* Something had been forced into her mouth. More drugs?

Probably.

She'd likely been injected with a variety of sedatives as well including truth serums. Sodium . . . Sodium thiopental. That would explain the dry mouth and eyes. The brain cobwebs and headache, too.

Had she told them everything? Were they on their way to collect Viktor's evil cache she had hidden?

And Marco? Dear God! Did Dante know he had a son? Did he care? Jesus, what had she done? Marco was a complete innocent, and yet he seemed the one most likely to be hurt. And it was all her fault.

The ache she had carried for too many months grew unbearable. Desolation swamped her and she started to cry without noise, without tears.

"Good. You're awake."

She drew in a sharp breath at the sound of Dante's voice. Still unable to see clearly, she concentrated on sounds. But all she could hear was her own ragged breathing.

She jerked involuntarily when his fingers brushed her neck. She tried to form words—*no more drugs!*—but her desiccated larynx couldn't muster a sound.

He pressed against her carotid artery. "Pulse is even."

A light snapped on beside the bed, blinding and disorienting her.

"Glad you decided to rejoin us," he continued.

Us? How many people were here? He touched her again, his hand sliding behind her neck, lifting her head.

"Open your mouth. It's water."

Her dehydrated body obeyed. It would lap up poison if it were in liquid form.

"Swish some in your mouth first."

She resented his orders, but had to follow them. She wet her tongue, her teeth, rehydrating the tissue of her mouth. Water escaped and dribbled down the side of her face. She panicked, afraid she'd choke as it seemed she'd forgotten how to swallow. Then she did and it hurt worse. Her throat was raw. Greedy for more, she took another swig, and then the bottle was withdrawn.

"That's enough for now."

She wanted to cry out for more, knew that was what he wanted. He was in control.

His fingers poked at her eyes next. Again she instinctively struggled. Cold water dripped onto her cheek.

"Eye drops. Hold still."

The artificial tears felt divine. As she blinked, things came into focus. She met Dante's gaze. He turned away, his expression inscrutable.

While he wasn't exactly gentle, he wasn't cruel either. Did he feel he could afford to be nice now that he'd gotten what he wanted out of her?

But it was hard to look at him when all she saw was her son. *Don't let him see you cry.* She forced her gaze elsewhere.

Stop. Breathe. Assess.

Her prison was a small room, maybe eight by eight. A private house belonging to the CIA, she'd guess. But where? And how long had she been held? The windowless walls were a dark gray, giving her no sense of day or night. No noise permeated the walls. A soundproof chamber.

She was tied down to a twin bed. Beside it was a table with a lamp. Two straight-back chairs were across the room. Had Dante sat there while she was questioned?

The air was stale and rank. From her own body odor, she realized. *Interrogation for Dummies, Page 1: Keep the subject uncomfortable and self-conscious.*

Dante lifted her head again, offered water.

She thought briefly of refusing, knew she didn't dare. She needed to get her faculties back online ASAP. Whatever she'd been given had severely dehydrated her entire system. That and the fact she hadn't drunk much in how long now? The time lapse pressed heavily. If Sister Dores didn't hear from her in seven days . . .

"I was beginning to think you were taking the coward's way out," Dante said.

She ignored his coward jibe. If she'd actually been close to death, it was their fault for overdoping her.

As the silence grew, she realized he was waiting for her to respond. He knew she'd have questions: Where was she? Was it night or day? What would happen to her next?

Dummies, Page 2: Being granted answers from her captors indebted her.

But all Cat cared about was Marco. What would happen to him?

That Dante hadn't mentioned her son made her wonder if he even believed the child was his. God, she was an idiot ever to think he might have cared.

"Don't feel like talking?" Dante said. "Fine. Let's move on."

She heard a ripping noise. He bent over her long enough to press duct tape over her mouth.

Page 3: Keep the upper hand. It was no longer a case of her refusing to speak. He had now denied the opportunity. Reasserted control.

"You yakked up a storm while you were sick." Dante pulled a chair closer, turned it backward and straddled it. "Though honestly, I doubt you'd want your precious Marco to see you right now. Unless your lover has a strong stomach."

Cat stared at him in disbelief. He thought . . .

Dante sneered at her reaction. "You were crying for him. Marco! Marco!" His voice raised in falsetto. "So does lover boy work at the brothel, too? A male prostitute perhaps? Ernesto said they'd cater to anything."

In spite of his crude comments, elation swept through her. *He didn't know.* He thought Marco was a boyfriend. Did that mean her other secrets were safe, too?

Possibly.

If he knew what she had, he wouldn't be sitting here playing head games.

"Hope your memory is good, because you'll never see him again, Cat." Dante's demeanor went from cold to heartless. "As much as I'd like to prolong this, we've wasted enough time. I know you probably think this is part of an official interrogation, but that will come later. This is about payback, Cat. It's between you and me. Let's start with the video."

The video. She'd suspected he'd known, but hearing him say it—

"I spent months trying to figure out why you did it. Seemed like there was more to it than money. But after I escaped—"

Escaped? Cat struggled to lift her head but couldn't.

"And started putting together all the pieces, I realized you and Giselle must have been crooked from the start. There was nothing that turned you bad, you were rotten from the get-go. You've probably been selling secrets all along. And when Remi decided to close shop, you figured you had nothing to lose. Until I returned. Then you and Giselle decided to permanently cover your tracks. Starting in London. MI6 and the Mossad are waiting their turn at this, too, Cat."

Cat had no idea what Dante was talking about, but she recognized disinformation when she heard it. Spin a false tale, the more embellished the better, obliging her to correct it.

Wait, you've got it all wrong, was what he wanted to hear.

No. What he wanted to hear was, *Let's make a deal: Zadovsky's notebooks in exchange for . . .*

For . . .

Cat looked at the ceiling, felt a single skimpy tear roll down from her eye. The only thing she wanted in the whole wide world was for Marco to live and be happy. To be safe.

Her son had a chance at that now.

Without her.

Even if Cat did the unthinkable, bartered Zadovsky's secrets for her freedom, she'd never really be free. They'd follow her—certain she'd kept a copy somewhere, sure there was more.

It would never end.

She'd be on the run the rest of her life. Dear God, Sister Dores was right. Her past would haunt Marco forever.

And yet . . . *never* to see her son again? To lose the last person she loved. Marco.

She'd lost Remi.

She'd lost Giselle.

And she remembered the day when she'd first heard Dante had died. A part of her had died then, too. The part that had loved him as no other. The part that had dreamed of a happy ending for the three of them.

The part that hoped.

Now she'd lost . . . everything.

Her shoulders shook as sobs overtook her, setting off a new and painful round of muscle spasms. But the physical agony was nothing compared to her heart shattering.

She heard the door open and close, hating that there were now two people watching her cry. She breathed deeply through her nose, ordering herself to stop. To not feel. To go blank.

She glanced at Dante, ready for him to do his worst.

But he was gone.

* * *

Dante's hands shook. He white-knuckled the kitchen counter. He couldn't tell himself it was *contained rage* any longer. Or that the trembling was a side effect of a barely controlled fury that wanted only to strangle her, to snap her in half like a twig. To make her feel all the things he'd felt in prison. Desperation. Betrayal. The bleak hopelessness.

Right now none of that applied, though, because the damn truth was *he was shaking because he wanted to hold her . . .*

Yes, a part of him still wanted to hurt her, but a bigger part was horrified by that thought.

Where was the elated vindication he thought he'd feel from exacting revenge? From the joy of payback?

Was this what Rocco had been trying to tell him?

His friend had been concerned about Cat's condition for the last two days. When they'd first brought her here and she hadn't roused, they'd been concerned she'd had a reaction to the drug.

But it quickly became apparent she was sick. Dante had insisted on caring for her—telling himself, telling Rocco—that he wanted her well enough to witness his revenge.

Now the thought of her suffering sickened him. Jesus, he sickened himself.

He closed his eyes, remembering the hell he'd been through in prison. The beatings, the savage humiliation, the endless suffering—

Stop. He wasn't a prisoner anymore.

Or was he?

It dawned on him that every time he remembered what they'd done, he surrendered. It was like he walked back in the cell and closed the door. No more! This had to stop. No. Fucking. More.

He opened his eyes. He heard Cat's ragged cries come across the monitor and felt like scum. He'd denied her the basic right of presumptive innocence. Worse, he'd judged her guilty and was meting out *his* definition of punishment. That wasn't justice.

He had a choice to make. Do the right thing. Or—

Shit. There wasn't another choice. Not for him. Not if he ever hoped to reclaim that part of himself that was honorable, decent, compassionate.

Rocco had been correct; Dante had no objectivity when it came to Cat. But it wasn't because of what he had suffered overseas. *It was because part of him still cared for her.*

What she did—or didn't do—would be sorted out by others and dealt with via proper channels. He tugged out his phone; called Rocco. His friend had left a short time ago under the auspices of doing a perimeter sweep. The truth was they'd been close to coming to blows.

Rocco had been torn between loyalty and decency. Dante felt ashamed.

"You were right," he said when Rocco answered. "I'm not removed enough from this. I want you to take her in. I'll call Travis."

Rocco cleared his throat. "Man . . . I . . . I don't know what to say. I feel like I let you down."

"Don't go *Brokeback* on me." Dante had to clear his own throat now. "See you in a few."

After disconnecting, Dante headed for the bedroom.

He'd call Travis after he settled one final score with Catalina Dion.

Chapter 33

Mexico City, Mexico
July 15
(Present Day)

Rocco drove away from the small roadside market. A jet rumbled overhead as it swooped in low to land at the airport.

The small house they were using was located in a mostly vacant commercial subdivision not too far from Mexico City's airport. *Not too far* meant the bigger, newer commercial complexes farther up the road were closer, so the other place had steadily lost its tenants.

But considering the clandestine nature of their business, *mostly vacant* worked really well.

The watermelon he'd just purchased started to roll across the front seat when he turned. He caught it, then used the seat belt to secure it. They'd been in town only two days and still had plenty of food. Nothing fresh, though. And after going this long without food, Cat would have to be coaxed to eat.

The relief Rocco had felt after receiving Dante's call had surprised him. *St. Travis of the Franks* had been right again.

Travis had told Rocco to let Dante handle Cat and to step in only if things got out of hand. Problem was Travis hadn't defined "out of hand." In his typical Obi-Wan Kenobi fashion, Travis had simply said, "It'll work out."

Rocco hadn't given it much thought at first. The desire to see someone pay for what Dante had gone through had clouded reality. Reality settled in when he saw Cat tied down to a bed and he found she was burning up with fever.

That's when Rocco had discovered his own inner conflict. He knew better than to let gender distort his judgment—women were capable of evil, too. But seeing Cat so damn sick . . .

It had bothered Dante, too. Though the other man hadn't wanted to admit it, Rocco could see that Cat's presence reminded Dante of all those horrible months in prison. To watch his friend suffer once again kept Rocco torn.

He'd left, using the excuse he was scouting the area. In truth, he'd needed distance to sort out his own feelings. When Dante had called, Rocco had already been on his way back, having concluded that *both* of them were too close to this situation to handle it impartially.

Rocco had worked with Cat once way back when and had liked her. But Dante had lost his fucking heart to the woman. Cat had been The One. Rocco sighed. *Been there, done that, have the tattoo.*

Bottom line: If Catalina Dion was guilty of even a tenth of what they claimed, she deserved a harsh sentence. But if Rocco and Dante had meted it out, they would have proved they were no different than those motherfuckers Dante had escaped in Thailand. Heavy shit.

He slowed as he turned back into the complex. Now, that was interesting. The brown Taurus was back, parked at the side of the Gutierrez Ice building. The deserted ice building.

He'd noticed it yesterday and had the tag run. It had come back registered to a local handyman. By the time Rocco had crept back for a closer peek, the car had been gone.

Tugging out his cell phone, he dialed his Mexican contact, the same one who'd rented this place to Rocco. "Yo. That tag you ran yesterday. Can you find out what they're doing at Gutierrez's?"

"Sure. What was the name of the handyman service again?"

"Angel or Angelo—"

His contact snorted. "Never mind. I'll look it up myself."

Rocco had barely closed his phone when it rang again. He glanced at caller ID. "That was fast."

"*Sí.* That's why I charge more. I just pulled up that record again to get the name and found that tag was reported stolen this morning."

"*Gracias.*" Disconnecting, Rocco continued past and turned right.

Someone was spying on them, but who? He quickly discarded the Brits and Israelis. MI6, and the Mossad for that matter, wouldn't be this careless. Nor would they need to steal car tags. Taking another right, he pulled over and climbed out. On foot, he followed the overgrown hedgerow that ran behind the ice building.

Hidden by the bushes, he had a clear view of the Taurus now. It was empty, making him wonder who was inside the building.

Rocco heard a voice. Ducking, he slipped closer and found a better position. A balding, sandy-haired man, fifty-something, finished taking a leak. When the man turned and headed back toward the Taurus, Rocco realized he wasn't talking to his dick after all. A Bluetooth earpiece was stuck in the man's ear.

And he was talking in Russian.

Dante carried Cat, free of all restraints, into the bathroom and lowered her into the tub of warm water.

She still hadn't spoken, but her wariness and distrust were evident in her eyes. While Dante was in the kitchen having his big epiphany, Cat seemed to have come to some resignation as well. That or she'd simply cried herself out.

She hadn't struggled when he'd free her—not that she was strong enough to do much of anything.

He had massaged her arms, knew they'd cramp from being tied down. He suspected she was hurting in other places as well. Dehydration could trigger muscle cramps. He'd gotten her to drink more water, though not nearly enough, which he'd deal with later.

Dante had told her he would be leaving and that she would be turned over to other agents, at which time formal charges would be pressed.

"But I'll get you cleaned up and dressed first," he'd said.

She had looked wild-eyed when she first spotted the tub of water, clearly expecting to be drowned. Or perhaps electrocuted. Her attempted struggles confirmed that she wasn't strong enough to bathe herself. Hell, she couldn't even stand. And he wasn't about to dress her and leave her so filthy.

Dante knelt down beside the tub, a washcloth in one hand and a bar of soap in the other. She exhaled noisily. Embarrassed.

"I figured it might be easier to have me do this than Rocco," he said.

She closed her eyes. If the tables were turned—hell, they had been—Dante knew he wouldn't trust his captor either. *Nice* was always a setup.

Just get it done and over with.

Picking up her limp arm, he realized just how weak she was. Guilt stabbed him again.

He washed her hair first. The ends were blunt cut, as if she'd hacked it off herself, but the thickness surprised him. The color was almost as dark as his. Even though he'd adored her as a blonde, he had to admit she looked even more gorgeous with the longer, darker hair.

And as much as Dante tried to be impersonal, lathering and rinsing efficiently, he noticed everything about her. While she had good muscle tone—workout?—she was at least fifteen pounds lighter than he remembered. The missing weight showed in her breasts, which he avoided staring at; her ribs and hipbones showed, too.

Her slender hands—which had always moved with expression when she'd talk, with passion when she'd stroke— seemed as if they belonged to someone else. The nails were short, chipped, and framed with ragged cuticles. Calluses covered her palms and fingertips.

What the hell had she been doing the last year? Digging ditches?

He wished she'd open her eyes; talk. But maybe that would make them both too self-conscious. Him, because he'd realized he wasn't detached. And her because . . . Shit. She had a fucking boyfriend.

He moved up her leg, realized he'd never seen her with anything but silky smooth gams and a Brazilian bikini wax. He swirled the washcloth along her inner thigh. And higher—expecting *that* to get a reaction.

It did. But not at all what he'd expected. Her face had tightened with fear. Jesus, did she really think he'd—

That was when he saw the scars high up on the inside of her thigh. Both thighs. The thin horizontal ridges had faded to white and were probably only visible at certain angles. Anger trickled into his bloodstream.

Unable to stop himself, he lifted her breast, her armpit. More scars there. There were probably matching ones behind her knees, and under the cheeks of her ass.

Someone had taken a razor and made cuts in the places she'd typically perspire. Nothing serious, except it stung like hell with sweat and movement.

Dante knew, because he had similar scars. The cuts had healed quickly enough—which called for another. And another.

He met her eyes. They were open, vulnerable.

"I don't suppose you want to tell me where those came from?" he asked.

She didn't speak, but at least she shook her head. Dante finished bathing her, noting the scars on her feet as well. These were rougher, deeper. What the fuck was going on here?

He turned and grabbed the bottle of water he'd set on the counter. "Drink." He held the bottle, coaxed her to finish it.

She was trembling again and Dante realized the water

had cooled. He lifted her from the tub and wrapped her in clean towels before carrying her back to the bedroom. He'd already dug out clean clothes from her confiscated backpack.

Dante set her down in one of the chairs and began toweling dry her hair. He was trembling now, too. The thought that she'd been subjected to what he'd been through ate at him. And made no sense.

He moved to dry her legs. Immediately, the wariness returned to her eyes.

"It was the last job we worked," Dante started talking again, wanting to put her at ease. He also hoped that maybe if he offered some explanation first, she'd reciprocate. "Harry, Max, and I. I don't remember what happened right after the shack caved in. There are big chunks of time that are . . . gone. It seemed like one day, I just woke up in prison. Wasn't even sure who I was. Or how I got there. Or what I'd done."

He slid her threadbare white cotton underpants up her legs. These belonged to the woman who claimed to have trained silkworms who spun her underwear? He quickly slipped her bra on and covered it with a shirt.

"Better?" He knelt, guiding her feet into a pair of khaki trousers. "The guards' only job seemed to be to torment me. I escaped once, later learned it was in-house training for new guards."

He had to lift her to fasten her pants. She looked even tinier dressed. And while she was sitting up on her own, her arms shook with the effort. The look on her face— confusion, fear, pain . . .

He dropped his hand, realized he'd been about to stroke her cheek. "I don't understand what the hell's gone on—

maybe you're as perplexed as I am. But I swear to you, Cat. Nobody's going to hurt you again. Especially me."

She swayed sideways off the chair then. Dante caught her, swinging her up in his arms before hugging her close to his chest.

"Jesus. We need to get more fluid in you. Some food, too."

He carried her into the main part of the house and set her in one of the dilapidated recliners that faced a television.

Back in the kitchen, he grabbed water, a straw, and a can of warm ginger ale. The ginger ale sprayed like a geyser as he opened it.

Ignoring the mess, he poked a straw in the can and offered what was left to Cat. "The sugar will do you good. I'll get another in a minute."

She took a sip, grimaced.

"Throat pretty sore?" he asked.

At her nod, he wondered if that was part of the reason she remained so silent.

"Look, you're pretty dehydrated. When Rocco gets back, I'd like him to start an IV of saline."

She shook her head violently, refused to meet his gaze. Shit! She had every right to be scared of him.

"After what you've been through, after what I've done—" He rubbed the back of his neck uncertain how to apologize. "I'll get another ginger ale. And we'll try some soup in a few minutes."

In the kitchen, Dante's cell phone vibrated.

It was Rocco. "I'm pulling in now. But heads up. I've got company."

Dante straightened. "Who?"

"Not sure. Caught him down the road. Spying on us."

The garage door opened with a muffled whine. Dante returned to the living room and set another can of soda on the table next to Cat.

Behind him, in the kitchen, he heard the door open.

"Rocco's coming in," Dante said to Cat. "Don't be alarmed."

There was a shuffle of feet. Dante turned back just as Rocco shoved the man into the room ahead of him. The man's hands were cuffed behind him.

"Whoa! Shit! I didn't know she was up." Rocco looked at Dante for an explanation.

Then Cat made a noise. A whine.

Dante twisted around, catching a few words of Russian as Rocco's prisoner lunged for Cat.

Chapter 34

Rio de Janeiro, Brazil
July 15
(Present Day)

The sun would soon set on The Marvelous City. Bringing Viktor one sunset closer to triumph.

He eyed the burned ruins from the backset of the car. How clever of Catalina to pick a church—an orphanage and a brothel—such a combination to hide behind.

"The arrangements are complete?" Viktor asked as soon as Karl closed his cell phone.

"Yes. The jet is on standby. Alexander will be here any moment."

They'd been in Rio less than thirty-six hours. Catalina had fled two days before with Dante Johnson right behind.

Grigori had finally picked up their trail again in Mexico City. That Johnson hadn't taken Catalina back to the United States was temporary. He was probably extracting the revenge that he'd been programmed to seek. Which made Viktor nervous since he wasn't present to control the variables.

What if Johnson got too heavy-handed? Viktor wasn't overly concerned about Cat telling everything. Grigori would be moving in on them as soon as the reinforcements arrived.

"You're confident Grigori will follow my instructions?" Viktor asked.

"To the last detail," Karl said. "He needs you."

Viktor nodded. Actually, Grigori needed the protection Viktor offered. And Viktor did intend to make good on his promise to let Grigori have Catalina—eventually. Fortunately, Grigori was more obedient, more tractable than his brother, Jeter.

After listening to Jeter's bullshit excuse about how Catalina and her friend had escaped back in Berlin, Karl had killed him. But of course, Grigori believed Cat was responsible for Jeter's death.

Cat would be Viktor's in a few more hours. Dante Johnson would be dead. Rocco Taylor would be dead, too. Taylor's death would be a nice bonus, since he, too, had been involved in Belarus. Sure, at one time Viktor had agreed to leave Taylor alone, but at this point all bets were off.

Especially now. Viktor had high hopes that he would have his stolen data back in his possession before he even saw Catalina.

Wouldn't that be sweet? Viktor was eager to retrieve his stolen property. He chuckled at the thought of Cat begging to make a deal, while Viktor already had reclaimed his data . . .

He knew Cat wouldn't have fled with the data and

risked being captured with it. Hidden, she could use it as a bargaining chip. A bargaining chip Viktor would recover first.

Finding where she lived had at first appeared to be a challenge. Then Karl's connections to the crime cartel in the brothel's area had located a woman who volunteered at the orphanage where Cat spent so much time.

The old woman, Zetta, had been a fount of information when Karl visited. The woman had claimed that Cat— or Luzia, as she was known—lived at the orphanage, only leaving to go to work.

Especially interesting to Viktor, though, was Zetta's babble about one child, Marco Lopez, who had shown up at the orphanage around the same time Cat did. Apparently, the nun who ran the orphanage consulted Cat on everything about the child.

"Had the old woman ever questioned the nun on the child's parentage?" Viktor asked now.

"I didn't get a chance to pose that question." Karl met Viktor's gaze in the rearview mirror. Zetta had a heart attack before Karl finished their interview.

"Alexander has secured the body?" Viktor asked. They didn't want the woman's death, even though from natural causes, to alert anyone.

Karl nodded. "The woman did say the child looked like Luzia. And when the child was hospitalized, the nun immediately dispatched a message to Catalina, who then stayed at the hospital until the child returned to the orphanage."

The thought that Catalina Dion could have a son— when poor Adrik was dead—infuriated Viktor. If he had only known that a year ago.

Karl's phone rang. He spoke briefly, then turned toward Viktor. "That was Alexander. He will meet us there."

Viktor opened his car door and climbed out, suddenly eager.

The young nun who answered the door at the orphanage wore a habit of navy blue. She looked from Viktor to Karl to Alexander with unconcealed suspicion.

Viktor held up a hand when Karl began to speak.

"Forgive the interruption, Sister." Viktor offered a slight bow, before continuing in polite Portuguese. "We are looking for Sister Dores. We have an urgent message from Luzia—regarding Marco."

The nun's brow furrowed in recognition. She waved them inside. "Wait here, please. Sister Dores is with the children. I will get her."

Viktor's gaze swept the austere interior. While the building's exterior was crumbling in disrepair, the inside was spotless. The small front window was draped with white lace and kerchiefs. A chipped vase with fresh flowers sat on a table beneath a large painting of the Virgin Mary. A narrow staircase went up to the top floor.

The sounds of children crying and laughing drifted through the wall in front of them.

An older nun wearing a similar dark-colored habit bustled though the open doorway. Her face was lined with worry. "I am Sister Dores. You have word from Luzia?"

At Viktor's nod, Karl withdrew a large handgun and pointed it toward the wall that separated them from the children.

"I understand you have thirteen children here, Sister Dores," Viktor began. "I'm sure you want to protect them all."

The nun gave Karl a calm stare. "The gun is not necessary."

"He takes orders only from me, Sister. Remember that," Viktor said. I know *Luzia* lived here. Where is her room?"

The nun tipped her head toward the staircase. "Third door on the left."

Alexander took the stairs two at a time.

"Now." Viktor took a step closer to the nun. "I want to see the child, Marco."

The nun shook her head. "I'm sorry, we have no one here by that name."

"Where did you learn subterfuge, Sister? From Luzia perhaps?" Viktor tugged his chin. "Zetta mentioned that you and Luzia were quite close."

The nun's eyes flickered at the older woman's name, but she remained mute.

"Enough," Viktor barked. Behind him, Karl clambered around. "Tell the other nun to bring Marco out here now."

"Please don't."

"You can spare twelve lives in addition to your own by cooperating. The child will not be harmed."

"Sister Lolita!" Sister Dores had to shout to be heard. "Bring Marco here to me, please."

The younger nun, Sister Lolita, came around the corner and paused when she saw Karl's gun.

Viktor couldn't take his eyes off the dark-haired child. Adrik had been four months old at his death. What would he have looked like at this age?

There was no denying this child was Catalina's. *Because he looked just like . . . the father.* Dante Johnson. Catalina's former lover.

Viktor did the math. He'd been told that Johnson and

Catalina had split up a few months before Johnson's disappearance. "Marco is about sixteen months old?"

The younger nun spoke. "Fourteen."

That meant Marco would have been only a few weeks old when Viktor had captured Catalina . . . And she'd suffered in silence, protecting her son. If Viktor had only known!

Alexander came down the stairs. "I found nothing. I searched all three rooms. If I get an axe—"

Viktor raised his hand. "That won't be necessary." He stepped closer to the nun holding the child. Marco was fretting, rubbing his eyes.

Come and kiss your son, Viktor. Adrik is getting fussy.

"Sister Lolita, in the interest of the other children's safety, you must do everything I say." Viktor held out his hands toward Marco.

The child scowled and clung to the nun. Until Viktor reached into his pocket and withdrew a piece of brightly wrapped candy. Marco leaned forward and allowed Viktor to hold him, distracted by the prize in his fist.

"Quickly now, Sister Lolita, go upstairs with Alexander." Viktor rocked Marco in his arms. "Pack a few things for the child."

Sister Dores started to protest, but Vicktor tuned her out. A year ago, he had thought he was on top of the world. It had been great, but that feeling was soon to be eclipsed.

Chapter 35

Western Thailand Jungle
July 4
(Twelve Months Ago)

Viktor was alone in the prison's guest wing. He poured another glass of wine and toasted himself.

After all he'd endured—his injuries in the car wreck, the loss of his family—his hard work and persistence had paid off.

Viktor read the report a second time, jotting notations in the margins. Now he was more eager than ever to return to Berlin. These facilities were crude, meant for testing, so he only kept the barest essentials and supplies—and certainly no records—here.

The irony that this latest drug permutation was based on an older *failed* experiment that he'd stumbled upon in his notes made this victory all the sweeter. Yes, it needed refinements. And more human testing. But what he'd seen today! The promise it held . . . To think that he'd almost gotten it right all those months ago in Belarus.

He would love to see the faces of his former colleagues who'd labeled his vision impossible. Viktor's Folly.

You will prove them wrong, my darling. You always do. Now come to bed.

His beloved Lera had never understood the first thing about his work. But, oh, her blind faith in him.

He missed her. And Adrik. They were the only shadows in an otherwise perfect life. And alas even those shadows had faded.

The people responsible were paying. That some were even helping with the very experiments they'd sought to destroy made Viktor smile. Perhaps he'd bring Catalina here next trip.

He moved back to the television and rewound the video he'd been given upon arrival. Taking a sip of wine, he pressed PLAY and tried to imagine what Catalina would think if she ever saw this.

The screen showed a naked, unconscious Dante Johnson chained to a wall, his wrists and ankles manacled. A guard moved in and sprayed Johnson's genitalia with a clear liquid—another trick Viktor would have to borrow.

A portable television was rolled in front of the prisoner and turned on.

An ammonia capsule was waved under Johnson's nose as his face was slapped. Johnson came to life with a virtual roar, lunging against his restraints, exhibiting the same characteristics that Viktor had observed during the other tests. A warrior indeed.

The guards had cranked up the volume on the ancient television and Cat's laughter filled the air. At first, Johnson stared at the television in complete disbelief. His expression grew hungry, desperate, as his erection swelled.

Then Johnson started writhing in pain. Viktor had been told the spray created a sensation of the skin being on fire, a feeling that amplified with swelling.

Johnson seemed to realize just then that Cat was discussing him—the jobs they'd worked. She was promising her off-screen lover that she'd tell him more after they fucked.

Johnson strained against his restraints, cursing Cat, unaware that one of the guards approached with a riding crop . . .

A loud knocking interrupted. Viktor paused the video. He'd been expecting Karl to confirm their arrangements to leave in the morning.

"Come in and enjoy a glass of wine, comrade," Viktor said as he opened the door. "We have much to celebrate."

But the look on Karl's face destroyed Viktor's perfect day even before he heard the words.

"They've escaped."

Chapter 36

Mexico City, Mexico
July 15
(Present Day)

Cat had been horrified when Grigori came in with Rocco Taylor. And here she'd begun to think—

"You will die, whore, for killing my brother," Grigori shouted in Russian as he charged.

Dante jumped in front of her, landing in her lap and knocking over the side table. For a moment she felt a crushing weight. But it lifted as Dante sprang back to his feet. Then Grigori crashed against the far wall, cursing Dante in Russian as he fell.

Rocco grabbed Grigori and yanked him to his feet, pulling him farther away. That was when Cat realized Grigori was handcuffed. That Dante had tried to protect her.

"You okay?" Dante and Rocco addressed her simultaneously.

Feeling sick, she nodded. Grigori's presence could mean only one thing.

"You know him?" Dante asked.

Cat looked from Dante to Rocco. Jesus, didn't they know? "He works . . ." Cat's voice was a croak. She swallowed. "He works for Viktor Zadovsky."

Rocco must have twisted Grigori's arm then because Grigori grimaced.

"Guess that explains the Russian," Rocco said as he looked at Dante. "I found him not too far from here. High-powered rifle and scope in the trunk."

"Where is Viktor?" Cat asked in both English and Russian, her voice nearly nonexistent.

Grigori glared but didn't respond.

Cat tried to control the trembling that threatened to overtake her. How had Viktor found them?

Dante exchanged glances with Rocco. Immediately Grigori was hustled into the bedroom, the door firmly shut.

"I'll be right back." Dante disappeared into the kitchen for all of two seconds before returning with bottled water and another ginger ale. "Would you like some ibuprofen for your throat?"

She took a couple sips of water, uncertain whether to trust this man. Nothing made sense. "No, thanks."

"How do you know this guy works for Viktor Zadovsky?" Dante pulled a chair close and sat directly in front of her. "My intel has Zadovsky in a nursing home in Belarus."

"You need new intel," Cat whispered. "Viktor's been fully recovered for nearly two years."

"Did he do that?" Dante's eyes dropped to her thighs. The scars.

Cat shut her eyes, debating what to tell him. What if this was all an elaborate scheme? What he'd told her in the bathroom, that he'd been held prisoner, could have been fabricated.

She opened her eyes. To her surprise, Dante was unbuttoning his shirt.

"It's not what you think. I wanted you to see these," he said, pulling one arm free and lifting it. While the dark hairs covered most of his scars, the thin white edges extended beyond his armpit. *Just like hers.*

"I wanted you to know that what I told you in the bathroom was true," Dante said.

Cat nodded, unable to stop staring at the other scars on his chest. Burns, whip marks. Other deeper cuts that had been crudely stitched together with thick thread as if to maximize the scarring. "Did Viktor do that?"

"Not directly." He stuck his arm back in the sleeve. "If Zadovsky was somehow involved in my capture, I wouldn't have known. I only saw the Thai guards." He rebuttoned his shirt. "That wasn't a ploy for sympathy, Cat. I know you have no reason to trust me now or to believe anything I say—but I really need to understand what's happened. Would you please tell me?"

The stark sincerity in his voice moved Cat. "Fourteen months ago—" Her voice cracked and she took another sip of water. "I had just heard that you and Max had died. I'd . . . I'd dropped out for a while before that—" She skipped the part about being pregnant. *About Marco.* "I'd heard conflicting accounts about your demise, so I asked Giselle to dig a little. She found a source who claimed to have been an eyewitness. But it was a setup. Viktor Zadovsky captured both of us."

Cat had to look away from the sympathy she saw in

Dante's eyes. She wanted no one's pity. She had lived. Giselle's hadn't.

"Viktor made it clear that he blamed me for his wife and son's deaths. But Giselle bore the brunt of his rage. He tortured her to punish me. I did everything he asked—everything—but it only won her the briefest periods of relief."

"Is that when the videos were made?" Dante asked.

Cat remembered the very first time Viktor brought her in the room where the camera was set up. He had explained what he expected and she had refused. Giselle was brought in and whipped until Cat agreed to do anything Viktor said. And when they finished . . . Giselle was whipped again. *But what have I done?*

"Viktor already knew who I worked with in Belarus," Cat said. "He had all the names, dates and places already. And I thought you . . . were dead."

"How long were you held?"

She looked at the closed door where Rocco and Grigori had disappeared. "Two months. Grigori's brother Jeter had been left to watch us. Viktor was gone on one of his trips. I managed to overpower Jeter, kill him. Then Giselle and I fled. Giselle didn't—" Cat stopped, pretended her throat hurt too much to speak.

There was much she hadn't told him. About Marco. About the data she'd stolen from Viktor. Because the one part she still couldn't reconcile was Viktor's claim that the CIA had turned Cat over. And Cat knew Dante still worked for the Agency.

"That's enough for now." Dante leaned forward and grabbed the ginger ale. "Here, drink. Rest your voice and just nod or shake your head. Giselle died, right?"

She nodded.

"Was that her body recovered from the Seine?"

Again, she nodded.

"And you've been hiding in Rio ever since."

With Marco. She dropped her eyes and nodded.

"That explains how Viktor got your cologne."

My cologne? Cat mouthed the words, not understanding.

"My sailboat blew up a week ago in Key West. Two clues were left that pointed to you."

The bedroom door opened just then and Rocco came out.

"He claims he followed us here from the airport," Rocco said to Dante.

"Alone? And with the precautions we took?" Dante shook his head. "Somebody's feeding him information. How reliable is the owner of this place?"

"Does Grigori know you were in Rio?" Cat interrupted. If so, did Viktor know she'd been in Rio, too?

"More than likely," Dante said. "But that doesn't explain how—"

"Viktor had you tagged," Cat said. She remembered what Dante told her earlier about not recalling all of his imprisonment. Giselle had forgotten, too. If Viktor had somehow been involved with Dante's capture, too, did that mean the CIA had sold out one of their own?

Or had Viktor lied about the CIA's involvement to compound Cat's anguish? Disinformation . . .

Dear God! Where was Viktor now?

"What do you mean 'tagged'?" Dante asked.

Cat pointed to the underside of her left upper arm. "Viktor implanted a microchip in case we escaped. I cut mine out."

Dante unfastened his shirt again, ripped his arms free. Rocco moved in to help look and immediately pointed to a spot.

"Small, round scar? From a large-gauge hypodermic?" Rocco asked Cat.

She nodded.

Dante and Rocco swore simultaneously. "Grigori was probably waiting on backup. Cocky bastard," Rocco said. "We need to lose that chip and get out of here."

"Can you cut this one out, too?" Dante asked her.

Cat held up a trembling hand. "No. He'll have to do it."

"We'll need to make it quick," Rocco said. "Let me get a medic case."

"I need . . ." Cat turned to Dante and spoke slowly in an effort not to cry. *Marco.* She needed to contact Sister Dores. "To make a phone call."

She watched hesitation cloud Dante's eyes, knew he struggled with trust as much as she did. They both had unanswered questions.

"If you want to warn your lover," Dante began.

She could no longer hold back tears. "Marco," she whispered. "Is my son. Have to warn them."

The color drained from Dante's face and was quickly replaced by a hard-edged anger. "Viktor raped you, didn't he? Jesus! I'll fucking kill him. Did he know . . . you were pregnant when you escaped?"

Cat shook her head. "Not . . . Viktor's." She swallowed. "*Yours.* Need to call. Now."

Dante stood outside the hangar at the airport three hours later. The stars he'd seen hundreds of times before shone brightly overhead. Except now they were different. He was different.

He and Cat hadn't spoken much since she'd dropped her bombshell. She'd rasped out the explanation that Marco was in an orphanage and Dante had immediately jumped to conclusions.

"You gave up our son!"

If Cat had had the strength, she surely would have kicked his balls in again. And he deserved it. She'd explained it was only a cover and that she lived at the orphanage, too.

Then they'd had to flee the house, forcing Dante to focus on other matters.

He had a son.

Behind him the hangar door opened. Rocco stepped out. "We leave in five."

"How's Cat?" Dante asked.

"She let me hook up an IV—it'll help rehydrate her quicker. She's upset that there's no answer at the orphanage. I reminded her it's the middle of the night there, but . . ." Rocco shrugged. "How's the arm?"

"Fine." It had hurt like hell, but Dante had let Rocco probe and remove the encapsulated chip. They'd dropped it in a FedEx box for Travis.

And after finding the tracking device, both men had drawn the same conclusion. If Zadovsky had been involved in Dante's capture he probably knew what happened to Harry and Max. Jesus, if they were alive . . .

Travis had been stunned to hear about the turn of events and immediately began sifting for dirt on Grigori. He struck gold. Grigori was a former KGB explosives expert, Yuri Stanis. Another piece of the puzzle fell into place. If Grigori had blown up Dante's boat, that meant he was also linked to the explosions that killed the foreign operatives, too. That Zadovsky seemed to have had access to information leaked from the Agency was also of top concern.

Travis was en route to Mexico City to personally collect Grigori from his new and secure hiding spot. Dante, Rocco, and Cat were on their way to Rio to collect Marco. *His son.*

"Still in shock, Dad?" Rocco asked.

"I never thought I'd have kids." Dante had given Rocco the broad strokes before they left. Of course, at this point all Dante had were broad strokes. That, and a million questions.

The pilot came out just then, signaling he was ready.

Inside the jet's cabin, Rocco replaced Cat's IV. "You're looking better already. Wake me when this drips out."

As Rocco moved to the rear of the aircraft, Dante motioned to the seat beside Cat. "Do you mind?"

"No." She still had his cell phone gripped in her hand.

"Still no answer?" he asked.

"No, but it's two a.m. in Rio. I'll try later."

Her voice sounded better. The throat lozenges they'd picked up were working. And she'd finally agreed to take some ibuprofen.

"Can we talk, Cat?" Dante hated asking, knowing she needed to rest.

But he had to know the rest of the story. He'd been relieved to learn she'd left their son at the hotel in Paris, to know that Viktor hadn't gotten ahold of Marco.

The plane was moving now. "What did you do after leaving Berlin?" he asked.

Her eyes darkened, remembering. "I was desperate to get back to Paris. To find Marco. But Giselle was so sick, and we were in a stolen car."

"Running for your life, by the way," Dante added. Cat had probably been in poor physical shape herself.

"I called Remi. He'd just had surgery—I didn't even know. Alfred, his butler"—she smiled—"yeah, like Bruce Wayne. Alfred came immediately, but Giselle had already died." Cat grew quiet. "He helped me stage her death; I claimed her body later. Alfred has connections at the morgue and handled everything. He found that Marco had been placed in a state home, as a ward of the French courts. I broke in one night and basically kidnapped him. I suspect the French have kept it quiet rather than face more outcries over another child falling through the public welfare cracks."

She paused and drank water. "Alfred took care of passports for Marco and me and got us out of Europe. He also gave me money, but then he had to back away. We knew Viktor would watch to see if I went to Remi for help."

"Did you go straight to Rio?" Dante asked.

"No. I hid several places before coming up with the Rio plan."

The orphanage. "Were you raised at Saint Maria's?"

At first she didn't answer. Finally she nodded, but offered no further explanation.

"I guessed that," Dante admitted. "For Marco to have been taken in there, you would have had to known someone."

"I worried the French authorities would publicize the kidnapping. That Viktor would figure it out." She looked at him, cleared her throat. "How did you find me?"

"I got your Luzia name by following up on Remi's death." He also told her about tracking down Pearl Patterson.

"I didn't want to be the one to help Remi," Cat blurted out. "But Alfred's health has been declining due to Parkinson's. I couldn't tell them no. They would have done it for me."

Dante noticed that she was out of water. "Be right back." He got up and got them both a chilled bottle of water. He brought back a box of tissues, too. She was trying so hard to hold it all in.

He opened her bottle, passed it to her.

"Thanks," she said.

"Have I thanked you for protecting our son?"

Her eyes grew moist. "Right now, I don't feel like I've done such a great job."

"Did you know you were pregnant in Belize?" He remembered their argument. God, he'd been such a dickhead.

"Yes. But everything seemed stacked against us. And you'd said—we'd both said—we didn't want children."

"If I had known . . ."

"You'd have what? Not gone on that mission? Come to Belize and celebrated?" Cat blinked back tears again, grabbed a tissue. "It's too late to play what-if."

Was it too late for them to start over? "You're right." Dante met her gaze. Then he reached for her hand and clasped it in his. "Now, will you tell me about the day our son was born?"

Chapter 37

Rio de Janeiro, Brazil
July 16
(Present Day)

By the time they touched down in Rio, fifteen hours later, Cat was frantic that there was still no answer at the orphanage—

"Don't think the worst," Dante said. "You said the nuns stay busy. And now they're down one volunteer."

She prayed he was right.

Dante hadn't left her side on the plane. They'd talked for hours last night, mostly about Marco. The shock of learning he had a son showed in the way he shook his head frequently.

At some point she'd fallen asleep, waking to find her head on Dante's shoulder. That he'd been asleep, too, spared both of them new awkwardness.

They were in a private hangar again. She felt better than she had in a while. The IV and sleep had helped revitalize her body. But the biggest difference she felt was the lightness about her shoulders. That Dante knew . . . That he shared her worry.

Don't read anything into it.

She sighed and tried calling the orphanage again. As the phone rang and rang, she suddenly remembered that Zetta had been packing the church office for the move to Saint Bernadette's. *God, how could I be so stupid as to forget that?*

"I'm going to call Saint Bernadette's," Cat told Dante.

He and Rocco moved away, speaking quietly. Cat's first attempt to contact Saint Bernadette's netted a busy signal. A woman answered the second time.

Cat cut her short. "I'm trying to reach someone from Saint Maria's," she began.

Dante looked at her and mouthed, "They answered?" At Cat's nod, he started moving back toward her.

"Saint Maria's is now closed—" the woman began.

"I need to get in touch with Sister Dores from the orphanage. It's urgent."

There was a too-long moment of silence, that awful hesitancy that telegraphed bad news.

"You haven't heard," the woman said.

"Heard what?" Cat asked. Dante had reached her side, but she couldn't look at him. "Please, I volunteered at the orphanage and helped Sister Dores and Sister Lolita with the children, but I've been away."

"I'm sorry to tell you this then, but Sister Dores is in the hospital."

Cat's heart stopped beating. "Where is Sister Lolita?"

"Sister Lolita is—missing. Someone kidnapped her and one of the children."

"Marco."

"Yes! That was the child's name," the woman went on.

Cat felt as if she were dying, felt Dante's hands on her shoulders, shaking her slightly. "When . . . did this happen?"

"Last night. The doctors think the stress caused Sister Dores to suffer a brain aneurism."

"What hospital is she in?" Cat's voice grew hoarse.

"Antonio's Public Charity."

Dante's grip tightened almost painfully as she disconnected. "What's happened? Tell me."

"Marco and Sister Lolita were . . . abducted last night." Her voice broke.

His arms encircled her, holding her close. She pulled away, afraid that if she broke down now, she'd never stop crying.

She wiped her eyes on the backs of her hands. "We have to get to the hospital. I have to see Sister Dores."

Rocco stood behind Dante. Cat knew by his grim expression that he'd overheard. "I'll get a cab." Rocco hurried off.

Viktor had Marco. That thought repeated nonstop in Cat's mind all the way to the hospital. She was vaguely aware that Dante was having the airports monitored in an effort to determine if Viktor had left Rio. She prayed they weren't too late.

When they finally reached the hospital, Dante stayed with her while Rocco took off to "check things." Before she climbed out of the car, Rocco squeezed her hand in unspoken reassurance.

"This is all my fault," Cat began as she and Dante hurried toward the entrance of one of the city's poorest hospitals.

"Stop." Dante's hand cupped her chin and forced her to meet his eyes. Her son's eyes. "There's one person at fault here: Viktor Zadovsky. And I promise, Cat, we will get Marco back. But I need you—our son needs you—thinking and acting with clarity right now."

She nodded, mostly to get him moving again.

Inside, they learned Sister Dores was on the fourth floor. Rather than wait for an elevator, they took the stairs. When they reached the fourth-floor landing, Dante touched her arm. "Sister Dores may be impaired from the aneurism."

Like Remi. She hoped that was not the case. They found Sister Dores in a room with twelve other patients—the beds practically touching. The room was Spartan. No televisions or telephones.

"I'll wait here," Dante whispered. *Here* was a chair by the door.

Cat crept into the room, her attention focused on the gray-haired figure in the fifth bed. She'd never seen Sister Dores without her headpiece. As a child she'd once seen a strand of the nun's hair work loose, but Sister Dores had swept it away as if embarrassed.

Seeing the nun's chest rise and fall left Cat wanting to cry with relief. Sister Dores was so still, her complexion so ashen that Cat had thought the nun was dead.

Her eyes took in the IV, the scuffed blood pressure cuff hanging over the bed rail. There was no high-tech beeping equipment like she'd seen with Remi. The beds weren't even electric.

She slipped her hand into the nun's. It felt icy.

"Mama." The word popped out from a childhood long forgotten. A childhood steeped in the desperation of being abandoned by someone Cat couldn't remember.

She'd been three years old when she first met Sister Dores passing out bread. The older children always beat back the younger ones, but the nun had spotted Cat that day, huddled behind a garbage pile.

The nun coaxed Cat out from of her corner using a crust of bread. But it had been the kindly smile that had encouraged Cat to take the nun's hand and walk to the orphanage.

Few children stayed at Saint Maria's more than a few years. Most ran away rather than follow the strict rules of school and church. Cat had thrived, had worked to become the nun's right hand. At one point she had even imagined joining the convent, but Sister Dores had known it wasn't the right choice. *"You need to see the world."* Still, the nun had wept when sixteen-year-old Cat announced she was leaving the orphanage.

Sister Dores stirred now. "My little Rosa." The nun whispered the name of that abandoned child, then grimaced with a fit of coughing.

Cat grabbed the cup of water beside the bed and gently lifted the nun's head to help her drink. Only one side of Sister Dores's mouth seemed to work and Cat realized the nun had indeed suffered some paralysis.

"M-M-M-Marco." Sister Dores blinked back tears.

"Can you tell me what happened?" Cat asked.

"Three men." Each word seemed to drain the nun. "Sister Lolita, too. They said—" Sister Dores started coughing again, but she refused another drink.

"Rest a minute," Cat urged.

"No time. Have phone number." The nun's speech was slurred. "You must call."

"They left a number?" Cat's hopes soared. "Where is it?"

"He wrote it . . . on m-m-m-my hand. Said I couldn't . . . lose it."

Cat carefully unfolded the hand she held, but saw nothing.

"The other one," Sister Dores whispered.

Hurrying around to the opposite side of the bed, Cat gingerly drew back the sheet and lifted the nun's hand. The skin here was clean too, except for the faintest mark of dark ink—a 1 or a 7—the rest had been scrubbed away. *Marco.*

"Did you find it?" Sister Dores asked.

"Yes." Cat bent and pressed a kiss to the top of the delicately veined hand, unable to stop the tears.

"That's good," Sister Dores exhaled with relief. "There are . . . angels . . . waiting. They will guide you now."

"Don't leave me!" Cat begged.

The nun's grip went lax.

"No!" Cat shouted out.

The single word echoed in the room as Sister Dores's final breath left her body. Desperate, Cat looked around, but this hospital did not have call buttons, or fancy crash carts, or intercoms spouting CODE BLUE.

"I'll get a nurse." Dante moved away.

Cat hadn't even realized he'd come up beside her.

And then he was back, gently releasing Sister Dores's hand from Cat's grip as a nurse moved in and bent over the nun.

But even before the nurse said, "I'm sorry," Cat knew.

The angels had left the building.

"This is the worst," Dante said to Rocco as he paced. "I want to find that bastard now."

They were in the finest part of Rio, staying in a penthouse that included its own three-man security team. Travis had pulled out all the stops.

It had been four hours since Sister Dores had died. Cat had been inconsolable, grieving for the nun while worrying about their son and Sister Lolita.

Her love for Marco, for all the people she'd loved and lost, amazed and humbled Dante. He eyed the closed door to the bedroom, where he hoped she was resting.

His cell phone vibrated. It was Travis.

Travis was in Mexico City, interrogating an initially uncooperative Grigori. "He changed his tune when his fingerprints confirmed that he is Yuri Stanis," Travis said. "Turns out he's more afraid of returning to Moscow than of Viktor Zadovsky. Now he's suddenly eager to remain in U.S. custody."

"What are you getting out of him about Viktor?" Dante asked.

"Zadovsky arrived in Rio two days ago, accompanied by two men. Grigori says one of them, Karl Romanov, another ex-KGB agent, has contacts there. The original plan was for Grigori to nab Cat and turn her over to Viktor. Of course, since Grigori hasn't checked in, Viktor will know something's wrong. Grigori says Zadovsky is obsessed with the idea that Catalina stole something from his lab before she escaped. Grigori thinks it's wishful thinking. Apparently Zadovsky's had some cognitive issues since the accident."

Dante's mind flashed back to that job in Belarus. Zadovsky's notebook. *They want that recipe book. The whole fucking enchilada. At any cost.*

"Zadovsky didn't know about Cat's son, did he?" Dante asked.

"Grigori thinks no. He says the main objective was to search her room. For what it's worth, Grigori thinks Viktor will remain in Rio now, waiting for Cat to contact the nun."

"Any luck getting Viktor's phone number?"

"Not yet. Grigori claims he won't talk more until he's on U.S. soil. I'm arranging transport now. I'm having his cell phone analyzed, but the damn thing had a dead battery and the chargers for it are only sold in BFE. As soon as I get something, I'll call. Tell Rocco I'll have an ETA on reinforcements shortly."

After disconnecting, Dante relayed the conversation to Rocco.

"Jesus," Rocco said. "What if Cat doesn't have this data that Viktor's after?"

"We may need to make Viktor think she does so we can delay long enough to set a trap. I'm going to talk to Cat," Dante said. He moved to the bedroom door and knocked.

Cat answered, her eyes immediately searching his face. "Is there word?"

"A little. I just spoke with Travis."

Cat motioned him into the room. He looked at the bed. The duvet was untouched. She'd probably been pacing, too.

"It turns out Grigori is a KGB sellout who is eager to cooperate with anyone but Moscow. Travis is working on getting Viktor's phone number, too."

"Oh, thank God!"

"Grigori thinks Viktor might have stayed here in Rio, knowing you'd return for Marco. We're expecting backup and then we'll work out a plan to contact Viktor."

Cat's eyes filled with tears. "There's something I need

to tell you—that I should have already told you. I have something of Viktor's."

"Don't tell me its his notebooks," Dante said.

She nodded. "I took those notebooks on the spur of the moment—thinking they'd be an insurance policy if Viktor ever threatened me again. And by the time I realized it only made me a bigger target, there was no undoing it."

"Jesus! You could have sold them," he whispered. "Made a fortune." Instead of scrubbing floors in a brothel, living in fear.

"That wouldn't have made the danger go away." She brushed her hair back, held it. "The stuff he was doing, the viruses he talked about creating. What he did to Giselle. No one should have that kind of knowledge, that kind of power."

Dante stepped closer, but she backed away. "Let me finish or I'll never get this out. We need to set up a trade with Viktor. My son and Sister Lolita in exchange for me."

"What! You? If we do any human exchanges, it'll be *me*, Cat." Dante's temper flared.

"I've given this a lot of thought and it has to be me. Viktor will want proof that I still have his data. I can give him sketches of what I saw, and then take him to where the data is hidden."

"I could do that just as easily."

"But you're the only one who can keep Marco safe. You've got the CIA behind you and now you've got Grigori, too. After Marco is secure, you can come after me."

"No. We'll find another way, Cat."

"There's not another way that is fast enough." She moved to the desk, picked up a sheet of paper, and held it out to him. "This is just in case."

Dante took the paper and read the top line. *Last Will and*—He ripped it in two, let the pieces fall to the floor.

"I won't lose you again, Cat. I love you. You hear me? And I'm as prepared to love our son as I am determined to get him back safely. You have to trust me."

"No! You have to trust me!" Cat launched herself at him then pounded his chest with her fists as she wept. "I want Marco, I want my son!"

Dante didn't stop her. He understood that right now there were no words that could make this better.

As her anger subsided, she leaned into him, her arms wrapping around his waist. He pulled her close . . . and then he was kissing her fiercely. Cat's arms raised and entwined around his neck now, tugging him closer.

His body responded, growing hard as Cat rubbed against him, making soft sounds as her hands tugged at his shirt, pulling it loose.

To hold her, to kiss her again, was heaven. And after all the hell they'd been through . . .

Jesus. He broke the kiss, remembering what Viktor had done to her. And now here he was—

"Please." She rose onto her toes, trying to pull him down, wanting to continue the kiss.

"Cat, baby, listen. I don't want this to get out of control." *To hurt you any more than you've already been hurt.*

She dropped her head to his chest and started crying once again. "I'm so tired of control. Of everyone else's control."

"Shhh. Then I won't tell you no." Dante caught her chin and held her gaze. "We'll do anything you want, Cat. But if you feel uncomfortable at any point—just tell me to stop."

And then he caught her mouth again in a kiss that went

on and on. Their movements grew frantic as they stripped off their clothes, kissing, touching, moving closer to the bed.

Her hands skimmed down his sides, then closed over his erection.

Dante cupped her, found her wet, ready. He picked her up and laid her on the bed, covering her body with his.

"Don't stop, don't stop," Cat whispered. "Don't ever stop."

He pushed fully into her. She moaned, raising one leg to wrap about his hips, taking him deeper. And then she pushed up, grinding, rubbing, already on the verge.

He answered her demands for harder, faster, and felt her begin to shake with release.

Dante slowed, watching her, wanting to prolong the moment—only to lose it when she whispered, "I love you, too."

Chapter 38

Rio de Janeiro, Brazil
July 16
(Present Day)

Knocking sounded on the bedroom door. Cat looked at Dante, embarrassed to realize that for a moment she'd forgotten everything. *Marco.*

"I'll be right out," Dante called. The knocking ceased, but he made no move to get up.

He was still buried inside her, still hard . . . or hard again.

"Are you okay?" he asked.

She nodded, then shook her head. She wouldn't be okay until . . . She pressed a hand against his shoulder. "Maybe he's heard something."

"Yeah. We'll get dressed." Instead of moving away, he pressed the softest, gentlest kiss to her lips. "We didn't use a condom. And I'm not apologizing for it."

Cat wasn't sure what he meant. What any of it meant. And right now she had other things to think about.

He pushed up and began gathering their clothes. Cat noticed more scars on his back, his buttocks. He had suffered much, too.

She took her clothes and moved toward the bathroom.

Dante stopped her. "How do you want to handle this data you've got of Viktor's?"

"Is it really my choice?"

"Yes. You've got the most at stake here, Cat. And you've paid a hellacious price to keep this secret. For what it's worth, Grigori already expressed doubt that you even have it. You're the only one who can disprove that."

Cat felt tears threaten. "If I have to give it back to Viktor to get our son, I will. All that crap about the good of the many doesn't mean shit when you're on the side of the few."

"Agreed. Let's keep it quiet and see what we learn. I'll meet you out there."

Cat got cleaned up and dressed, grateful for a few moments alone. With her son's safety at stake . . . the line between right and wrong no longer mattered. It was frightening to think of what she'd do to free her son, to assure his well being.

Dante and Rocco were at the dining room table when she walked out.

"We got Viktor's cell phone number," Dante said. "Since he gave Sister Dores a number, he'll be expecting you to call. I suggest we make contact and see what we can find out."

"We don't have the means to track his cell phone," Rocco said. "But I'm set up to record the call."

"We'll use my cell phone," Dante went on. "On speaker-phone. Ask to speak with Sister Lolita. Even if he refuses, try to keep him on the line as long as you can. You ready?"

Cat nodded. Her hands shook as she dialed the number.

The phone rang three times and went to voice mail, with only a beep. She began talking.

"This is Catalina. I want my son and Sister Lolita released unharmed. Call me at . . ." She glanced at the piece of paper Dante had shoved at her with his cell number, then read it into the phone.

After disconnecting, she sat down. "How do we even know that's the right—"

Dante's phone rang, startling her.

Dante held a finger to his lips while Rocco activated the recorder.

Cat hit the speakerphone button. "Hello."

Viktor Zadovsky's voice came through as he greeted her in Russian. "I was beginning to wonder if you even cared about this precious boy."

"Where is Marco?" she demanded in Russian. "Let me speak with Sister Lolita."

"Make another demand and I'll hang up." Viktor switched to English. "I'm sure others are listening. Now, I have something of yours, you have something of mine. I propose a trade. I will call back in fifteen minutes with instructions."

"Wait—" Cat said. But it was too late. Viktor had already disconnected.

Viktor called back in ten minutes. Cat flew back to the dining room table.

"Told you," Rocco mouthed as he prepared to record the call. He and Dante had begun packing gear as soon as the last call ended.

They expected Viktor to make demands quickly, to

keep them off guard. The penthouse's three security agents had joined them, but now they, too, grew silent.

Dante came to stand behind Cat as she answered. "Yes, I'm here."

"I am eager to see you again, my pet," Viktor said in English across the speakerphone. "We have much unfinished business."

Cat felt Dante's fingers tighten at her shoulder. "All I care about is my son."

"And you think I did not care about mine?" Viktor's voice rose. "We will discuss that point in person, when we have more time. More privacy. Now how long will it take you to retrieve my property?"

"I have it now." She saw Rocco shake his head. He wanted her to delay. But Cat couldn't bear to stretch it out.

She wanted her son and Sister Lolita freed. Since the data she'd stolen was buried in Germany, she'd have to convince Viktor to take her there.

"Excellent," Viktor said. "Here is what you need to do."

Cat held a pen, ready to write. "Can I talk to Sister Lolita, please?"

"No!" Viktor snapped. "And do not ask again. Or the little nun will pay. Do you remember how that works?"

Giselle. "I remember."

"Here are the rules: No tricks, or your son and the nun die. You need to get in your car and leave now. Dante Johnson may drive—I'm sure he's listening in—but no one else! Or your son and the nun die. Bring my property, or your son and the nun die. Is that clear?"

"Yes."

"Now, then, head east on the *President Costa e*

Silva bridge, toward Niterói," Viktor said. "I will call in thirty minutes."

The line went dead.

Rocco wasn't happy. "This is a setup. And what happens when he sees you don't have his data?"

"I'll tell Viktor that it's hidden overseas," Cat said. "He'll have to take me with him."

Dante shook his head. "It's too risky."

"What other choice do we have?" She met his gaze and saw how torn he was.

God, she loved him. But she'd made peace with her own death long ago. Yes, she wanted to live, but not at the cost of her son's life.

Rocco had been talking with one of the security men. Now he rejoined them. "They'll follow in separate cars, running a pattern. The three of us get to use one of the owner's cars. It's bulletproof and has a sniper compartment."

"I won't take any chances with Marco's or Sister Lolita's lives," Cat said.

"Agreed," Dante said. "But Viktor won't play by the rules, so we have to take every advantage."

Dante drove in Rio's nightmare traffic, grateful for the distraction. Cat looked ready to jump out of her skin.

The Lincoln Towncar they borrowed had a hidden compartment between the backseat and the trunk, complete with shooter's holes. He and Cat also had on Kevlar vests, courtesy of their host's wardrobe. The magnitude of the *favor* Travis had called in was obvious.

Rocco was currently crouched on the floor behind

them, keeping in radio contact with the others. They were on the bridge between Rio and Niterói when Viktor called again, only to reverse his directions. It took twenty minutes to find a spot where they could turn and head back.

Viktor proceeded to run them around, back and forth, on the same stretch of interstate before finally telling them to head north, toward the city of Petropolis, on BR-040.

"About time," Rocco said as he relayed instructions to one of the men following.

But then Viktor didn't call for nearly an hour. Dante watched as Cat kept checking his cell phone, worried about the signal, but it remained strong. Maybe Rocco was a signal magnet after all.

When the phone finally rang at three o'clock, Cat let out a cry. "Hello!" she said, once again keeping Viktor on speakerphone.

"How far are you from Vila Bonanca?" Viktor asked.

Dante pointed to the GPS navigation screen that displayed an area map.

"Two, maybe three, kilometers," Cat estimated.

"You'll need to write this down." Viktor rattled off detailed instructions that would take them away from the main interstate. "You'll arrive at a private airstrip that can handle small jets. The combination to the gate is 3578. Park at the red flag and walk to the east end of the runway." The phone went dead.

"Did you all catch that?" Dante asked Rocco.

"Yes. And it means the others will have to back off," Rocco said. "Viktor will have a clear view of the entire area as he flies in."

"See if they can find another road that comes in on the opposite side of the airstrip," Dante said.

"And tell them to take no chances!" Cat added.

Dante reached across to take her hand. She grabbed it and squeezed. He knew they were both thinking about everything that could go wrong.

After relaying the information to the other drivers, Rocco put in an earpiece and tested the microphone Dante wore before rolling into the hidden compartment. Rocco had a rifle, but Dante prayed no shots would be fired. Not with Marco and the nun present.

Viktor would be pissed to learn Cat lied about having his data with her. But not having it there guaranteed that Viktor wouldn't kill her on the spot. He would keep Cat alive at least until he retrieved his data.

For the hundredth time, Dante wished they'd had more backup, more time. They didn't.

It took forty minutes to reach the deserted airstrip. At the gate, Dante punched in the code. With a quiet hum, it swung open. It was obvious this place was used for drug shipments and smuggling. Tucked in a valley, it was invisible from the road but well maintained.

A red wind sock hung on a pole a half mile in. He parked perpendicular to the asphalt airstrip.

"Test, test." Dante checked his earpiece and microphone a final time.

"Back at ya," Rocco said. "Got video feed, too. I want one of these fucking cars." A remote-control camera lens hidden in the grill fed footage back to the shooter's compartment.

Dante spoke to Cat now. "Ready to do this?"

She nodded and reached for the handle to open the door. He stopped her, wanting to go over their plan again.

Instead he held her gaze. "No matter what happens, know that I love you."

He climbed out of the car before she could reply. The small suitcase he retrieved from the backseat held a brick, for weight, and a few quick sketches Cat had made as "proof" that she had Viktor's data. If they were being watched, they didn't want to appear to be showing up empty-handed.

As they walked to the end of the runway Dante surveyed the scene. It didn't get any worse than this. Open fields on either side gave them absolutely no cover and made the Kevlar vests they wore feel even more inadequate.

Dante checked the time. They had less than an hour of daylight now. Viktor would probably fly in from the west— putting the setting sun right in their eyes. And then he'd fly off in the same direction, into the cover of darkness.

Cat scanned the skyline, then spun around. "Behind you!"

Dante heard the helicopter mere moments before it swooped in. The pilot swung around and buzzed the field before landing thirty feet away.

Dante turned his head away from the kick of grit and dirt. The pilot slowed the rotors, but didn't shut off the engine.

The man who climbed out of the front seat of the helicopter brandished a large handgun as he moved to open the rear door.

"That's Karl Romanov," Cat whispered. "I'm not sure who the pilot is." She drew a sharp breath. "I see Sister Lolita . . . and Marco!"

Dante saw a woman holding a child. Both were seated

behind the pilot. He touched Cat's forearm, felt her tension and knew she wanted to run forward.

"There's Zadovsky," he said.

Viktor had stepped out then leaned back into the helicopter and took Marco from Sister Lolita, leaving Karl to assist the nun. That both the nun and the child appeared unharmed relieved Dante. But when the nun tried to take Marco again, Viktor refused and continued to hold the child.

The drumbeat of fury pounded in Dante's ears as he watched Viktor. *My son.*

"Send Catalina over with the suitcase," Viktor shouted.

Dante shook his head and grasped Cat's wrist, stopping her short. "I'll bring it. As soon as the nun and baby are headed this way."

Cat struggled to free herself. "Dante, no!"

Karl lifted his gun and pointed it at Sister Lolita.

"That's not what we agreed to." Viktor started to turn away.

Cat screamed. "Wait! I'm coming." She turned to Dante and dropped her voice. "You have to let me do this."

"That is the man who raped you," Dante hissed. "Do you remember what he did to you and Giselle?"

"Yes. And if I want to protect Sister Lolita from that same fate, I have to go."

Dante reluctantly released her.

As she reached for the suitcase, she whispered again. "Tell Rocco to take out Karl as soon as he gets a clear shot after I get Sister Lolita and Marco to the ground."

"You copy that?" Dante breathed.

"Check," Rocco confirmed in Dante's earpiece.

Letting Cat walk away was one of the hardest things Dante ever did.

She walked straight toward Zadovsky. Marco grew animated as Cat drew closer.

Cat held out her arms for her son, but Viktor turned and handed Marco back to Sister Lolita. Then he took the suitcase and opened it. Immediately, he threw it to the ground. Cat's sketches blew away as the brick fell out.

Viktor slapped Cat, knocking her to the ground.

Dante watched through a haze of deadly red. "Now," he said to Rocco. "Take that bastard down!"

"I can't," Rocco said. "Viktor and Karl are right in front of the nun. I can't get a shot without endangering Marco."

Cat pushed back to her feet and faced Viktor. "I will take you to where I hid your stuff . . . after you release—"

Viktor grabbed Cat's arm and slapped her again. Marco started crying now. Sister Lolita instinctively turned away, trying to shield the child from violence.

"Kill Johnson," Viktor said to Karl. Then he tugged Cat close. "You and your son can both watch him die!"

From the corner of her eye, Cat saw Karl shift. She screamed at Sister Lolita. "Get down!" Then Cat spun into a low drop kick, landing a solid blow to Viktor's ankles.

She hit the ground herself and rolled toward Sister Lolita. Gunshots erupted and she heard Dante yell. Then the helicopter blades cranked back up, the noise level deafening.

As the chopper began to lift, Cat used her body to shield Sister Lolita. Marco was crying in earnest now, struggling to get out from under the sobbing nun as the chopper spun off into the night.

Cat looked over her shoulder, saw that Karl was on the

ground, half of his head blown away. Just beyond that bloody mess stood Dante and Viktor, locked in a classical standoff. Each had a gun pointed at the other.

Dante looked like a madman, his face distorted in rage. With the chopper gone and Karl dead, it was over. But Dante seemed locked in an internal struggle between killing Viktor or letting him live to get answers. To pay for his crimes.

"We're okay," Cat called.

Dante nodded, but didn't look away from Viktor. "My sniper's got you in his crosshairs, Zadovsky. But I'm calling dibs on your forehead."

"Where are the fancy deals? The promises of amnesty in exchange for an explanation of what I did to you? All those things you can't remember?" Viktor snorted. "And what I did to your comrades?"

"I don't give a shit what you did to me," Dante said. "But to find my friends . . . yes, you'll get a goddamn deal. Now drop your gun. It's over."

"You're right. It's over." Viktor turned his gun toward himself and fired.

Cat heard multiple shots fire. "No!" she shouted as Viktor fell to the ground. Then she realized that Rocco and Dante had both fired as well. Viktor Zadovsky was dead.

Dante yanked the gun from Viktor's hand before moving to help Cat and Sister Lolita.

Cat scooped Marco up into her arms, hugging and kissing him. Marco was squalling at the top of his lungs, and it was the most beautiful sound Cat had ever heard.

"Is he hurt?" Dante asked.

Cat shook her head. "He's scared, but fine."

"Let's get him away from here."

Rocco was there now, too, one arm around Sister Lolita as he shielded the nun from the carnage. "Let's get them to the car," Rocco said. "In case the helicopter pilot decides to buzz by again."

Inside the safe confines of the bulletproof Town Car, Dante pulled Cat and Marco across the seat and into his arms. Marco had quieted, sniffling back tears as he looked curiously at Dante.

Tears shimmered in Dante's eyes as well. "Care to introduce us?"

Cat boosted her son, *their son,* slightly closer. "Marco, this is your daddy."

Dante's mouth opened and closed. Marco touched his cheek, then drew back shyly and buried his face against the crook of Cat's neck.

"You guys ready to go home?" Dante asked Cat.

Home. Cat shook her head. "I don't know where home is anymore."

"I know mine is here." Dante touched Marco's head, then cupped Cat's cheek. "I'll follow you anywhere, Cat. Forever."

It was too much. Tears filled her eyes again. Tears of joy. She sniffed. "Right now, sailing off into the sunset and just disappearing for a while sounds perfect."

Dante laughed. "Have you ever been to Key West?"

Epilogue

Key West, Florida
September 5
(Two Months Later)

Iris had insisted on hosting a Labor Day weekend bash
when she heard Dante was bringing Cat and Marco to visit
Key West.

Dante was grateful Iris agreed to keep the guest list
small. It would make doing what he needed to do easier.

The delicious smells of barbecue permeated the air.
Truman had been up since dawn smoking ribs, chicken,
and beef briskets. Dante helped him carry the platters of
food to the tables set up beneath an open tent.

"We finished just in time," Truman said. "People
should be showing up anytime. Guess I'll go change."

Dante's gaze drifted back to where Cat and Marco were
walking with Iris along the seawall. D-dog followed Marco
everywhere. The dog still hated men, but as it turned out,
he went marshmallow for women *and* little boys.

As Dante watched, Marco threw a stick into the water

and pointed at it, clearly wanting D-dog to fetch. For a moment, Dante thought the dog might actually do it, then . . . nope.

Dante chuckled. Adjusting to fatherhood had been surprisingly fun. Marco was as easy to love as his mother, and it was impossible to imagine life any other way.

The three of them had spent the last eight weeks at a beachfront villa in the Caymans. It had been a quiet, secure place for them to decompress and get to know each other again.

Dante and Cat had agreed to take it one day at a time as they worked through the aftermath of Viktor's reign of terror. Much of it was still being sorted out. That Cat felt ready to meet people, to come to the States with Dante, was a huge step.

She still hadn't decided what to do about the information she had hidden—and that was okay for now. When she was ready to discuss it, she knew he'd be there.

Travis had worked behind the scenes to clear Cat's name of any wrongdoing. And while she was officially free to travel, Dante knew it would be a while before either of them stopped looking over their shoulders.

"Dada!" Marco came running toward Dante with arms wide.

Dante scooped him up and hugged him, then admired the shell his son had found.

His son.

Dante caught Cat's gaze as she walked toward him. She looked gorgeous. Tanned and rested, she'd even begun to put a little weight back on.

"Mama!" Marco waved at Cat, but shook his head

when she held up her arms, quite content to stay in *Dada's* arms.

"The food smells awesome." Travis Franks came up behind them and kissed Cat's cheek. Then he tickled Marco.

Marco rewarded him with giggles and held out his shell. Travis was a familiar face after visiting them at the Caymans several times.

"Rocco and Maddy pulled in right behind me," Travis said. Then he turned to Cat. "I have some papers for you to look over later. For Marco."

"His Canadian birth certificate?" Cat asked.

Travis was also helping to untangle the rat's nest of legalities they faced in establishing Marco's real identity.

"Actually it's a copy of Remi St. James's will. He left a third of his estate to one Marco Lopez. Another third goes to charity. The last third went to Giselle Barclay." Travis met Cat's gaze. "And you were named as the primary beneficiary of Giselle's estate, but we'll tackle those details later."

Dante wrapped an arm around Cat's shoulders. "You okay?"

She looked at him and nodded. "A little stunned, I guess." She turned back to Travis. "Thank you. For that . . . for everything."

Behind them, Rocco called out as he and Maddy Kohlmeyer joined them.

Rocco held out his arms for Marco. "Geez! What are you feeding this kid? He's grown three feet."

Rocco and Maddy had spent time with them in the Caymans, too. They were definitely *on again* and Dante hoped this time it stuck.

"Don't want to come to Uncle Rocco, huh?" Rocco

had just hugged Cat. Now he poked a finger at Marco's belly. "Fine, be that way."

Marco did his Tickle Me Elmo imitation, then hid his head against Dante's shoulder, suddenly shy.

Iris and Truman came up, and after a round of introductions, Iris waved everyone toward the tent. "Chow's on. If you leave hungry, it's not my fault."

Cat reached to take Marco. "I'll go change him quick."

Dante twisted away, playfully keeping Marco from her. Then he bent forward and gave her a kiss. "I can handle that. Go and save us a seat, okay?"

She nodded and stepped backward. Dante was the only person she allowed to take their son out of her sight.

Inside the bathhouse, Dante changed Marco's diaper. Then he stood him up on the countertop by the sink and cleared his throat. "Got time for a little man-to-man talk?" He reached in his shirt pocket and withdrew a ring. "I'm going to ask your mama to marry me. What do you think?"

"Mamamamamamamama." Marco grabbed for the ring.

"I take it that's a yes." Dante slipped the ring back in his pocket and kissed his son. "You ready to try some barbecue, sport?"

Outside, Dante paused. His friends were all gathered at one table, laughing and talking. For the first time in a very long time, he felt . . . blessed. His thoughts drifted briefly to the people he'd loved and lost. His parents. Max. Harry.

But his son's hand patting his cheek brought him back to the present. "Dada. Eat!"

Cat had prepared plates for both of them. Marco squirmed to be put down as soon as he spotted food. He sat between Cat and Dante in a booster chair.

"Kid gets his appetite from me," Rocco said as Marco

stuffed a handful of green beans in his mouth before climbing back onto Dante's lap.

Snatching a rib off Dante's plate, Marco settled back and studied it intently before attacking it with an "aarghh" growl.

"He got your table manners, too," Dante laughed.

"I'm finished." Cat pushed her plate back. "Want me to take him so you can eat?"

Shaking his head, Dante held up a rib. "Aarghh." He mimicked his son.

The conversation drifted to the latest tropical depression forming in the Gulf. "The way it's tracking, we may be under an evacuation order within forty-eight hours," Truman said. "Figures, you just getting here and all," he said to Cat.

Dante watched as the expression on Cat's face shifted briefly to *where do we go now*. They had planned to spend two weeks in Key West. She shrugged. "Guess we go to Plan B." She looked at Dante. "Do we have a Plan B or do we need to wing it?"

"Actually . . ."

Shifting Marco in his arms, Dante got ready to stand, suddenly nervous. What if she said no? Or even *I'm not sure*? God, he didn't want her to feel pressured. Maybe doing this in public wasn't such a great idea.

"Mama." Marco thrust his fist toward Cat.

"Yuck." She held out a napkin to wipe the barbeque sauce from her son's hands. "What's this?"

She held up a diamond ring that was now covered in red sauce and mushed bits of green bean. Everyone at the table grew still.

Rocco's cell phone rang, shattering the silence.

Dante reached for the ring. "Guess he's not real good with secrets yet." When he tried to move Marco off his lap and onto the seat beside him, his son started to whine. "I'll get down on my knee when he takes his nap, okay?" Dante cleared his throat. "Cat, I love you. I love our son. And I'd be honored if you'd marry me and be with me for the rest of our lives."

Cat's eyes filled with tears and he knew before she said it, that the answer was yes. All the other questions like where they'd live and what he'd do didn't matter.

"Yes," she said. And again he felt . . . *blessed.*

Rocco stepped away to check his cell phone. Damn thing had rung twice more since his best friend had proposed. Jesus, he was happy for Dante. And Cat. And Marco.

He pushed buttons to retrieve the message, curious to see who had called three times in a row. What in the hell was that damn important?

Diego Marques's voice came across from voice mail. "I've been contacted by a kid claiming to have a blood chit. Says it's for Travis Franks. Kid also says his father worked at a prison in the jungle. He may be running a con; I understand the kid owes money to the wrong people. Which, for that matter, means this may be a moot point if they've already found him. But I figured you'd want to know anyway. You know how to reach me."

Rocco glanced toward Dante and Cat, who were collecting congratulatory hugs. He caught Travis's eye and nodded imperceptibly.

Travis broke away from the others. "You look rather serious given the festive occasion. What's up?"

Rocco pressed a button and held out his cell phone to Travis. "You'll want to hear this message. Then I've got a favor to ask. If I need to disappear, can you make certain Maddy gets back to D.C?"